A WHIFF OF SULPHUR

Also by Gillian Linscott:

Murder Makes Tracks
A Healthy Body

Gillian Linscott
A WHIFF OF SULPHUR

St. Martin's Press
New York

A WHIFF OF SULPHUR. Copyright © 1987 by Gillian Linscott. All rights reserved. Printed in the United States of America. No part of this book may be used or reproduced in any manner whatsoever without written permission except in the case of brief quotations embodied in critical articles or reviews. For information, address St. Martin's Press, 175 Fifth Avenue, New York, N.Y. 10010.

Library of Congress Cataloging-in-Publication Data

Linscott, Gillian.
    A whiff of sulphur / by Gillian Linscott.
       p.   cm.
    ISBN 0-312-01531-3 : $15.95
    I. Title.
PR6062.I54W48 1987
823'.914—dc 19

First published in Great Britain by Macmillan London Limited.

First U.S. Edition

10 9 8 7 6 5 4 3 2 1

CHAPTER ONE

'Comfortable sort of island, is it? Golden beaches and so on?' The man in the deep armchair opposite Birdie leaned back and sipped a malt as mellow and expensive as his voice. Birdie, wondering if he'd have to pay for the second round, fingered the few pounds in his pocket.

'Well, not comfortable exactly, but then that isn't the point.'

'No golden beaches?'

'No beaches of any kind. Basalt cliffs right down to the sea. That's why it hasn't done so well with conventional tourism.'

'What do the locals do?'

'Apparently there's only one local. He's a sort of nature warden.'

'No bars then, no restaurants, no attractions.'

'Well, not what most people would call attractions.'

Birdie racked his memory for anything good he'd heard about Diabola. After all, the man opposite him was paying a substantial sum for his son to join the jungle survival course (Tooth and Claw Adventure Holidays Limited) run by Birdie's current employers. Chances were, judging by the wealth and position of Daddy, and sonny boy's own track record, that he'd be a pampered little sod from monogrammed cradle onwards.

'There's the sulphur springs and the moustached peccaries.'

The man opposite raised elegant eyebrows and signalled for a waiter. A waiter came and the eyebrows indicated his own empty glass and Birdie's. The waiter left.

'The only island with peccaries in the Caribbean,' Birdie floundered on. 'Endangered species. Apparently they've got this white stripe across their muzzles. That's why they call them . . .'

He couldn't go on. Here he was in one of the most expensive hotels in London, maundering on about wild pigs of all things to an MP who was sitting there with the same polite interest he'd give to a constituent with a sewage problem.

'How very interesting.' This in the kind of voice that said, Of course it wasn't. 'And the sulphur springs?'

'There used to be a volcano. It blew itself away but left some hot springs and a pool called the Devil's Bath Tub. They thought at one time it might attract tourists, but it didn't much.'

The waiter arrived with two more doubles. Justin's father gave no sign of noticing him.

'So, to sum up, this place has got no home comforts, and not much in the way of scenery except rain forest, which is probably teeming with poisonous snakes and malarial mosquitoes.'

He waited for comments.

'Not many snakes,' Birdie said, trying to remember what the guide book said. 'And the mosquitoes aren't malarial, at least I don't think so.'

'But there are mosquitoes and snakes and so on?'

'Yes.' Then, as he was getting tired of being defensive about it, 'And giant toads, and slugs eight inches long and cockroaches to match.' After all, if he was going to withdraw his precious son, he might as well do it now as later. 'In fact there's probably no more uncomfortable island in the whole of the Caribbean.'

He took a good gulp of malt and sat back, waiting for the polite regrets.

'Excellent,' said his host. 'Excellent. It sounds as if Justin's going to have the most uncomfortable week of his young life.'

Which, after a fashion, made sense. Birdie knew about young Justin. The name had seemed familiar as soon as the booking form came in. The father's name was familiar too, but only in the way of any moderately well known MP. If the papers printed his photo it was usually a smudged single column on the parliamentary pages. In that respect, at least, Justin at twenty-three was doing a lot better than his father. When he was photographed, usually coming down the steps of a London court, it got at least six inches by two columns in the gossip pages. 'MP's son in dock again. Prison next time, says judge.'

'He's been too comfortable for too long,' Justin's father said. 'When I saw your firm's advertisement, I thought, Let him be shit scared and uncomfortable for a day or two. Let him get hunted through the rain forest by some gorilla of an ex-NCO or failed police officer . . .'

He'd been getting enthusiastic, but stopped suddenly when he saw Birdie's face.

'I didn't mean . . .'

'Don't worry. They were both a long time ago.'

Justin's father at least had more sense than to waste time trying to recover it. 'But you see the point? We've tried everything else: tutors, psychologists, drying-out clinics. This is worth a try.'

'Does Justin want to go?'

'Justin! Want to go on a rain forest survival holiday? He thinks a weekend in Gloucestershire is a survival test.'

'But if he won't come . . .'

'Justin will come.' The voice was grim and determined. 'Justin will be there or I cut off his allowance. I've told him that.'

Birdie must have looked as unhappy as he felt about that. Organising the survival holiday on Diabola looked like being difficult enough without a rebel in the party.

'I'm afraid it's going to make it more difficult for you,' Justin's father said.

'It's bound to.'

'I realise that. Of course, I wouldn't expect you to take on extra responsibility for nothing.'

A cheque had suddenly appeared on the table. Coutts bank, five hundred pounds, made out in Birdie's name.

'What's that for?'

'The extra work. You earn it by keeping Justin busy, uncomfortable and scared out of his wits for a week. You keep him away from drugs, drink, abnormal sexual liaisons and all the other things he seems to think make life worth living. Above all, you keep him on the bloody island.'

'That bit won't be difficult. We get marooned there for the week.'

'And the rest?'

Birdie looked at the cheque. 'I'll try.'

Drugs and drink must be in short supply on an almost uninhabited island, and surely even Justin wouldn't pursue abnormal sexual relations with a moustached peccary.

'If it works, there's another five hundred for you when you get back.'

For bringing back a bright-eyed boy scout instead of a cocaine-sprinkled hell raiser?

'A week's not long.'

'It might be a start. There's got to be a start somewhere.'

When he said that, Birdie pitied him, in spite of the hand-stitched lapels and the confidence. He was worried about that son like any father would be, desperate even.

'I'll do my best.'

When he picked up the cheque, Justin's father relaxed and smiled properly at last. He glanced at his thin gold watch but seemed to have all the time in the world for Birdie, a politician's talent. 'Have you done a lot of this sort of thing before?'

Birdie decided it was adventure holidays he had in mind, not the rehabilitation of prodigal sons. Even so, it was tricky territory.

'A bit. I helped look after a school ski-ing party a couple of years ago, then there was a sort of historical project down in Somerset. Oh, yes, and I did a stint as a gym instructor at a French nudist colony.'

'It must be interesting work,' said Justin's father. He'd have said the same to a clerk in a tax office, but Birdie didn't mind that. At least the man gave no sign of knowing that his earlier forays into the travel trade had all ended disastrously. No sense in scaring the customers.

'How do you get into that sort of thing?'

That answer needed some care as well.

'The . . . the woman I live with, Nimue, she's in the holiday business. She . . . um, got me started.'

Which up to a point was true. One of the things it left out was the furious argument when Birdie told her about the job with Tooth and Claw. She'd been scathing about their ethics, prices and personnel and unimpressed by Birdie's usual argument that he needed the work.

'And what does she think about you going off to the giant toads and so on?'

'She knows it's all part of the job.'

In fact, the last thing she'd said to him on the subject was that it would serve him damned well right if he got cannibalised by the clients. No sense in passing that on either.

'Do I gather you used to be in the police force?'

Birdie took a good gulp of whisky and closed his eyes. The man was only trying to be civil, for goodness sake. It wasn't his fault that all his questions led into a minefield. Birdie's past, after all, was mostly minefield.

'Yes, I was on the force for nearly twenty years. Then I'd had enough.'

If Justin's father had done his research on Birdie he might have found out a lot about that departure from the force. Or perhaps he had and had decided to keep quiet about it. Not that there was anything to be ashamed of, after all. But still he hoped that Justin's father didn't know.

The next question led to what Birdie hoped would be less explosive ground.

'This holiday – what will the rest of the party be like?'

Birdie could answer that, because Tooth and Claw holidays went in for a sociable kind of survival and had a big space on their booking form for personal details.

'Quite a mixed lot. Nine besides your Justin. A married couple in their thirties, Ellie and Simon, from Birmingham. Toby and Peter, they're brothers who keep their own zoo somewhere near Norwich and I gather they're mainly interested in the wildlife. The rest are around your son's age. Two blokes with the same sort of background I should think, public school, working in the City. Then there's a girl called Annabel and her friend from Chelsea and Russ from the Isle of Dogs who works on oil rigs.'

'And you in charge. Any more staff?'

Another awkward question. Tooth and Claw didn't lay out unnecessary money.

'The man I told you about who lives on the island, Morton, he'll be helping with the survival side. Then there'll be somebody along to do the cooking and generally help out – my daughter, in fact. She's seventeen.'

He could tell Justin's father was weighing up her age. Forty-five and looking it in the face, although not in the body. The cheque for looking after Justin had come just in time to pay his gymnasium subscription.

'Your daughter's making herself useful already then?'

Birdie hoped it was a trace of envy in the question, rather than a patronising of the lower classes whose kids started in the job mines at sixteen.

He said hastily: 'She's just in the middle of her 'A' levels. At a bit of a loose end, to be honest.'

That was putting it mildly. Suddenly German was boring and history of art was boring and even tennis, at which she'd excelled, was boring. When she'd accepted the holiday job with him she'd managed to give the impression that wild Caribbean islands were boring as well.

'I think it's a late reaction to the marriage breaking up. She seemed all right at the time. Got a scholarship to boarding school on the strength of her tennis. Stays with us for some of the holidays and gets on really well with Nimue, only . . .' He was talking too much. His time, however smoothly measured, was up. Justin's father was signalling to the waiter while making polite sympathetic noises.

'Difficult at that age, aren't they?'

'Difficult at any age.'

They wiggled their eyebrows sympathetically at each other while Justin's father signed the drinks chit; two concerned fathers with only a few million pounds to tell them apart. Even without the cheque in his pocket, Birdie would have wanted to help.

CHAPTER TWO

Eight o'clock on Tuesday morning. The sun was mounting through an intense blue sky. The rum level in Morton's glass was falling almost as rapidly. He sipped at it at pauses in his lecture, standing there with a pointer like an old-fashioned school teacher, and with his home-made large map of the island slung on the outside of his bungalow. Around him on the balcony the ten members of the survival holiday spread themselves in varying degrees of comfort. Toby and Peter, the two brothers who ran a zoo, were perched on the rickety balcony rail like two parrots. Their bald heads and their knees, showing below baggy khaki shorts, were already pink from the sun. They took neat notes of what Morton was telling them into two spiral-bound notebooks.

'The first thing to remember about the geography is that there's the sulphur side, that's to the east . . . (tap tap with the pointer on the map) . . . from the pool they call the Devil's Bath Tub up here down to the sea here. The geology of it's complicated, but I'll tell you about that later if you want to know.' (Another gulp from the rum glass.)

Annabel looked across at Birdie, grimaced, smiled and looked away. Since the party had met at Gatwick, he'd been wondering whether Annabel or her friend Helena was the better looking of the two and suspected that every man in the party was doing the same – except perhaps Toby and Peter who seemed to be interested only in endangered species, and the Helibels – as Debbie called the two of them – certainly weren't that. Helena was smaller and rounded, adding strokeable contours to her camouflage suit that even to Birdie's eyes looked more likely to have come from a boutique than a quartermaster's store. Her hair was chestnut brown and silky, piled up on her head in an artless way that let little tendrils escape and stray down the nape of her neck. She'd tucked a pink hibiscus flower behind a neat ear. The only jungle Birdie could imagine her surviving in for more than five minutes was one on a pantomime backcloth, and even then she'd need the handsome prince to rescue her pretty damn quick.

Annabel, on the other hand, would give the rescuing prince a run for his money. She too wore a camouflage suit, but her long body was making a successful escape attempt. Trousers rolled up to the knee revealed long, golden calves, sleeves pushed up to the elbow let the sun glint off the golden down of her tanned arms. The top was unzipped far enough to show she didn't believe in wearing a bra and she had a way of dabbing on mosquito repellent that looked like a welcome signal for anything higher up the animal chain. She was doing it now and Morton, noticing it, faltered in his geography lesson.

'The other . . . the . . . the western side of the island is the freshwater side.'

Birdie supposed he wasn't used to women, not after years of living alone on Diabola with the peccaries.

'The freshwater side. That's where you'll find most of the wildlife and that's where you'll be making for yourselves when you come to the escape exercise. Water and shade. Remember that: water and shade.'

The Helibels were sitting on the bare boards of the balcony. So were the pair Debbie called the two Hoorays – Mal and Henry – closer to the Helibels than they'd been at the start. Mal was square, russet-haired and open-faced, Henry tall and prematurely plumped out with business lunches, floppy hair already receding a little from a long, horse-like face. They both played rugby and talked with confident braying accents that Birdie was trying hard not to dislike. He couldn't help being fascinated, though, by their sideways shuffle across the floor to their objective. Mal's hand was just a few inches from Helena's bottom. One more shuffle and it would be within patting distance. The girls didn't seem to have noticed.

'You could lay up by day and travel by night.'

Morton hadn't expected to be interrupted. Surprised, he stood blinking at his audience.

The interruption had come from Russ. It would. Every party had one, and Birdie had already identified Russ as the one. Russ the know-all, seen it all, done it all.

'You lay up by day and travel by night,' Russ repeated. 'That's what we did in the desert.'

Derisive noises from the two Hoorays. Mal muttered something about Lawrence of Arabia. Russ was about their age and played rugby too from the look of him, but there'd been dislike on sight. Russ had an East-End accent, tattooed arms swinging from broad shoulders, blond curly hair and a good opinion of himself that he took no trouble to hide. Mal and Henry kept their good opinions of themselves tucked away like a silk lining to a suit.

'Russ is quite right. Why don't we travel at night?'

That came from the other woman in the party, Ellie, wife of Simon. You could tell they were husband and wife from the way they sat as far apart as the balcony would let them and never looked at each other. Simon was wispy haired and skinny, in his late thirties but still with the wistful look of a boy who never gets invited to parties. Ellie, looking at least five years younger, was electric with energy, determined not to miss anything. Her small, wide-mouthed face, framed by red-brown hair cut as short as an athlete's, was avid for conflict as she glanced from Russ to Morton and back again.

'Because we'd keep bumping into the trees, that's why not,' her husband growled from the other end of the balcony.

'Don't be silly, Simon. You wouldn't expect . . .'

'Have you brought your camel along then, Russ?'

'We're not actually, sort of literally, going to have to spend the night out there, are we?'

That was from Helena. Her bottom and Mal's hand were now near enough for him to try a comforting pat. The others went on bickering at each other while Morton stood looking weary already and drinking rum. Birdie caught Debbie's censorious eye and looked away. He'd noticed it before, that look assessing the adult world and finding it not up to standard. His eye fell on Justin, sitting apart from the others and pointedly taking no notice of what was going on. He'd been in a state of passive sulks ever since the trip began, when Birdie had more or less frog-marched him on board the plane.

Birdie looked away from him, wondering whether to try to get him involved with the others or leave him as he was. Below them, a dense cover of forest sloped to a sea more violet than blue. St

Lucia, the nearest island, was a darker violet smudge five miles away. Yesterday the boat had dropped the party – the ten holiday-makers plus Birdie and Debbie – at the scoop in the grey basalt cliffs that was the island's only harbour before sailing off with promises to return on the following Sunday. The sulphur smell had hit them before they landed. Morton, an upright figure in faded trousers, teeth and shirt yellowish, as if the sulphur had got to them too, was waiting to welcome them. He looked as if he had both Caribbean and European in his ancestry, face tanned almost to blackness, with a mulberry tinge to the nose.

'Welcome to my island,' he'd said, like a reigning monarch. Now he was looking like a monarch faced with a serious case of lese-majesty. Birdie clapped his hands. 'Hadn't we better let Morton get on with it? You'll be needing all this soon.'

'Wildlife,' Morton said. 'The thing to remember is, most of it here, you mustn't eat.'

'But is it allowed to eat you?' Henry enquired, while Toby and Peter turned over new pages in their notebooks. Henry was still making steady progress towards Annabel and Mal had his arm around Helena's shoulders. Morton went on, taking no notice of them.

'Nearly everything you see on this island's protected, mammals, birds, reptiles. The only things not protected are rats, mongoose and fer de lance snakes. Rats you can eat if you catch them. Mongoose you can eat if you catch them. Fer de lance – I wouldn't advise trying to catch them. Anything else – taboo. You eat it and you answer to me.'

From the rum, or their inattention, his attitude had changed. He was angry with them now.

'What about toads?' asked Henry.

'Yuck,' said Helena.

'We once stewed an iguana,' said Russ.

'There aren't any iguanas in the desert,' said Henry.

'Don't be silly, he doesn't mean in the desert,' said Ellie.

Birdie, trying to keep the peace, said: 'Tell them about the peccaries.

Mal sniggered. 'I thought that was what they put up your bum in France.'

The Helibels giggled.

'That's pessaries,' said Ellie coldly.

'Peccaries,' said Morton. 'To be precise, the moustached peccary, variant of the white-lipped peccary found on the South American mainland. The moustached peccary exists in only one place in the entire world and that's here on Diabola. And, if it weren't for me, it wouldn't even exist on Diabola.'

Birdie noticed Toby and Peter were scribbling away even faster.

'Fifty-seven moustached peccaries when I came to this island, and how many now?'

A silence that should have been dramatic, but Henry was whispering something to Annabel, who giggled.

'A hundred and three,' said Morton. 'That's nearly a hundred per cent rise in the peccary population since I got here.'

'Jolly good effort for one man,' Henry drawled.

Annabel slapped him playfully on the shoulder. Morton's mulberry nose turned loganberry-colour with annoyance. Birdie said hastily, 'I think you've got one of them here.'

'That is so. Hamilcar, a young adult male.'

As Birdie had intended, Toby and Peter asked to see him and the party followed Morton off the balcony and round the side of the bungalow to a large wire enclosure with a wooden shelter. They crowded round the wire and Morton made clucking noises that brought on another fit of the sniggers in Mal and Henry. After much clucking, a slim pig-like creature covered in coarse black hair emerged from the shelter and turned its face curiously towards them. Two narrow white stripes extending from its tusks round to its neck, with two mean little eyes above them, gave it the air of the moustachioed villain in a Victorian melodrama. When it had taken a good look at them, it pressed itself against the wire and pissed copiously over Simon's boots.

'Oh, isn't it sweet,' said Helena.

Toby and Peter too seemed entranced, staring at the beast as it rooted round in the trough. Their admiration put Morton back in a good humour.

'Found it by the water hole with a broken leg when it was just a few weeks old. Brought it up myself.'

'It's a pity for the poor thing to be shut up,' Annabel said.

'He's not going to stay shut up, are you, Hamilcar? Got your duty to do out there.' He put a finger through the wire to scratch the peccary behind the ears.

'Big boy now. Aren't you, Hamilcar?'

From the tone of voice it was clear it was the animal's potency, not his size, he was talking about.

'You're going to release him then?' Toby asked.

Morton nodded. 'Any day now. Next time the herd comes back to this part of the island.'

Morton, Peter and Toby would have clearly been happy to stay admiring the peccary all day, but Birdie moved the party along. Before the sun got too hot to move around comfortably they were to walk back two miles or so up the rough dirt track that was the island's only road to the lodge where they were staying, and from there half a mile further on to the volcanic pool the maps called the Devil's Bath Tub. Then a survival lecture from Birdie over what might otherwise be siesta time. Day one, 'general orientation' was what the brochure called it. But, before they left, Toby and Peter had to go into Morton's bungalow to borrow a paper on peccaries and, out of curiosity, Birdie followed them.

It was a simple room, just a wooden-walled rectangle, with a camp bed against one wall and a dresser with plates and saucepans against another. On a table in a corner was the modern radio set that was Diabola's only contact, via St Lucia, with the outside world. A shelf under the window held a few dozen books, most of them looking like scholarly studies of Caribbean wildlife or geology. Morton picked out a thin pamphlet and handed it to Peter.

'Professor from Cambridge wrote that. His name on it anyway, but most of it's me. Hadn't even seen a moustached peccary till I showed him.'

When Birdie managed to get the party on the road, Toby, Peter and Morton strode in front, talking peccaries. The two Hoorays and the Helibels followed more slowly and Simon, moaning over his urine-spattered boots, already perspiring more than all the rest of the party put together, attached himself to them although they didn't look as if they wanted him. His wife, meanwhile, was either chatting up or being chatted up by Russ. That left only Justin and Debbie. Justin, still in his state of sulk, hadn't even bothered to follow the rest of the party when they went out to see the peccary, and, now Birdie thought about it, he didn't remember seeing Debbie there either. That meant they'd stayed on the balcony together and now they were walking up the road together, some way behind the rest of the party, deep in conversation. He wondered what they were talking about and might have gone back to find out if Russ hadn't called him.

'Here, Birdie, we're wondering when the tough stuff starts.'

Ellie nodded, glancing at Russ then Birdie, in the eager way he'd noticed when there was the chance of an argument. Russ, shirt open to the waist, heavy gold medallion glinting in a thicket of golden-brown hair on his broad chest, smiled down at her. 'Ellie here's waiting for the Tarzan and Jane bit.'

Birdie, unwisely, couldn't help glancing up the track towards where her husband trailed the Helibels and Hoorays. It looked as if he was limping, but perhaps he always walked like that.

'Simon's a martyr to athlete's foot, Ellie said. She didn't sound sympathetic.

Birdie explained laboriously that the first day was a matter of acclimatising and learning the geography of the island. From Wednesday onwards they'd be working on survival, living in the open, leading up to the escape and evasion of the last three days.

'Shall we be spending nights outdoors?' Ellie asked.

'That depends.' Birdie wasn't going to commit himself until he saw how they all got on.

'I spent three nights in a snow hole once,' Russ said. 'Arctic survival.'

'I wanted to go on a sledging holiday,' Ellie said, 'but Simon gets chilblains.'

'It was your idea to come here, I suppose?'

Russ smiled down at her again and moved closer so that his arm was touching hers as they walked. Birdie, beginning to feel superfluous, wondered why he wasn't trying it on one of the Helibels instead. Both of them were more obviously attractive than Ellie and, from their point of view, Russ looked a better prospect physically than either of the two Hoorays. But perhaps Russ knew what he was doing.

'Our marriage guidance counsellor suggested it,' Ellie said.

'Uh?' From Birdie and Russ together. She smiled up at them, pleased.

17

'She agrees with me. What Simon's suffering from is premature middle age. Jolt him out of it, something with a bit of risk in it, that was the idea.'

Russ said: 'So when you get carried off by a randy gorilla, he strips to his red jockey pants and comes swinging down a vine to save you, that it?'

'Something like that,' she said.

Their hands were touching now. Not far to look for the randy bloody gorilla, Birdie thought, feeling sour.

'This marriage guidance woman suggested you booked for a jungle survival holiday?'

'I think what she had in mind was rock climbing in the Lake District, but then Simon came into a bit of money from his father and I saw your advertisement, so I said we'd try that.'

'I' not 'we'. Birdie was beginning to feel sorry for Simon. He'd fallen behind the Helibels and Hoorays now and was walking on his own, still limping. At the front of the crocodile, Morton, Toby and Peter were out of sight. They'd come to the end of the dirt track and disappeared into the thicket of crotons and hibiscus that surrounded the narrower path up to the lodge. Years before, when somebody was trying to run the place as a proper hotel, the thicket might have been a shrubbery. But even the lure of a bubbling sulphur pool and moustached peccaries hadn't been enough to draw tourists from the more comfortable islands, so the lodge was hovering just a stage above dereliction, deserted except when parties of naturalists visited for a night or two. Tooth and Claw Adventure Holidays had got it cheap.

The Helibels and Hoorays had reached the thicket now. Annabel, then Henry, disappeared into it. Helena made a fuss about something, and Mal put on a great display of holding branches back for her. Had she really got an insect down her cleavage? Either that, or holiday affairs grew as quickly as everything else in the place. Simon, plodding along behind, seemed not to notice and disappeared into the bank of greenery without looking back at his wife and Russ. When it came to Birdie's turn he let Ellie and Russ go first and stood to wait for Debbie and Justin. They were walking very slowly, heads down and deep in talk.

'Come on, you two.'

Debbie, after all, was there to work. She should have been ahead of the rest, boiling sterilised water on the camp stove for their morning coffee. She raised her head when he shouted and gave him a vague wave, then went on listening to Justin. He'd have to have a word with her, warn her that her holiday job was catering, not psychotherapy for moneyed yobs. When eventually they arrived at the top of the track he said to her: 'Run on and get the coffee going, love.'

She went skipping neatly as a deer up the narrow track. He heard the jokes and insults as she passed the rest of them on the way. A good kid, active as they come and hard working when she put her mind to something. Many worse these days. Which brought him back to Justin. The young man was standing there staring at Birdie in a meaningless way, making no move to follow the others.

'Not far now,' Birdie said.

He found it hard to know what tone to take with Justin. Apart from the physical scuffle at Gatwick when, at the very last moment, he'd staged a half-hearted rebellion against getting on to the plane, they'd hardly said a word to each other. Justin had eaten, slept and sulked, and that was that. Now he stared some more and said: 'You go first.'

Birdie didn't like the tone, but wasn't eager for unnecessary arguments. He went first into the tunnel between the dark green leaves and could hear Justin walking behind him, slipping and sliding on the mud.

'Is Morton with you?'

The question came suddenly from behind him. The tone was bored, but with something underlying it.

'With Tooth and Claw? Not permanently. We're paying him a guide fee for the week.'

'I didn't mean that.'

A few more steps.

'I meant, is my father paying him as well as you?'

That was awkward. Birdie had assumed, without anything being said, that the conversation with Justin's father would stay a secret between them. Had Justin been told or had he guessed? Either way, Birdie wasn't going to take the trouble of lying to some workshy public school reject half his age.

'No, as far as I know, your father's not paying Morton.'
'But he is paying you?'
So he hadn't known for sure. Birdie said nothing.
'How much?'
'Five hundred pounds now, same again on safe delivery.'
A whistle from behind him.
'My father is a cheap skate.'
This amused Birdie, that Justin didn't resent being nurse-maided but bucked at the level of the fee. 'Isn't that the going rate then?'
'I wouldn't know what the going rate is. You'd know that better than I do.'
If he wanted to think Birdie made a profession of it, then let him.
'But I'll tell you one thing,' Justin said. 'He's wasting his money.' The voice had gone higher, with a squeak in it, like a finger dipped in champagne and rubbed round the rim of an expensive glass. A classy-glassy whine.
'We'll see about that,' Birdie said.
Twelve days, counting the journey out and back, of keeping Justin off drugs, booze and – what was it? – abnormal sexual liaisons. He still reckoned he could manage that. No reply from behind him, which meant Justin was sulking again. That was all right by him.
When they got to the lodge, the rest of the party were spread around the balcony waiting for their coffee. Morton, standing by the rail that couldn't be leaned on heavily because of wet rot, was pointing out some of the features of the island to Annabel. His other hand was straying towards her haunches, watched with open interest by Russ, Henry and Mal, less openly by Simon, who was sitting on a stool in the corner pretending to look at a map of the island. Only Toby and Peter were absent and Birdie found them as soon as he wandered round the corner of the balcony to the open platform that served as a kitchen. They were both there, talking to Debbie. Between them on the floor was a blue plastic ice box of the sort people took on picnics, its lid open.
I'm sure you can find room for it,' Toby was saying. 'It's not as if it's very big.'
He was holding out to her a bright blue floppy thing. Birdie

recognised it as the refrigeration pad from the ice box. Debbie, looking harassed, seemed relieved to see her father.

'Have we got room for it in the fridge, Dad?'

It was a moot point. The fridge ran off a precious bottle of camping gas and was full almost to bursting with the things any civilised adventure holiday couldn't do without, like tubs of margarine and processed cheese.

'I suppose we could make room for it,' Birdie said, 'but why do you want it?'

'Films,' Peter said. 'We have to keep them cool.'

Toby nodded. 'It's the steamy heat that does it. We've lost important negatives before.'

Birdie took the pad and found room for it in between the cheese and the slabs of chocolate. The brothers departed, full of thanks.

'Honestly, they are a pair of old sheep,' Debbie said.

She was sitting on the edge of the cooking platform, waiting for the water to boil. Her camouflage overalls, like the Helibels' only more battered, were too short for her long legs and she scratched casually at mosquito bites on her ankle. Her hair was a grown-out crew cut, pale pink.

'You should use the mosquito stuff.'

She said automatically, 'Don't fuss, Dad,' and went on scratching.

He opened the kitchen's only cupboard. 'The cockroaches have got at the milk powder again.' There was a long trail of it over the wooden floor.

She said, 'I suppose Ellie was telling you how hopeless her husband is.'

'Well . . .'

He still didn't know how to deal with them, these plunges into adulthood.

'She was going on about it in the dormitory last night. Honestly, I don't know why she married him if she feels like that about him.'

Girl talk in the dormitory, Ellie, the Helibels and Debbie. He hadn't thought about that when he'd decided to bring her with him.

'People change,' he said vaguely, sweeping milk powder between cracks in the floorboards. It was dangerous territory.

'She meant it for Annabel and Helena. I mean, with them wanting to marry the Hoorays.'

'Already?'

'They sort of knew them before. You know, debby parties and May balls and so on . . .'

This from a world as remote from her as the moon.

'. . . so when they found out Mal and Henry had booked for this, they decided to book too, to have a chance to catch them.'

'They said all this? In the dormitory?'

She nodded. So, in addition to everything else, he was running a Sloane mating agency. He felt somebody should have warned him.

'I don't suppose it matters much,' she said. 'I mean, if they don't marry each other they'll marry somebody just like each other, so they might as well get on with it.'

Again, this feeling that, from a great height, she was looking at the adult world and finding it wanting. He was sure Ellie and the Helibels weren't a good influence.

Gusts of laughter drifted round from the main balcony, the loud brays of Henry, the deeper tones of Mal and Russ, giggling from the girls. Birdie, glancing round the corner, saw that Henry was clowning with Annabel's mosquito spray, aiming it under his arms like a deodorant. He went back and reported to Debbie.

'Like schoolboys,' she said.

'I don't suppose they've needed to grow up. Straight from public school to jobs their fathers find for them in the City. Just a change of rugby team.'

And yet, watching her as she sat there, sharp knees and shoulder blades jutting at the fabric of the camouflage overalls, he wished he could make the transition to adulthood as smooth for her. Regret turned to anger against the nearest irritant.

'One thing you can say for Mal and Henry though: at least they do a job. Not like young Justin.'

'Justin's had a hard life.'

With his mind on Justin, he didn't hear at first what she said. Then it sank in.

'Hard life? Young bloody Justin, a hard life? Got through more money at twenty-three than you'll ever see in a lifetime on cocaine and God knows what else. Thrown out of one public school after another. Going to inherit half of ruddy Gloucestershire. That's a hard life, is it?'

He'd raised his voice and it might have been audible on the main balcony. He didn't care.

She said quietly, 'His father's unfair to him.'

'Unfair? If it hadn't been for his dad's influence, he'd probably be in Wormwood Scrubs by now. Come to that, if it hadn't been for Justin, his father might have been a government minister.'

'He told you that too, did he?' Her voice was still quite dispassionate. 'About being in the government if it hadn't been for Justin.'

So that was what they'd been talking about so earnestly on the way back from Morton's bungalow. Not only had Justin known about the meeting between Birdie and his father, he'd made sure Birdie's daughter knew about it too.

'The little . . .'

He felt his fists bunching and his shoulder muscles tensing.

But she was going on, still calmly. 'Justin says it's an obsession with his father. He says his father should be grateful to him for giving him an excuse. He's just a second-rate MP and they wouldn't have wanted him in the government anyway.'

'Well, I'll be . . .'

The thought of Justin pouring all this out to her, of her taking it seriously, made him speechless.

'The water's boiling,' she said.

Mercifully, for the next ten minutes or so he had something to do, helping her fill enamel mugs with coffee and distribute them around the party. But it didn't do anything for the way he was feeling and when the argument came between Morton and Justin he was glad of it. The two of them had drawn apart from the others, taking their coffee mugs to a corner of the balcony, and at first it looked as if Justin had come out of his sulks and was asking Morton questions about the island. But, to Birdie, watching them, it was soon clear that Morton was getting annoyed. He moved closer.

'There must be some out there,' Justin was saying. The tone was a combination of bullying and wheedling. He stretched an arm in a wide arc, indicating the miles of heaving greenery between them and the sea.

'In all that lot, there's got to be something smokable.'

Morton shook his head.

'Oh, come on, man. You're not telling me you don't grow a bit for yourself. I won't tell anybody. I'll pay you.'

Birdie moved closer. This, after all, was what Justin's father was paying him for. Justin may have noticed him because he dropped his voice, though not enough.

'What about all that sugar cane and stuff around your bungalow? You must have some in there, haven't you? Go on, you can tell me, man.'

Morton straightened up. 'I told you, nothing doing.'

'What's up?' Birdie asked.

'Nothing to concern you,' Justin said.

'He thinks I'm growing cannabis,' said Morton. 'He won't believe me.'

Birdie, glad of his height, looked down on Justin. 'Just one more word about it, to Morton or anybody else, and you're out there for the week. On your own.'

He pointed to the sea of green under the balcony.

'Out there getting your food and water, finding your own place to sleep and everything that crawls and flies out there feeding off your precious skin. Behave, or you're out there. Understood?'

Justin gave him a look, but didn't reply. Instead he turned to Morton. 'I knew you were in this together. He said you weren't, but I knew you were. And I'm saying to you what I said to him: my dear father's wasting his money. He thinks I've ruined his career, does he? Well, I haven't started yet. You tell him, the next time you're speaking to him, I haven't started yet.'

He stalked off to the opposite corner of the balcony, taking his coffee with him, and stood staring down at the trees.

'What was all that about?' said Morton to Birdie.

Birdie had no intention of explaining his private arrangement. 'He's got funny ideas about his father.'

'I don't like him,' Morton said, as if it came as a surprise.

'Neither do I, but we're stuck with him. I meant what I said about the rain forest, though.'

'He wouldn't last a day out there,' Morton said. 'Not his sort.'

The rest of the party were restless, aware that something had been going on but not sure what. Birdie, making himself calm down, told them it was time to finish their coffee and move on to the sulphur pool before the sun got too hot. They followed a narrow path of yellow-grey clay that led from the side of the lodge furthest from the road. As they went along it, a smell of sulphur that had been no more than a hint on the balcony got stronger, crawling along the path to meet them like some slow, malevolent animal. It sank deep into their lungs. Simon had a choking fit and was banged on the back by Russ. He didn't appreciate it.

'Simon's allergic to nearly everything,' Ellie said.

It was getting hotter as well. The ground steamed from overnight rain and there was a smell of peaty, fermenting earth underlying the sulphur. Morton strode along easily in front, grinning back at them occasionally with a flash of large yellow teeth. Birdie noticed he was breathing deeply, as if the sulphurous fumes were a luxury to him. Half a mile from the lodge the bushes began to thin out and a grey reptilian rock showed between them.

'From the volcano,' Morton said.

Soon there were no bushes at all on their left-hand side, just a wall of the reptilian rock, and the rain forest straggling away to their right.

'I'm not enjoying this.'

That was Helena's voice. Birdie reassured her that they wouldn't be coming there much after this first day. Their game, after all, was survival, and for that they needed the clear waters on the west side of the island, not the sulphur-tainted streams to the east.

'Most of the wildlife's on the other side too,' Toby said.

Birdie said, 'We couldn't miss the Devil's Bath Tub, though. It's supposed to be one of the wonders of the Caribbean.' And it was in their brochure.

They made it up a kind of natural rock staircase to a plateau of grey rock and sand. The sulphur smell came at them in a wave and there was a slow globbing sound like a giant toad.

'Here it is,' Morton said.

Birdie saw that part of the rock plateau was on the move. It was a sheet of grey, yellow-scummed water, about thirty feet across, with dirty bubbles slowly rising and bursting with the toad-like sound. More grey water was welling into it from the base of a fissured rock face, like pus from a decayed tooth.

Helena said, 'Yuck, these rocks are hot.'

'Ooh, flattering me again, ducky,' Henry squealed.

Even through his heavy boot soles Birdie could feel the volcanic heat. Ellie was gazing at the pool, lips parted. 'There should be legends about a place like this.'

'There are,' Morton said.

He was standing, legs apart, his back to the pool. His proprietorial attitude seemed even stronger here than on the rest of the island and he was smiling more, as if the thing had been made to his specification.

'What legends?'

That was Helena, coming close.

'They believe in the Devil round here,' he said. 'You've heard of Obeah?'

Silence.

'Like voodoo. Magic. Black magic. The slaves brought it with them out of Africa.'

'Slaves. On this island?'

There were tones of an outraged liberal conscience in Ellie's voice.

'There was a plantation here. At one time, it was supposed to be the strongest place for Obeah in this part of the Caribbean. Because of this.' He nodded towards the pool.

'What did they do with it?' Helena asked.

Birdie noticed that Ellie and the Helibels had formed a little group around Morton, hanging on his words, and he seemed to be enjoying it. The men were standing back, looking sceptical but not missing a word either, all except Toby and Peter who'd taken themselves off to the edge of the plateau and were looking at something down in the forest.

'What did they do?' Helen persisted.

Morton grinned, took her by the shoulders and made a sudden pushing movement towards the pool. Her screams set the birds off on the far side of the island and brought Mal lunging forward, grabbing her in his arms.

'You shouldn't play about like that,' he told Morton.

Morton shrugged. 'She asked.'

'You mean, human sacrifice?' Ellie asked. 'Sacrifice to the Devil?'

'I think he's making it up,' Mal said.

'Why would he do that?'

Ellie disregarded the interruption, staring at Morton like a student at a lecture.

He shrugged again. 'If you wanted something very much, you had to pay for it. Some things came cheaper, like a goat or a pig. Some things were more expensive.'

'What sort of things?'

'Revenge. Or if you wanted to make somebody love you.'

'He's making it up,' Mal said again.

'If you say so. On any of the other islands, though, you buy people a drink or two then ask them about Obeah. There was a case just last year – man sent to prison for possession of fingers.'

'Fingers?'

'Somebody else's. You don't necessarily need a whole body for Obeah spells, just some parts of it.'

'Parts?' Henry, still clowning, asked it in a strangled voice, knees together.

'That's right,' Morton said. 'Those parts as well.'

'Yaargh.'

Henry walked over to the edge of the pool, pretended to be sick into it, had a choking fit.

'Be careful,' Morton warned him. 'You wouldn't live long in there.'

A few of the bolder ones joined Henry near the pool; Russ, and Ellie and Annabel.

'How hot's the water?' Ellie asked.

'It's around seventy degrees centigrade. They measured it over six weeks when they came to do the geological survey.'

Ellie crouched at the edge of the water.

'Be careful, dear,' Simon warned, from a safe distance. She disregarded him.

'You wouldn't put your hand in it then,' she said. Her voice was wistful.

'I went swimming in a hot spring once, in Iceland.'

That was Russ.

Mal said: 'You would, wouldn't you?'

Then, very slowly, with all of them watching him but not believing it, Russ unbuttoned the cuff of his camouflage suit, rolled the sleeve back and, kneeling beside Ellie, plunged his arm up to the elbow in the steaming water.

There was a scream from Helena and a disgusted sound from Henry. Russ stayed there, unmoving. His face, turned towards Ellie, was as calm as a mask.

'Make him stop it,' Helena shouted at Mal.

Mal did nothing but stare.

Ellie said, very quietly, 'That's enough Russ. You've proved your point.'

And slowly, still looking at her, he withdrew his arm. It was fiery red and he winced as he re-buttoned the cuff round his wrist.

'What was that supposed to prove?' Mal asked.

Birdie, disconcerted by the way Ellie was looking at Russ, said, 'That wasn't very clever. It's meant to be about survival, not playing games.'

To his surprise, Russ looked a little shamefaced, but covered it with a painful salute with his right arm.

'That's it, sergeant major. You put him on a charge.'

Henry, stirring things as usual. It was about the tenth time already Birdie had heard the sergeant major joke. Even first time round, he hadn't missed the point that the Hoorays, like Justin's father, had him tagged as strictly non-commissioned.

'If we can get on with things,' Birdie said, 'there's a good view of most of the island from here.'

And of a fair part of the Caribbean. Miles away, a white yacht moved over the flat violet sea, making for St Lucia. Further out still, a cruise liner slid past on its way to Barbados. Nothing was heading for the scanty harbour of Diabola itself, which wasn't surprising. The next boat there would probably be the one that came to pick up the survival party in five days' time. From the harbour, seven miles of uninterrupted rain forest sloped steeply up to the plateau where they were standing. Even the dirt road from the harbour to the lodge was invisible under the trees, although you could, if you knew where to look for it, pick out the roof of Morton's bungalow down to the right. Behind them, the grey rock heaved itself abruptly into jagged crags. Below and to their left the same rock ran off into a long grey spur about half a mile long, sloping to the level of the forest. Toby and Peter were sweeping it with binoculars.

'Iguanas.'

'They come here to sunbathe,' Morton said.

'Yuck,' said Helena.

Birdie noticed that Morton, of all people, had an arm round Helena's waist and a hand resting casually on the camouflage patches over her bottom. He suspected it had got there when Helena was shivering over Obeah, and she seemed in no hurry to shake it off, although Mal was looking daggers. If the ploy was to make Mal jealous, he thought she might have chosen a likelier candidate than the sulphur-fanged Morton. Wondering how many were actually listening, he went on pointing out some of the landmarks of the island they'd need to know when it came to the escape and search exercise, but his mind wasn't entirely on it either. He couldn't help being conscious that, under a big rubber tree at the edge of the plateau, Debbie and Justin had their heads together again and seemed unconscious of everything else.

CHAPTER THREE

Evening. The tree frogs were throbbing away like an amplified heartbeat. They started well before the sun was setting, just two or three of them, no bigger than blowflies, sitting in the angles of the lodge walls, miniature throats pulsing. Then, as the sun got near the tops of the trees, other frogs began answering them from the forest until the noise was as persistent in human ears as the smell of sulphur in the nostrils, so much a part of life on Diabola that they hardly noticed it any more. There'd been a diversion at the end of dinner when Henry had put a frog down Annabel's neck and she'd stripped to her underwear to get it out, there at the table in front of them all. Birdie was pretty sure that an all-in-one satin garment with white lace trimmings wasn't standard survival gear under a camouflage suit, but over Annabel's long browm limbs it had been enough to make even Toby and Peter look up from their nature diaries.

Now, the excitement over, they were back at their diaries again, working side by side at the communal table by the light of a paraffin lamp, like a pair of middle-aged schoolboys. Simon, who had a headache and had taken a Paracetamol, was sitting at the far end of the table, eyes closed. Henry and Annabel were in a corner giggling about something and Mal, making up for lost time now Morton had gone home, was leaning dangerously out over the balcony, picking hibiscus flowers for Helena to make into a garland.

Justin was sitting on his own, out of the lamplight, turning over the pages of what looked like an address book. Only Russ and Ellie seemed to be taking his survival lesson of the afternoon at all seriously. They were at the opposite end of the table from Ellie's husband, making something from a pile of creepers and sharpened sticks they'd collected in the rain forest. Ellie was holding a pliant stick about ten feet long across the table while Russ tied smaller sharpened stakes to it at right angles, cursing when the creepers kept breaking.

'What's that supposed to be?'

Mal, leaving Helena to thread her flowers, strolled across.

Russ didn't look up. 'Monkey trap. We used to use them in Borneo.'

Birdie decided he'd better take an interest. 'How does it work?'

'Surprised you don't know about it, Birdie. End here goes in the ground, bent right back with these short stakes pointing up. You tie it down to a peg, with a bit of slack that you take up with a short stick here.' He pushed back Peter's notebook in his eagerness to demonstrate. Peter frowned but said nothing.

'Then you've got these other stakes leaning over at forty five degrees, with a crossbar between them. You tie a creeper to the end of the stick with the spikes on it, loop it over the crossbar, tie a banana on the end of it, then there you are.'

'Where?'

By now he had the interest of everybody on the balcony except Justin, though Henry and Annabel had broken down in giggles again.

'The monkey,' Russ explained, 'grabs the banana. That pulls up the short stick which lets the slack go, then up come the spikes, slam, straight through your monkey.'

'Yuck.'

'I'll bet it tastes perfectly foul.'

'Why don't you just eat the banana?'

Mal said, 'You got that out of a book. It doesn't work anyway. We tried it at prep school with the first years.'

'No I didn't.' Russ, more bothered by their ridicule than he'd been by the heat of the sulphur pool, appealed to Birdie. 'It could save your life, couldn't it? You've got to have protein.'

Ellie, tense as if it mattered very much, was looking at Birdie too. He tried to let them down gently.

'Well, yes, I think it could work in the right circumstances, Russ. The trouble is, there aren't any monkeys on Diabola.'

And the most explosive of the giggles raised came not from the Hoorays or Helibels, but from Ellie's husband, still sitting, eyes closed and forehead creased, at the far end of the table.

Russ's face was as flaming red as his arm had been, but he wasn't retreating. Instead, he attacked Birdie. 'That's the point, though. It's all bloody unreal. I mean, we've been here for a day and a half now, and all we've had is a nature walk with Morton and an afternoon piddling about around the lodge learning to make shelters. We shouldn't be sitting about here. We should be out there, experiencing it.'

His wide gesture took in the whole of the throbbing darkness outside the circle of lamplight.

Birdie said pacifically, 'And so we will, Russ. But we can't rush into it, you know that.'

No way was he releasing the Hoorays and Helibels into the rain forest on their own at night. He'd have to arrange something to keep Russ happy, though.

Helena said unexpectedly, 'It would be great to try it, really oohsome.'

She was wearing her garland of red and white hibiscus and had twisted some of the flowers into her chestnut hair.

'You'd be scared,' said Mal indulgently.

'No I shouldn't. And you'd be there to protect me.'

Birdie said: 'We might consider a night walk tomorrow night, keeping together.'

He'd have a talk with Morton and make it as trouble free as possible.

'It'd be something,' Russ said. He went round the party and, to Birdie's surprise, got an almost unanimous vote for a night walk in the forest. Toby and Peter wanted to find a particular sort of moth, Henry thought it might be a good giggle, even Simon groaned a reluctant yes.

Only one person hadn't been asked. Justin, still riffling through his book although it might have been too dark to see much, hadn't seemed to notice what was going on. Russ, walking up to him, had to repeat his question twice. Suddenly a smile spread over his face, a wide but cold smile as if something had just become clear to him.

'So we're going out at night. That will make it easier for them, won't it?'

'Easier for who?' Russ was puzzled, suspecting a joke, but Birdie, with a sinking feeling, thought he knew what was coming.

He hoped Debbie, still in the kitchen washing up after supper, would be out of earshot.

Justin said loudly, 'Easier to lose me.'

Birdie couldn't let it go unchallenged. 'Don't be daft, Justin. Who wants to lose you?' He thought, but didn't add, Except everybody.

'You should know.'

Justin was standing up now, swaying a little from side to side as if to disco music only he could hear.

'You should know, Birdie. You and Morton. And my dear father, of course.' His voice was high and carrying, as for amateur dramatics.

Russ turned away. 'What's he talking about?' He walked back to the table and began fiddling with the monkey trap. The others stared but, after a second or two of silence, started talking among themselves again.

'Don't take any notice of Justin,' said Helena to Birdie, kindly. 'He's always like that.'

In her circle, he supposed, they were used to Justin and people like him. He thanked her and walked round into the kitchen to find Debbie, sure she must have heard. She was putting things into tins against the cockroaches, as he'd told her.

'Did you hear any of that? Justin thinks Morton and I are being paid to get him lost.'

'What about the coffee?' she said. 'Would they eat that as well?'

'They eat anything.'

The coffee went tidily into a tin.

'He's obsessed,' he said. 'He thinks everybody's out to get him.'

'You can't blame him.'

She was kneeling to stow the tins away.

'What do you mean, I can't blame him? Nobody wants to do him any harm. His mind's rotted from all that cocaine.'

He had to keep his voice down, but it was an effort.

'Nobody ever listens to his side of things,' she said.

'That's just plain daft, love. He's had tutors and child psychiatrists and probation officers listening to him ever since he was in his pushchair.'

'Perhaps they didn't listen properly.'

'You've been making up for it then, have you? That's what you've been doing all the time since we got here, listening to Justin properly?'

She nodded, ignoring the sarcasm. 'Somebody's got to.'

He made himself calm down. This was more serious than he'd thought.

'Look, love, he's six years older than you. He lives in a world you've got nothing to do with, thank God. He'd mess up your life without giving it another thought. You keep clear of him.'

She'd turned away from him, stacking plates. The nape of her neck was white and vulnerable under the arrowpoint of pink hair. He wished he could still hug her.

'Talk to him just as much as you have to for the job, that's all. Don't spend a lot of time with him.'

She still hadn't turned, but one thing he had learned in seventeen years was when to stop. He hoped she'd got the message. There was another message to be delivered though, and for that one he didn't have to be tactful. His step quickened as he came round to the main party on the balcony.

'Where's Justin?'

He'd gone from the corner where he'd been sitting. He wasn't in the bathroom or either of the dormitories. Peter remembered something.

'I thought I saw him going down the side steps.'

The side steps went down to the path leading to the Devil's Bath Tub.

Birdie stared. 'What was he doing?'

The idea that Justin, of all people, would take a voluntary walk in the dark struck him as odd. He got no more help from Peter, so, without saying anything to the rest of the party, he found the torch in his pack and went down the rickety wooden steps to the start of the path.

The moon, an almost full one, was coming up over the trees, and the pale trodden clay made the track easy enough to follow. When he thought he was out of earshot of the lodge, he stopped and called Justin's name softly, but there was no reply. Moths, disturbed from the bushes, flopped past him and he heard a whirring sound from some night bird or insect. Even if the path had been less clear, he could have followed the sulphur smell. At first, when he got to the plateau, he thought there was nobody there, then a figure stood away from the rock wall to the left.

'Is that you?' it said.

Justin's voice.

'No. It's me. Birdie.'

Whoever the little sod was expecting, it certainly wouldn't be him.

'Oh.'

Justin's voice let it be known that Birdie was a disappointment.

'You shouldn't go off on your own like this,' Birdie said.

'Not supposed to let me out of your sight, is that it?'

'A rain forest is a dangerous place, especially at night.'

'I'm sure you'd know about that.'

His face was turned away and shadowed, but the sneer in his voice was clear enough.

'I wanted a word with you, about Debbie.'

Justin said nothing.

'I don't know what you've been saying to her, but don't. She's just a kid and I'm not having her upset.'

'Who's upsetting her?'

'You are. All this silly talk about your father. You solve your own problems; don't go pushing them off on a kid of seventeen.'

Justin turned his back. The abrupt rudeness of it made Birdie fight harder to keep his temper.

'You just keep away from her. Understood?'

Justin said, over his shoulder, 'I don't know what all the fuss is about. She's over the age of consent, isn't she?'

'You little . . .'

Birdie was on him in a bound, grabbing his shoulder, pulling him round so that Justin's face was only inches away from his own. A flaccid shoulder, a pale face trying to register amusement, showing alarm.

Birdie said, loudly and slowly, 'You lay a finger on her and I'll mash you into something you could spread on toast.'

He stared down at the pale face for a good minute, while the alarm on it spread into real fear, until he could smell the sweat breaking under Justin's armpits, then gave the unresisting shoulder a contemptuous shake and released it. Justin's other hand went to the shoulder where Birdie had gripped and his face was twisted with pain and anger.

'I'll get you for this, Birdie, you and my father. I'll get you both for this.'

Birdie laughed and turned away. He was almost ashamed of himself now he remembered what a poor thing Justin was after all. He walked away, calling over his shoulder, warning that Justin shouldn't stay out in the forest past his bedtime, and found the track leading back to the lodge. The moon was so bright now he didn't need his torch. Because he was thinking about what had just happened, asking himself if he should have handled it differently, his ears were picking up the noises coming in the other direction long before his mind registered them. Something on the path, coming towards him from the direction of the lodge. The clay was too soft for footsteps, but whatever it was brushed against bushes as it passed and set off the whirring night birds.

At first he wondered if it might be a herd of peccaries and, in spite of his mood, was pleased at the idea of seeing them. He stood aside off the track, hoping they wouldn't catch his scent. Then he found his hand was resting on a thorn bush and moved suddenly, making a rustling of his own, and the noises from the other direction stopped. The peccaries had heard him. But, then, what would peccaries be doing, trotting along a track that led to hot, sulphurous water? Their place was on the other side of the island where the streams were drinkable; Morton had said so. He was, all of a sudden, quite sure it wasn't an animal at all but another human being coming along the path from the lodge.

'Who's that?'

There was no reply, just a moment of silence, then the rustling again but going in the other direction away from him, faster than it had come.

'Who is it? Wait.'

But whoever it was wouldn't wait, was walking away from him as fast as it could, running even. He started to run after it, skidded on the clay, slipped and went sprawling, giving a bad tug to his knee with the dodgy ligament. He sat there in the path, massaging it.

'Wait,' he shouted again. Then, more quietly. 'Wait . . . Debbie.'

The last word was almost a question.

He got up and, knowing he wouldn't catch up with whoever it was, walked on slowly. Had it been Debbie, coming out by arrangement to meet Justin at the sulphur pool? If not Debbie, then who? He was reluctant now to get back into the circle of lamplight on the lodge balcony. When he arrived there, Debbie was at the big table with the rest of them, listening to Toby giving an impromptu talk on moths. She could have been there for minutes or all the time he'd been away. He wasn't going to ask. Half an hour or so later, Justin appeared and went straight through to the dormitory without a word to anybody.

'Where's he been?' Mal asked.

Nobody else seemed concerned.

Soon after that there was a general movement towards bed. There were just two big habitable rooms inside the lodge and they were used as dormitories, men on one side of the passage, women on the other, a communal bathroom with a primitive shower and more primitive lavatories at the far end. Birdie had chosen to sleep on the balcony under a mosquito net, with the idea that this would help him adapt to the rain forest more quickly than the rest. He lay awake for a while, worrying, listening to the sounds of the rest of them settling for the night behind the wooden wall: Henry's bray of laughter, the twittering giggles of the Helibels from the other side. He wondered, suddenly and sharply, what the four of them were talking about in the women's dormitory. Was Debbie telling them how she'd set out to meet Justin by the Devil's Bath Tub and nearly bumped into her father on the way? Was that what they were giggling about? Then he told himself she wouldn't do that.

Later, when it had all gone quiet inside, rain came battering down on the stiff leaves all around the lodge. After the rain a colony of toads somewhere down near the sea started making a noise like a huge dynamo and fireflies flashed bright green against the dark. Listening and watching, Birdie dozed. He was woken suddenly by the noise of footsteps on the balcony, coming from the direction of the dormitories; bare footsteps of somebody padding carefully on the wooden boards. They came towards him, then stopped, and he knew that somebody was watching him.

'Hello. Who's that?'

He spoke quietly, not wanting to wake the others. There was silence at first, but he could hear breathing. It was still deep, rain-smelling dark all round them.

'What do you want?'

Annabel's voice said, out of the darkness, 'It's the mosquitoes.'

He groaned and sat up. He'd lit mosquito coils in both dormitories before they all retired to bed and didn't see what else he could do.

'Are they bothering you?'

'Um. They like my blood. I'm always the one they sting.'

He looked at his watch. Nearly two o'clock.

'I'm surprised they're so active at this hour.'

'There's one keeps dive-bombing me. Or perhaps they're a kamikaze squadron taking it in turns.'

He could see the pale gleam of her long legs. She was wearing something white that knotted over one shoulder and skimmed the tops of her thighs, a kind of sarong.

'I don't know why it's me they fancy so much.'

Birdie swung his feet to the floor. 'I'll light another coil.'

'Don't do that, you'll wake the others. They're all sleeping like babies in there.'

He was starting to say there wasn't much he could do about it when she advanced towards him, holding out something he couldn't see.

'I've been rubbing on this stuff, but I couldn't do the bit between my shoulder blades. That's where they always go for. It's tender, I suppose.'

Then she was kneeling on the boards beside his bed with her back to him and the thing she'd been holding was in his hands.

'So would you be a darling and do it for me?'

'Er . . . You want me to just spray it on?'

'Yes, please.'

He sprayed the creamy expanse of skin between her shoulder blades. Her head was bent, blonde hair hanging down. She gave a little shiver when the spray hit her, but stayed kneeling.

'Some more?'

'No. Would you rub it in, please.'

His brain was inclined to be indignant about it, asking if this was really supposed to be part of his job, but his hand had other ideas. It liked the idea of touching that luminous skin and was already on its way. He smoothed the lotion in with long, firm strokes, up to the tips of the shoulder blades and back again, and she gave a little wriggle with her whole body, like a pleased cat.

'Thank you.'

Her voice was thanking him for more than he thought he'd given, but he liked it. She turned round, still kneeling, but as she turned something seemed to go wrong with her sarong. The knot on the shoulder came unhitched, she gave a little gasp, made a grab at it, and the whole thing cascaded down into her lap.

'Oh, dear,' she said, biting her lip and looking up at him, but the words had a giggle in them. Her breasts were round and firm. Against the dark, her skin was the colour of pale clover honey. He looked up again and saw the giggle had spread to her eyes and realised he was smiling too.

'Are they mosquito-proofed as well?'

She shook her head, smiling.

'We'll have to do something about that, won't we?'

He reached for the can.

He knew this wasn't the kind of adventure holiday he was supposed to be giving the customers, but what the hell. His self-esteem had been taking a battering over the past few weeks, what with the row with Nimue, the patronage of Justin's father and the Hoorays, the boasting of Russ, not to speak of playing the responsible father all the time. If Annabel wanted a bit of fun, and she could hardly have made it more obvious if she'd spelled it out in fireflies, that was fine by him. It was him she'd come to, which was one in the eye for that rich twit Henry. He didn't stop spraying until her breasts were glistening with mosquito repellent and by the time he'd finished rubbing it in they were both sprawled on the bare boards by his camp bed.

He started running his hands down over her ribs and stomach but she caught him by the wrists. Her grip was surprisingly strong, nearly as strong as Nimue's.

'No. It's your turn. We don't want the mosquitoes to get you.'

'Annabel, there aren't any mosquitoes. Not out here.'

He didn't want to be diverted, but she was insistent. A jet of spray hit him on the chest, then the stomach, then the tops of the thighs.

'Now I've got to rub it in,' she said, and did, very slowly. By the time she'd finished he was in a state of groaning desperation. He tried to pull her down on top of him but she resisted, giggling. In their struggles the canister of mosquito spray rolled away across the balcony and crashed into the bushes.

She giggled. 'Shh, we'll wake them.'

'Come on then.'

They wrestled, giggling and slippery, and then somehow she was the one underneath, pulling down on him, not resisting any more. Later, when they were still locked together, he felt a sharp sting in the buttock.

'Ow!'

'What's up?'

'Bloody mosquito.'

He felt her stomach heaving under him in another fit of giggles. 'I told you so.'

She was still laughing when she got to her feet and draped the sarong round her. She looked as fresh and full of energy as if she'd just got out of bed, but Birdie was feeling the tiredness of days creeping over him.

'I must go,' she said. 'You all right?'

'I've never been . . .' He stopped, listening. 'What was that?'

'I didn't hear anything.'

'It sounded like somebody moving about inside.'

'Probably one of the men going to the loo. I'll say I was out looking at the moonlight or something.'

A final wave of the hand from the doorway and she was gone. He knew he should be worrying more about the footsteps, but a wave of warm tiredness came over him and it was as much as he could do to get back on his bed before he fell asleep.

He woke some time after dawn after the deepest sleep he could remember for weeks. If it hadn't been for the lingering smell of mosquito repellent on his skin, he'd have thought he'd dreamt the whole thing. He had a thirst like a furnace and thought longingly of a little pile of green coconuts in the kitchen, so he pulled on his underpants and padded in bare feet to find one.

He chose a coconut and weighed it in his hand, but couldn't find the machete. He knew he'd hung it back on its nail the day before, but now there was no sign of it. Baulked of his drink, he put down the coconut and hunted. The cockroaches had been at it again. Debbie had put some cold water detergent in a plastic box by the sink. Now there was a scurf of white plastic shavings on the floor and, when he picked the box up to look at the jagged hole in its side, one of the insects fell out, its armoured body hitting the floor with a sound like a pan scourer. He stamped on it with his bare foot, but the thing was proof against more than thirteen muscular stone of Birdie and dragged itself away, only dented. Debbie had told him that, after the bomb had killed off everything else, cockroaches would inherit the earth. They were already staking a pretty strong claim to Diabola.

He scuffed the plastic shavings over the edge of the terrace and went on with his hunt. No sign of the machete but, puzzlingly, indications that somebody had been at the stores the night before. He'd watched Debbie stacking things neatly away in tins after supper, and could swear some of the tins had been disarranged since. A tin of biscuits had been turned round and, when he opened it, there were fewer biscuits inside than he remembered. He hadn't counted the tins of fish, but there didn't look as many as there'd been before. Midnight feasts then. The Hoorays or the Helibels, or probably all four of them, giggling in the dormitory. Typical. He'd have to have a serious word with them. They'd brought just enough food with them and if people ate more than their share others would go hungry. He was surprised he'd slept through the raid on the kitchen. That must have given them a good giggle.

Then he saw the letter. It was on the top shelf of the cupboard, propped up by the boxes of water-purifying tablets. It was addressed, in green felt-tip, to 'Mr Linnet'. For Birdie, the first and most immediate hurt was that she hadn't put 'Dad'. It was at least 'Dad' inside, once he'd torn the envelope open, but by then it was no consolation.

'Dear Dad,
    I hope you won't worry about this, but I've gone with

Justin. You said people shouldn't go off in the rain forest on their own, so I'm going with him. He says it's the safest place for him. Don't try to find us, Dad, and don't 'fuss'. I'll be all right.'

Then, 'lots of love from Debbie' and three kisses, the way she'd always signed letters as a kid.

CHAPTER FOUR

Birdie's first reaction was guilt. It came to him as a certainty that it must have been Debbie he'd heard moving about the night before, that she'd seen him making love to Annabel and gone off, hurt or disgusted. Even when the words in the note sank in and fury against Justin flooded through him there was still self-reproach under it. If he hadn't been making love to Annabel, he wouldn't have slept so hoggishly, would have heard them going, wrenched the little runt's balls off before he'd let him take Debbie away. Fury kept him paralysed, unconscious of time. He was still standing there, staring at her note, when he heard Russ's cheerful voice.

'Morning Birdie. Any coffee going?'

Russ was in shorts, bare hairy chest and a grin full of gleaming white teeth. The grin went, though, when he saw Birdie's face.

'What's up?'

'My daughter Debbie. She's gone off with that little bastard.'

Russ whistled.

Sense was beginning to return to Birdie, though not much of it, along with a desperate need to do something.

'Did you see him go? You must have seen him go.'

Russ wrinkled his forehead. 'I heard people going out to the lavatory a couple of times. I didn't stay awake waiting for them to come back, though.'

'He didn't come back. He went off with Debbie, into that.' Birdie made a flailing sweep of his arm over the waves of green falling down to the sea, the snakes and the insects and the sulphur smell.

'She'll be all right,' Russ said. 'She's a sensible kid.'

'With him?'

Russ was looking ill at ease, not able to respond to Birdie's anger and grief.

'They won't get far, Birdie. We'll find them, when we're doing the escape and evasion bit today.'

The plan for the day had been to divide into groups and track each other through strictly limited areas of the forest, a practice for the larger exercise at the end of the week. Russ clearly expected it to be business as usual, and so, Birdie supposed, would the other customers.

'Russ, will you tell them to get their own breakfast? I'll be back in an hour.'

'Where're you going, Birdie?'

A good question. Seventy square miles of rain forest, most of it trackless.

'I'm going to walk down as far as Morton's bungalow; see if I can find them.'

They might be on the path. He couldn't imagine Justin hacking a way through the forest. There was the missing machete, though.

'Don't get lost, will you, Birdie? Do you want me to come with you?'

He shook his head. He wanted time on his own to think. The sound of voices from inside the lodge reminded him that the others would soon be up and he didn't want to deal with them yet. He mumbled a word of thanks to Russ and made for the steps.

The track to Morton's bungalow was steaming as the sun came up and the forest on both sides of him was full of the noise of birds. The sea below him was calm, with not even a single yacht to break the expanse of it. Could they be trying to get off the island, get down to the harbour and signal to passing ships? Justin would be crazy enough for that, but would Debbie? A couple of hours ago he'd have said not, but now he couldn't even guess what she'd do, this new person his daughter had become. He kept turning his head, looking into the banks of greenery on either side for machete cuts that might show two people had hacked their way into them, but could see nothing. Several times his heart leaped up when he heard something blundering in the trees, but when he shouted there'd be nothing but the whirr of a pigeon taking off again. He was sweating by the time he got to Morton's bungalow.

The door of it was open and the living room, with its radio set and its tidy shelves of books, empty. He went round the back to find Morton in trousers and a shirt so crumpled he might have slept in it, scratching the back of his peccary. He was talking to it, in a low crooning voice, and straightened up looking embarrassed when he heard Birdie's steps.

'You're early. Want a coffee?'

He was holding a mug, and Birdie caught the fumes of cheap rum from it, as well as good coffee. He shook his head.

'Have you seen anybody going past?'

Morton grinned. 'Escaping already, are they?'

Now it came to it, Birdie found it hard to admit what had happened. He said at last, 'My daughter. She's gone off in the night with Justin.'

Morton stared, then an uneasy grin widened, revealing first millimetres then square centimetres of yellowed teeth.

'They didn't waste much time, did they?'

Birdie fought down his fury. No good quarrelling with the only man who knew the damned island.

'I wondered if they might be going down to the harbour.'

Morton shook his head. 'I don't sleep much. I'd have heard them going past.'

'What about the back way, down the stream?'

Birdie was trying hard to remember the map of the island. Morton shook his head.

'I've been out by the stream watching the peccaries.' He bent to scratch Hamilcar's back again. He seemed more interested in the little beast than in Birdie's daughter. 'Got to keep an eye on them now. Soon be time for Hamilcar to join them, won't it, old son?' There was regret in his voice about that.

'And?'

'Oh, no sign of them. No footprints by the stream. I'd have noticed.'

Which meant they hadn't made for the harbour by the two most sensible routes, the road or the freshwater stream.

'Where else could they be?'

Morton shrugged. 'Practically anywhere.'

'He was by the Devil's Bath Tub last night.'

Birdie didn't mention his suspicion that Debbie had been trying to join him there as well.

'They won't have made for the sulphur side if they've got any sense. They'll need fresh water.'

'Yes.'

Had Debbie remembered water-purifying tablets? He'd told her about them often enough.

'So how do we find them?' Birdie asked.

Morton took a long gulp of coffee. 'We're supposed to be playing hide and seek with your people today, aren't we? Bound to come across them.'

This was more or less what Russ had said, and to an extent it made sense. The trouble was that Birdie needed somebody to share his sense of loss and urgency about what had happened, and neither Russ nor Morton showed any sign of doing that.

'She's only seventeen.'

Morton slapped him on the shoulder, splattering him with rum-flavoured coffee.

'These islands, the girls think they're failures if they haven't had their first baby by the time they're seventeen. Two babies, some of them.'

Birdie glared at him, speechless. Morton pointed at the peccary, rooting in his trough on the other side of the wire.

'Only natural. Look at Hamilcar there, getting restless, knows he should be out there with the rest of them, showing the sows what it's for. Any night now, before the moon goes, I'll leave the door open and off he'll go without as much as a thank you. I'll miss him, but you can't argue with nature.'

The man seemed honestly to put Birdie's daughter and his wild pig in the same category and Birdie realised there was no urgent help coming from that quarter. He had alternatives: to plunge off into the rain forest on his own, or to stay with the group and try to organise its activities to give the best chance of finding Debbie and Justin. The first option was the attractive one, but he had to admit to himself that the second was the more sensible.

By the time the sun was high, though, he knew that being sensible wasn't bringing results. The customers, as far as he could manage it, had much the sort of morning they were paying for, a kind of glorified hide and seek with much shrilling of whistles and good advice from himself and Morton thrown in. He suspected that the absence of Justin and Debbie was discussed when two or three of the fugitives congregated under the same tree, but not much was said to him about it. Now and then Russ would appear from the trees, put a confiding hand on his shoulder, shake his head regretfully and melt into the trees again. He was getting tired of Russ. With some vague idea of protecting Debbie's reputation, Birdie had tried to give the rest of them the idea that it was all part of the plan, that Debbie and Justin had gone off together on his instructions and it was part of the exercise to look for them. If they believed it, they weren't taking it too seriously. Now that the sun was too hot to move around they were more concerned with playing houses or – as the brochure put it – constructing survival shelters – in the part of the rain forest sloping down to the freshwater stream between the lodge and Morton's bungalow. Birdie, perched high on the end of a tree trunk, looked round and saw reluctant smoke rising from a couple of their fires, heard snatches of talk that told him how they were setting about the business of survival.

'Do you think it could be oregano? I mean, seriously Annabel, it does smell a bit like it.'

The Helibels had made their shelter like a couple of bower birds, delicately woven from creeper and some of the more handsome varieties of leaf; about as much protection from the elements as Annabel's lacy underwear. Now they were inflicting haute cuisine on the standard survival soup cube.

Not far away, well within calling distance, Mal and Henry had put together a rather more substantial effort from branches and their two permitted pieces of polythene sheeting. Wild hunting noises rose from it, then Henry's announcement to the rain forest at large: 'Mal's caught a rat.' A united 'Yuck' rose from the Helibels' shelter, followed by a yelp from Mal, raucous laughter from Henry.

'Sorry folks. Rat's off the menu.'

Annabel called, 'You'd better come over for lunch with us. Helena thinks she's found some oregano.'

A short debate in the Hoorays' camp, then: 'Right, we're

coming over.' The equivalent of a phone call between two Gloucestershire mansions, green wellies in the back of the Land Rover and a drive through the beech woods. Birdie supposed it was survival of its kind.

At the Ellie and Simon camp, though, things were less friendly. Birdie had been listening on and off as they bickered about where the camp should go, whether the polythene was more useful as a ground sheet or a fly sheet, and, from Simon, whether they shouldn't have ignored the whole bloody thing and gone to Ambleside in a caravan instead. Ellie was all too obviously regretting that she was with her husband and not Russ, and it struck Birdie that, when it came to building a shelter, even of the roughest kind, the marriage lines still had some pull. While they were all going round as a party, Ellie could desert her husband in favour of Russ. When it came to their own front door, even if that front door was a polythene flap, she was back on the legitimate side of it.

Not that Russ seemed bothered. With a great show of independence he'd built his own shelter some way off and a trail of smoke had issued from it long before the others. Perhaps he'd succeeded where Mal had failed and even caught a rat for lunch. Birdie was realising reluctantly that some of Russ's good opinion of himself might even be justified.

As for the brothers Toby and Peter, they were being no trouble to anyone. They'd simply chosen their tree and, with magnifying glass and notebooks, were doing a bug count. Birdie could hear Toby's voice hypnotically rolling out polysyllabic Latin names which Peter was presumably writing down in his notebook.

Birdie sighed and stood up, supporting himself on a torn branch. He'd chosen this perch because the tree had lodged itself at a sharp angle when it fell, giving a lookout point over miles of the island. The sun beat down, bludgeoning even the birds to silence, turning the sea to an enamel plate. All round him, down to the sea, up to the grey crags behind the lodge, across to the sulphurous east side of the island, a heavy green cumulus of vegetation lay over everything that grew or breathed. He kept watching as if, like cloud, it might break apart and show him what he was looking for, but not so much as a leaf moved.

* * *

'It's hot,' Justin said. He looked at Debbie as if he expected her to do something about it.

'It's not so bad if you keep in the shade.'

Just as it was getting intolerably hot, they'd come to a rock face in the forest. Debbie, who had a good memory for maps, thought it might be part of the ridge that ran down from the Devil's Bath Tub, the one where Morton said the iguanas came to sunbathe. Justin didn't know or care. He was on his feet, fidgeting, pacing around on the patch of earth by the rock face, while Debbie sat with her back to it, in a few feet of shade. She'd made room for him beside her, but he went on pacing.

'I'm thirsty. Have we got any water left?'

'Just under a litre, but it's got to last till evening. We can get over to the stream then, when they've all gone back to the lodge.'

'We should have brought more with us.'

She said nothing. In their flight, she'd been the one who'd thought of food and water. He'd have dashed off with nothing. It was this impracticality of his, this incapacity for survival in spite of the fact he was six years older, that had decided her when, out of the blue, he'd suggested she should go with him. She knew he couldn't manage on his own.

'What do you think he's doing now?'

When they'd got to the rock ridge he'd helped her scramble to the top of it to see if there were any signs of people coming after them. All she'd seen were two wisps of smoke, close to each other, from the other side of the island near the clear water stream. 'I expect they're cooking lunch.'

Making shelters, making soup, making jokes. Silly, all of it, but half of her wanted to be back there, wanted to be found even.

Which was daft, because she'd been the one who'd made sure so far that they hadn't been found. Justin had no plans beyond getting away from the lodge and Birdie before daylight. She, knowing the programme would keep the party by the clear water stream all day, had suggested making for the sulphur side of the island. People wouldn't expect to find them there.

Justin had fished a tin of sardines out of her haversack and was making clumsy attempts to open it. He managed a jagged tear, cut his thumb, cursed.

'Let me do it.'

She finished off the job and handed the tin back to him. There were no more than a few fins and an inch of tail left when he asked, 'Did you want some?'

She shook her head. 'We've got to save food.'

She hadn't taken a lot because of not wanting to leave the others short, but the need to save food led to a question she'd been trying not to ask him.

'What are we going to do next?'

He looked down at her and munched sardine tail.

'Go to the harbour. Get a boat.'

'But there might not be a boat.'

'We can signal. Get somebody to pick us up on a yacht and take us to Barbados. I've got plenty of plastic. We can get a flight to London.'

'Oh.'

Creeping out of the lodge before daylight, softly down the side stairs so as not to wake her father; that had been all right. This was something different. He looked older now, much older, in spite of the dribble of sardine oil down his chin.

'First flight to London, then I walk into my father's office and say "Hello Dad" just when he thinks your father's shovelling me into a plastic sack in this God-forsaken compost heap.'

She said nothing. Druggies had fantasies, she knew that, and it was worse when they were coming off. What they needed was somebody to believe in them, stick by them, somebody strong enough to be there and take it all.

'Or perhaps I won't walk in straight away. I'll wait till they publish them and he's in a board meeting, then I'll go in and put the paper down in front of him and say . . .'

'What paper?'

It would help to know something about the fantasies.

'Depends who pays most. I should get twenty thousand at least.'

'Justin, what are you talking about?'

He laughed, threw the sardine can away and at last came to crouch behind her in the strip of shade. He smiled, the first real smile she'd had from him.

'Want to see a photograph of my father?'

He brought a handful of transparencies in yellow plastic mounts out of his pocket and handed one to her, carefully, by its edge. She had to lean out into the sunlight to get a good look at it and he watched, still smiling, for her reaction.

'Is it . . . Is it a fancy dress party?'

He laughed. 'Not quite.'

A man, quite an old man, older than her dad, in school cap and short trousers. You could see he was in short trousers because he was bending over. And there was a woman wearing a black mask and an academic gown like the head wore on speech days, and a black leotard under the gown, showing long bare legs. She was waving a cane like teachers always had in comics.

'Oh, it's one of those places,' she said.

She was pleased with herself for sounding so calm about it, bored almost, but the picture gave her a funny greasy feeling inside and she knew if Justin had tried to touch her at that moment she'd have edged away, although it wasn't his fault his father was like that.

Justin was watching her closely. He said, 'That's the man who thinks he'd be Home Secretary if it weren't for me. It's the hypocrisy of it that gets me.'

'Yes, the hypocrisy.'

She tried to hand the transparency back, but he wouldn't take it.

'I want you to keep it, and these others.'

'Why would I want it?'

It felt heavy, oily in her hand.

'Because they're safer with you. My father'll do anything to get his hands on them. That's why he hired your father to bring me to this place.'

'I thought you said he was paying my father to kill you.'

She could say that because she knew it was one of his fantasies. The picture was a different matter.

'Both. Get the photos, then kill me. He thinks he'll be safe then.'

He forced the other transparencies into her reluctant hand.

'So you take them. He'll never think of you having them.'

When she didn't move or answer an impatient look came over his face, then a smile that wasn't as open as the one before.

'You shocked?'

'No, of course not.'

Important not to be shocked, or he'd stop trusting her. That

51

was the problem, not being able to trust people.

'That's all right then. Wrap them up in a tissue or something and put them away in your pack.'

He watched while she did it, then the open smile was back again. 'You're a great kid, Debbie. You trust me, don't you?'

She nodded and he moved closer. His arm came around her shoulders and his hand slid under her overalls until it came to her collar bone. She held her breath, waiting for it to slide further, but it stayed where it was, massaging skin and bone, first gently, then with more force.

'Here, what are you doing? Looking for a secret compartment or something?'

The fingers turned gentle again and, after a while, she dozed, head on his shoulder. When she woke, the sun had started its track down to the west and his eyes were open, staring down at her.

'I've been thinking, we could give your father a run for his money.'

'How?' It bothered her that he should be thinking about that all the time she was asleep.

'Leave messages to get him confused. Split up even, so he doesn't know which of us he's following.'

'I don't want to hurt him.'

'Don't you? Well, he wants to hurt me. Got a pencil and paper?'

She passed over a spiral-bound pad and a red felt-tip from her pack and watched as he scrawled away. After a while he tore half a dozen pages off and passed them to her. 'To the Bargain Basement Hit Man. One of us isn't going to get off this island alive – and it isn't me.' 'I'm watching you, Birdie Linnet. You're not worth the blood money my father's paying you.' 'Birdie Linnet. This is to let you know that if you follow me it's at your own risk. I reserve the right to retalliate.'

She handed them back. 'There's only one "l" in retaliate.'

He took no notice, concentrating on flourishing his signature at the foot of each page.

'When you go to get the water tonight, you could leave a few of these around where he'll find them; stick them on trees and so on. Keep him worried.'

'It's a bit childish, isn't it?'

He stared and she thought this was going to be the moment when he decided that she was like the rest of them and couldn't be trusted. It was touch and go, she could feel it, but in the space of a dozen or so heart beats the hardness left his face, to be replaced by a disappointed expression that made him look younger than she was herself.

'I just thought it might be a laugh, that's all.'

He turned his head away, folding the sheets in half, stowing them in his pack. His disappointment went to her heart.

'I'm sorry, Justin. But he is my father.'

He nodded, still turned away from her. With the feeling almost of consoling a child she slid an arm around his shoulders, put her face close to his. Suddenly, with a convulsive movement, he had his arms around her waist, his face nuzzled against her chest. His shoulders were rising and falling and, after the first shock, a warm feeling like a sense of achievement spread through her body as she realised he was crying, sobbing like a baby and holding on to her as if she were his only safety in the world.

'Don't cry, Justin. Don't cry. I won't leave you.'

She patted his shoulder and went on murmuring until the sobs subsided, his head sank down into her lap and he slept. She was kneeling and her legs were cramped, but she made no attempt to move, only changing the position of their two packs so that they shaded his face from the sun, gently so as not to wake him. Once, from a long way off, she heard shouts and laughter that must have been the survival party, but they came from another universe.

When he woke at last the sun was low, not far above the trees, and the grey rock they were leaning on had turned gold in the light of it. That seemed to bother him and he scrambled up and away from her, with an abruptness that would have hurt if she'd let it.

'What time is it?'

His face had gone older again and his voice was harsh. She reminded herself that some men were embarrassed about crying.

'Nearly half-past five.'

He looked at her as if it were her fault.

'I've got to go. I've got to see somebody.'

'Go where?'

He grabbed his pack and she picked up hers, ready to follow, thinking the escape fantasy had got to him again.

'I don't want you to come with me. Just me.'

'You can't go off on your own.'

But he was already on the move, wild with impatience, going back the way they'd come, up the narrow path that led to the Devil's Bath Tub, then on to the lodge. She took a few steps after him, but he rounded on her.

'I told you not to come with me.'

The disappointment was the most bitter thing she could remember.

'Are you coming back?'

'Yes, yes, I'll be back.'

But there was no reassurance in the way he said it. He was turning away again when a thought struck him.

'Those transparencies; you've got them safe?'

'I don't want the bloody things.'

She was appalled at the anger in her own voice and even he seemed surprised. His voice became calming, wheedling.

'You won't lose by it, Debbie. I'll cut you in for ten per cent. Two thousand pounds all for yourself.'

There was a tenderness in the way he spoke when he promised her two thousand pounds that hadn't been there before.

'I don't want the money.'

'Of course you do.'

It was like an adult talking to a child now. 'You look after them and don't go running back to your father with them. Will you do that for me, at least?'

'But you're coming back? Back here?'

'Of course I am, Debbie. But I've got to go now, you understand?'

And, without waiting to see whether she understood or not, he was gone, hurrying up towards the sulphur smell, leaving her watching the bushes swaying where he'd pushed past them in his hurry.

CHAPTER FIVE

When the sun set, Birdie admitted to himself how much he'd depended on finding her while the daylight lasted. As the afternoon went on, his attempts had got more desperate. While the rest of them were having tea and resting, in preparation for the night exercise, he'd even run the six miles down to the harbour and back in case they were there, waiting for a boat. No sign of them. Six miles down and six miles back uphill in one hour and fifty minutes and, even with the sun past its peak, an atmosphere like a Turkish bath. Morton said he was mad. Morton was now down at his bungalow giving his bloody peccary its evening meal, and the night search – or the night exercise, keeping to the fiction – couldn't start until he got back.

He wasn't sure how many of the customers understood that finding Debbie and Justin was an urgent necessity for him, how many still believed it was part of the set-up laid on for them. Certainly none of them seemed to share his urgency. Now, when he'd have liked to see them lined up and ready to go the moment Morton got back, there were only three on the balcony with him: Simon, Mal and Henry. The rest were wandering off God knows where, and the three remaining were no help to him. Simon was wandering around bleating about where his wife had got to and his mood hadn't been helped at all when Henry had informed him breezily that he'd seen her going down the road with Russ for a look at the fireflies.

'But there are plenty of fireflies here,' he'd protested. 'They could see plenty of fireflies here.'

Mal and Henry in their turn were fidgeting around killing time till the Helibels got back and they, apparently, had gone off to the stream to wash their hair.

'On a survival exercise, for goodness sake,' Birdie groaned. But they'd told Mal they couldn't possibly survive with their hair all yuck. Birdie didn't even have to ask about Toby and Peter. He knew they'd be intruding on the privacy of some wretched animal or insect.

As the dusk came the rain switched itself on like a shower and this at least brought Ellie and Russ back, soaked and laughing like a pair of children. The laughter stopped when they saw Simon staring at them and Ellie, with a rueful look at Russ, went over to him and said something in a low voice. By the look of his hunched shoulders, if it was meant to be conciliatory, it hadn't worked.

Russ walked over to Birdie and asked in the hushed voice that was his idea of tact, 'Not back yet, then?'

Birdie shook his head.

'Don't worry. We'll find her for you.'

Soon after that, Toby and Peter got back, full of some night bird they'd seen, or nearly seen. There was an air of childlike excitement about them and they seemed as eager as Russ for the night walk in the forest, packing their haversacks with an assortment of small tins or tubes that Birdie supposed were meant to hold specimens. He'd have to watch those two. He didn't want them wandering off and getting lost to add to his problems. It was half-past seven and completely dark before Helena and Annabel got back and it was clear at once that something had gone wrong. Annabel stamped onto the balcony first, her sarong dripping wet and clinging from the rain, her long blonde hair flopping round her shoulders. Helena followed, equally soaked, shoulders hunched under a towelling beach robe, and rolled her eyes pathetically at Mal.

'Local salon up to standard?' Henry wasn't sensitive to atmosphere.

Helena said nothing, sitting hunched at the table with her back to Annabel.

'What's up, darling?'

Annabel said, through clenched teeth, 'She dropped the shampoo in the bloody stream.'

'It wasn't my fault,' said Helena, without turning round. Her voice sounded tearful and Mal put an arm around her.

Toby and Peter immediately started fussing about what shampoo would do to the fish life. Annabel asked them what was so special about a few fish, for goodness sake, it wasn't as if anybody was going to eat them. Russ launched into a description of a fish trap he was pretty sure would work if you had a mattress spring, and when Simon asked, reasonably enough, where you'd get a mattress spring in the middle of a rain forest, Ellie turned on her husband and asked why he had to be so bloody negative all the time. It was in the middle of all this that Morton appeared on the balcony, dark hair slicked down by the rain and a strong smell of rum about him. If he had to choose the perfect party not to go into the rain forest with, Birdie thought, he'd come up with something like this assortment. He was listening to them with only half his attention, wondering all the time about Debbie. Was she out in this rain? Had they made a shelter? If they had made a shelter, what were they doing in it?

Morton was, at least, managing to calm the argument about the shampoo and the fish. Helena and Annabel were typically vague about the point in the stream where they'd dropped it but he unrolled a map in the lamplight and was pointing out likely places, reassuring Toby and Peter that one bottle of shampoo in all that water was unlikely to do any serious ecological harm.

'You do know a lot,' Helena said seriously, looking up at him with great damp eyes.

Mal and Henry snorted with laughter, but Morton took the compliment as seriously as it was offered.

'There's nothing I don't know about this island. Every little stream I know, and where it goes to. The professors get their names on the books, but who told them, eh? Who told them?'

He'd dropped his paw of a hand over Helena's small white one and was looking soulfully into her eyes. Helena shrank away from him, but Annabel was there to rescue her.

'You did, of course, Morton. I suppose you introduced them to every rock and peccary.'

He managed to keep hold of both of them for a while, then, with a rum-billowing sigh, released Helena's hand in favour of Annabel's waist. He tottered and leaned back, head on her shoulders.

'Every rock and peccary, and their mothers and fathers. You believe me, girl?'

'I believe you.'

Birdie tried to break it up. 'We'd better be getting organised, Morton.'

He got a squinting glare for that.

'You get them organised. Your job. We've got better things to do, haven't we, girl?' He squeezed Annabel's ribs till she giggled.

'Morton . . .'

'It's all right, Birdie,' Annabel told him. 'I can look after Morton.'

'Perhaps he'll help you with your mosquito repellent.' He couldn't help it. He was conscious too of Henry's eyes on Annabel. If these were her tactics to bring Henry to heel, he wasn't flattered.

He clapped his hands to get the rest of the party's attention, trying to ignore the pair of them. 'Escape and evasion. We'll split into two teams. One goes with Morton and does the escaping. The other comes with me and tries to catch them.'

The rules, worked out beforehand, were simple enough. The escaping group would have two torches and a half hour's start. Their aim was to get to Morton's bungalow, grab a flag flying from his balcony rail, and get it back to the lodge before the other side caught up with them.

For Birdie, though, there was a different aim that he couldn't talk about. As far as he was concerned, Morton's team could capture all the flags in the Caribbean as long as, in the course of the night, he could find Debbie. Find Debbie, then reorganise the superior smirk on Justin's face. Still, he had to make a show of giving the customers their money's worth.

'Right, who wants to be an escaper with Morton?'

Russ did, of course. One pace forward, first to volunteer.

'I'll take care of it, Birdie.'

Birdie found his eyes drawn to Ellie and knew the rest of them were looking that way too. Her 'I'll go with Morton' was no more than a formality.

'So will I.' Simon's voice was sulky and too loud.

'Glad to have you aboard, Simon,' Russ said. Ellie ignored her husband.

Birdie, foreseeing trouble, looked for a stabilising influence and did the best he could with the material available. 'What about going with them, Mal?'

Morton, moving over reluctantly to join his group of escapers, tried to take Annabel with him but she wouldn't go.

'No. I want to be one of Birdie's bloodhounds.'

She whispered something in his ear, then moved herself firmly out of reach. She was bright-eyed and excited, possibly at the prospect of crashing around in the rain forest all night but more likely, Birdie thought, at her success in getting half the men in the place running round in circles after her. She grabbed Henry by the hand and pulled him up off the bench.

'Come on, Henry, you want to be a bloodhound, don't you? You too, Helena.'

This left only Toby and Peter unclaimed.

'One of you with Morton, one with me,' Birdie suggested, but they were inseparable. Russ, who seemed determined to take charge of Morton's party from the start, flatly refused to let them join it.

'They'll be stopping every time they see a bloody glow worm.'

So, like it or not, Birdie got them both. His tracker party now consisted of the Helibels, Henry, Toby and Peter.

Outside, the rain had stopped as suddenly as it started. The leaves were dripping and the full moon rising from broken cloud. As Birdie looked up at it, Russ came to stand beside him.

'You know Morton's pissed?'

'He's had a drink or two, yes.'

'Don't you worry, Birdie. I'll look after them.'

'Thanks, Russ.' He tried to sound more grateful than he felt.

'And, Birdie, don't worry about this other thing. I'll keep a look out too. We're bound to find her between us.'

He was ashamed his worry was so obvious and made himself concentrate on what he was supposed to be doing. He got Morton into a corner and impressed on him the importance of not trying anything too ambitious. The escapers were to keep to the paths and animal tracks whenever possible. If they needed to hide, they were to stay as close to the paths as possible and, for goodness sake, keep together. He noticed lamplight glinting on the machete stuck casually in Morton's belt.

'You'd better keep that in your hands. They'd only hurt themselves with it. And, watch Simon. He's your weakest.'

Morton promised, making an effort to concentrate, and Birdie reassured himself that, drunk or sober, the man really did know the island better than any of them.

The others watched as Morton's party went one by one down the steps and into the darkness of the forest, like swimmers into a pool; Morton first, then Russ with the big battery lamp, Ellie, Simon giving a departing glance at Birdie as if he blamed him for everything, and finally Mal with the smaller torch. For a few minutes they were visible as a patch of green light threading its way through the trees, then the torches went out.

'They don't want us to know which way they're going,' Annabel said. 'I'll bet they'll double back towards the Devil's Bath Tub to confuse us.'

Birdie agreed with her. It would be an obvious tactic to make a feint that way, in the opposite direction from their objective, just the sort of thing Russ would suggest and think he was being clever. Anyway, he had his own reasons for wanting to go to the Bath Tub.

'Why would they do that?' Henry asked.

He was fiddling with his digital watch, trying to set it to give an alarm when the escapers' half hour was up. Annabel took it and did it for him and Birdie noticed her fingers lingered a long time on his wrist when she strapped it back. Well, it was none of his business. Good luck to her, if that was what she wanted. Of the rest of his party, Toby and Peter were fussing with unnecessarily large packs, as if they expected to be out for weeks, and Helena was sitting at the table looking apprehensive. He went over to her.

'You don't have to come on this if you don't want to.'

'No, I'll come. I don't want to stay here all on my own.' She looked across at Henry and Annabel and Birdie guessed she was feeling shut out. He should have sent her with Mal and given her a chance to catch up.

'You keep with me. I'll look after you.'

He got a wan smile for that.

Ten minutes to go, and now Toby and Peter seemed to be having a brotherly argument. He heard them whispering ferociously to each other in the doorway to the domitories.

'You packed them,' Peter was saying.
'I know I packed them, and I know how many there were.'
'Well, there aren't now.'
They glared at each other.
'What's missing?' Birdie asked.
They seemed embarrassed.
'Specimen jars,' Toby said.
'You won't have much time for collecting specimens tonight. You'll have to keep up with the rest of us. Don't go wandering off.'

At five minutes to the half hour Birdie's team were gathered by the balcony rail, as ready as they'd ever be. He'd asked for silence so that they could listen for Morton's party, but there'd been no sound of them so far. It was possible even that they were hiding not far from the lodge, waiting to see his party go off in the wrong direction before making a dash for the road. That was a bit subtle for Russ and way beyond Morton in his present state, but Ellie might have thought of it.

'They could be anywhere.'
That was Henry, sounding aggrieved.
'But that's the whole point, darling.'
Birdie was aware of Annabel behind him, so close that he could feel her breasts against his back, through the fabric of their camouflage overalls.
'Perhaps we'll find Debbie.' Her voice close to his ear came as a shock because it echoed his own thoughts.
'I hope so.'
'Where do you think they are?'
'I wish I knew.'
Toby, roused from some private dream of bugs or peccaries, said, 'Are you still looking for her?'
'That's right, Toby.'
He didn't expect any sympathy from that quarter, but expected still less what he got.
Toby said, 'We've seen her.'
Birdie spun round. 'Seen Debbie? When? Where?'
'Earlier this evening. What time was it, Peter?'
Peter too took a while to surface. 'About seven, before it got dark. Near the sulphur place.'
'Why didn't you tell me, for heaven's sake?'

'We thought she must have come back.'

'Didn't you say something to her?'

'We weren't that close. We were up on the rocks looking for spiders. Anyway, we didn't like to interrupt.'

'Interrupt what?' Birdie was nearly frantic. It was as much as he could do to stop himself shouting at them.

They were silent, then Toby said in his precise little voice, 'They were embracing.'

The others were listening intently and Birdie knew it wasn't for noises in the forest. For Debbie's sake he had to keep calm.

'When you say they, you mean she was with Justin?'

'Yes.'

'You're sure it was them?'

'He's the one with the yellow hair, isn't he?'

'Yes.'

'It was him. I remember because my brother said it was funny because he thought he was probably a homosexual and I said he obviously wasn't.'

'And then I suppose you just went on looking for spiders?' The sarcasm got through to them and they both looked hurt.'

'We came back,' Peter said. 'We knew you wanted to go out on this exercise.'

Annabel said, 'You're sure it was Debbie he was with?'

Birdie was grateful to her for trying, but he had no doubts.

Toby said, 'We, um, didn't get a very good view of the female of the species but they had, um, paired off together, hadn't they?'

'You must have realised I've been looking for them all day.'

'We thought that was meant to be part of the game.'

Henry said impatiently, 'Shouldn't we be going? It must be well over the half hour by now.'

Distractedly, Birdie lined them up, Helena after him so that he could keep an eye on her, Annabel, Toby and Peter. He put Henry at the back with the second torch.

'We'll assume that Annabel's right and the other team made for the Devil's Bath Tub.'

If they doubted his motives for going there, they were right, but at least they were tactful enough not to say it.

After Justin left her, Debbie climbed to the top of the rock ridge.

When she was left on her own she'd felt as if the trees were pressing down and in on her, cramping her in a box of vegetation that would get smaller and smaller until there was no room for breathing or movement. She could breathe more easily up on the ridge and look down to the sea and the white sails of yachts making for St Lucia before it got dark. From there too she'd be able to see the bushes moving if Justin came back to her. He'd said he'd come back and she tried to believe he meant it, but the sea turned from blue, to gold, to deep purple, and still no Justin. When the rain came she scrambled down to shelter under the trees, but when it stopped she climbed back to her place on the ridge. She felt safer there, if she had to spend the night out on her own. Earlier, while it was raining, it had been in her mind that she should go back to the others at the lodge, but then if Justin came back and found she hadn't waited, that would be one more person who'd let him down. By the time the moon was up she knew he wasn't coming but, even if she could have found her way back without a torch, she'd have had to admit that Justin had gone off and left her on her own. She knew what her father would say about that, and what she'd say to him, so there'd be another argument.

Later, when she saw the torchlight below her moving through the trees, and when the first fear at its oddness was over, she thought it was her father come to find her and she was half glad, half sorry. Then she heard Russ's voice.

'We'll stop here for ten minutes and listen. If we don't hear Birdie's lot coming after us, we'll double back towards the road.'

So it was only another of their silly survival games. She felt detached and superior on her rock while voices whispered and torchlight made a green cavern just under where she was sitting. There was a complaining voice she recognised as Simon's.

'Shouldn't we wait for Morton?'

Russ said, 'He'll catch up with us if he wants to.'

'Yes, but he's meant to be in charge of us.'

Then Ellie's sharp voice. 'Morton's not capable of being in charge of anything.'

'Yes, but I don't see why Russ has to . . .'

'Well, someone has to.'

Then Mal's voice. 'If we're going to sit around here arguing at the tops of our voices, we might as well shout to Birdie to come and get us.'

Silence fell, while Debbie congratulated herself on not calling out when she first saw the torches. If there was anything she fancied less than a survival exercise it was more marital bickering between Simon and Ellie. After about five minutes of quiet, Russ decreed that they should move off, torches shaded and pointed downwards. As the forest swallowed them, Simon was still whispering complaints.

It seemed darker when they'd gone. She sat there wondering if her father would come and whether she'd call to him if he did. Within an hour, crashing branches and squawking night birds warned her they were on their way. She saw lights then heard the husky, penetrating voice of Annabel.

'You'll have to wait, Birdie. I've got something wrapped around my ankle.'

Helena squeaked that it might be a boa constrictor and her father's voice, sounding tired, said there weren't any boa constrictors on the island. She could hear him going back and unwrapping Annabel's ankle. It seemed to cause a lot of giggling and confusion and the impulse she'd had when she'd heard his voice to call out to him died away. She couldn't stand Annabel, or her ankles, or the way she had of sitting on the table and twiddling them so you noticed her long, high-arched feet. Feet were for walking on, not twiddling. She couldn't understand why her father got a job that involved dealing with the likes of Annabel. It occurred to her that she hadn't heard Henry's public school bleat, but where Annabel was Henry wouldn't be far away.

Helena was complaining that she was tired. She coughed pathetically and said her throat was all rough from the sulphur place. Why had Birdie dragged them all the way up there and down again?

Annabel said, very matter-of-fact, 'Because he hoped Debbie and Justin would still be there.'

Debbie nearly fell off the ridge. She shuffled forward on her bottom, not wanting to miss anything.

'You're quite sure it was them, Toby?'

Annabel's voice again, then a growling murmur from Toby that Debbie couldn't catch.

She didn't understand it at all. She and Justin hadn't been at the Devil's Bath Tub. Justin, she supposed, might have gone there after he left her, was even heading in that direction. But Annabel had talked about 'them'. Who had Toby seen and why were they all so certain it was her and Justin? She resented the idea that people had been spying on them both, spying and getting it wrong.

Annabel asked, 'So where do you think they are then, Birdie?' And Debbie hated the sympathetic tone in her voice.

'I wish I knew. It's her second night out in all this. I'll kill that little sod when I find him.'

After that, they started chattering about where Morton's team had got to. They guessed, correctly, that they'd have doubled back to the road and her father had a plan to follow the path down beside the ridge, then turn towards the road lower down and cut them off. When they were talking about it, she felt older than any of them. They were playing games, but it was the real thing for her. There were sounds of the group getting itself together, Annabel and Helena chattering, Peter and Toby talking to themselves in low tones. Then her father's voice, a little apart from the rest of them, so close to her that she felt she could touch his head with her toe if she stretched her foot down.

'Debbie. Debbie, love.'

But it was a defeated sound, as if he'd given up expecting an answer. She felt all mixed up inside and might have stretched out her foot, might have called to him, if it hadn't been for the others there and what he'd said about Justin. He gave up after a while, and they moved off towards the road. Or most of them did. It seemed to her that one of them had gone off in a different direction from the others, back towards the lodge or the sulphur place. But it might have been some animal intent on its own escape and evasion and in any case it was nothing to do with her. She listened until the sounds died away, then wrapped herself in a polythene sheet from her pack and curled up in a dip in the rock, wondering if iguanas found it more comfortable.

About an hour after their halt by the rock ridge, Birdie found that two of his party were missing. What with looking after Helena and worrying about Debbie, he hadn't given as much attention as he should to the rest of them, contenting himself with calling back every ten minutes or so to ask if they were all right. Invariably, Toby or Peter would answer that they were. Just before they got to the waterfall at the end of the rock ridge he stopped, casting round with the torch beam to find the narrow path back to the road. The battery was going, and rather than waste time replacing it he called to Henry at the back of the line to bring him the other one. No response.

'Henry. Where's Henry?'

There was no answer, except a little shuddering sigh from Helena.

'Peter, is Henry there?'

'No. I think he went off on his own.' Peter sounded quite unconcerned about it.

'Why should he go off on his own? When?'

Helena said, in a small, sad voice, 'Annabel's gone too.'

And so they had. Between the stop by the ridge and the stop near the waterfall the two of them had disappeared, taking the second torch with them. Neither Toby nor Peter would take an intelligent interest in how and when it had happened. As for Helena, when Birdie spoke to her sharply, she started crying.

'I didn't know she was going to do it. I kept looking back for her and she wasn't there.'

'Then why the hell didn't you tell me?'

No answer, only more sobs, but he could guess the reason. Annabel and Henry would have decided before the trip started that they'd take themselves back to the lodge at the first opportunity, to have it to themselves while the others were escaping and evading all over the forest. Typical. Annabel had, presumably, bullied Helena into not saying anything about it until too late.

Grimly he led his three survivors along the narrow path to the road. There was no question now of cutting the other team off or even looking for Debbie. His job, dangerously neglected, was to get straight back to the lodge and make sure the two half-wits had arrived there safely. If that involved dragging them off the nest, that was fine by him.

When they got to the road it was almost midnight, with the moon bright enough to cast shadows. There was no sight or sound of the other party, so he rummaged in his pack to find the green flare, their pre-arranged signal to call off the exercise and make for home. As it broke against the sky he shouted loudly to Russ and Morton, telling them the game was over and they could come out of hiding.

Toby, looking worried now and probably ashamed of his irresponsibility, produced a constructive idea for once.

'Peter and I will go down and see if they're at Morton's place. You can take her back.' He obviously couldn't even remember Helena's name.

Birdie was reluctant to split up the party any further, but he could see the sense of it. Helena was drooping and trembling with tiredness.

'All right, but for goodness sake keep to the road and don't go any further than Morton's bungalow. If they're not there, come straight back.'

He let Toby have the torch; there was enough moonlight to see himself and Helena home. They were about half way up the road to the lodge when they heard Russ's voice calling from bushes on their left. Birdie answered and Russ stepped out onto the road, followed by Ellie and Mal. Russ had leaves sticking in his hair. Birdie wasn't sure whether they'd got there by accident or were his idea of camouflage for a night exercise.

'What's up, Birdie? We saw the flare.'

Birdie explained about losing Henry and Annabel and having to go back to make sure they were safe. Russ looked cheated.

'That's a pity, Birdie. We'd have won easily. We were following the stream down to Morton's bungalow.'

The legs of his trousers and Ellie's were wet to the knees. Mal, who was standing back and saying nothing, looked as if he'd been going more carefully.

Birdie said, 'Call the other two. We'd better get moving.' Toby and Peter would have a fool's errand down to Morton's bungalow and back, but that was just too bad.

For once, Russ looked a little shamefaced. 'Easier said than done, Birdie. The fact is . . .'

'The fact is,' said Mal, 'he's lost them.'

Birdie stared. 'Lost Morton and Simon?'

Russ was blushing and fidgeting under his leaves. 'We didn't lose Morton, Morton lost us. He was too drunk to know what he was doing. You shouldn't have put him in charge in the first place.'

'But what happened?'

Mal said, 'Soon after we started, Morton just disappeared. Simon and I wanted to stay and look for him, but Russ and Ellie said he'd probably gone to sleep under a tree and we were better off without him.'

Russ gave him a glare. 'It was supposed to be an escape and evasion exercise, not an outing for Alcoholics Anonymous.'

'Where was this?'

'Not far from the Devil's Bath Tub.'

Ellie's strained white face told Birdie that worse was to come.

'And Simon? What happened to Simon?'

Ellie and Russ looked at each other, then at Birdie, then at the ground, leaving Mal to do the explaining again.

'We lost Simon later, about an hour ago. That was after we got over here by the freshwater stream.'

'Lost? He isn't a bloody dog, is he? How did you lose Simon?' He looked at Ellie again. 'I suppose you had an argument.'

She nodded, without meeting his eyes.

Mal said, 'Simon didn't like wading down the stream. He said it was bad for his athlete's foot. Russ was insulting about Simon's feet and . . .'

'I wasn't insulting. I only said if he was being hunted for his life through the jungle by communist gorillas, it wouldn't be any use telling them about his athlete's foot.'

'And I said, "Guerillas, not gorillas",' Ellie murmured.

'Then Simon said he didn't suppose Russ would know the difference and Ellie stood up for Russ . . .'

'Well, he shouldn't have said it.'

'. . . and Simon said something insulting about Russ and Ellie and stormed off, or squelched off, rather, back towards the road.'

'Why didn't you stop him? It's crazy to let anybody go wandering about on his own at night.'

'We thought it would only make things worse. Anyway, it wasn't far from where we were to the road. He's probably back at the lodge powdering his feet by now.'

It was some small consolation to Birdie that Simon, squelching back to the lodge in a temper, would at least spoil Henry and Annabel's arrangements. He was planning some strong words for all three defectors. As for Morton, when he eventually crawled out from behind some tree there'd be no mercy for hangovers. It was a silent and sulky group that trudged back up the moonlit road, with all the tropical night that they'd paid for wasted on them.

CHAPTER SIX

Annabel was waiting for them on the balcony, golden and satisfied as a sleek cat in the lamplight, perched on one of the wooden benches with bare feet, hands round her knees.

'Hello, had a nice exercise?'

Birdie said, 'You shouldn't have gone off like that. You know I told you to keep together.'

'Sorry, Birdie. Did I spoil your night?'

But she didn't sound in the least sorry. To his ears at any rate there was a suggestion in the way she said it that jealousy was what was biting him.

'Where's Henry?'

She waved a hand towards the dormitories. 'Would you believe I've just collected a fiancé who snores?'

'Fiancé?' Mal said.

'Um.' Annabel raised a hand towards the lamp, displaying twin trophies: Henry's watch and a twist of creeper round her engagement finger.

'You're engaged?' Helena said. 'To Henry?'

She sounded far from pleased about it and Birdie could guess why. It had been a race between those two from the start, and Annabel had taken an unfair advantage by disappearing with Henry, leaving her friend to do the Girl Guide bit through the jungle. Annabel rubbed it in.

'Your turn now, darling.'

What with that and the exhaustion, it was no wonder Helena broke down in tears. Annabel, repentant, insisted she must go to bed at once, but at once, and had got her as far as the doorway before they were stopped by Ellie's voice.

'Have you seen my husband?'

Annabel gave her a sunny smile. 'Never more than one a night, that's my principle.'

She disappeared, practically dragging Helena with her.

'Bitch,' Ellie said.

Birdie, without much hope, checked the men's dormitory but found only Henry, flat out on his back and mouth open. The volume of his snoring made Birdie wonder what income would make it worthwhile for Annabel to put up with it until alimony did them part. He shook Henry by the shoulder, as much to relieve his bad temper as with any hope of information, but he could hardly get him to open his eyes. He could smell mosquito repellent on his skin. It must have been some session.

On the way out he collided with Annabel in the corridor. 'Practising on me, were you?'

She looked quite startled at the question, but perhaps she'd already forgotten about it.

Ellie was waiting on the balcony, taut as a wire. 'Well?'

'Simon's not there. It looks as if he hasn't got back yet.'

'But he should have been back a long time before us.'

Russ was already shouldering his pack again.

'Search party. Ellie and I'll go down as far as the stream, then you can . . .'

'No. You two have done enough damage for the night. You're staying where you are. If there's any searching to be done, I'm doing it.' His hope was that Simon might have got to Morton's bungalow, in which case Toby and Peter should find him and bring him back with them. He put this to the party and told them not to stir as much as a yard from the lodge while he went down to look. Surprised by his anger, Russ and Ellie seemed to accept this quietly enough, but this time it was Mal who raised objections. He got Birdie in a corner, out of earshot of Russ and Ellie.

'Birdie, you don't think Simon might have done something silly?'

'Like what?'

'That was a real row he had with Ellie. Those two are playing it down. He sounded really, well, desperate.'

Annabel wandered over. 'I can't imagine Simon being desperate.'

'Well, he was. I mean, suppose he didn't keep to the road? Suppose he just wandered off into the forest and . . . well . . .?'

Birdie got a glimmering at last. 'You mean, he might have been suicidal?'

Mal looked embarrassed. 'I've been thinking about that time at the Devil's Bath Tub when Russ was playing the fool. I mean, that was when it got serious, this thing with Russ and Ellie. Simon's the type that broods.'

'You're seriously telling me you think Simon went to drown himself in the Devil's Bath Tub?'

Annabel said, 'I think that's crazy, Mal; just morbid.'

Birdie thought so too. In the face of their combined attack, Mal looked even more worried but stood his ground.

'We could go there for a look. I'll come with you.'

'Oh, no, you don't. I told you, I'm not having anybody else wandering off tonight.'

But once Mal had put the idea into his mind he couldn't get rid of the memory of Russ plunging his arm into the sulphur pool, the way Ellie had looked at Russ and Simon had looked at Ellie.

'I'll go and have a look at the Bath Tub first, then the bungalow.'

He collected a new battery for his torch, then, deciding he might as well have the machete with him, went to the kitchen for it, until the sight of the empty nail reminded him that Justin had taken it. In spite of the idiocy of everybody else's behaviour, he still had the idea that Justin was the source of all his problems. Trouble in a concentrated dose, that lad. He'd set the others off. He felt bone tired as well as worried by now and had to force himself to go, for the second time that night, along the slippery path to the Devil's Bath Tub.

The smell of sulphur came to meet him, the sparse vegetation fell away and he stepped onto the rock plateau. The moon was well down by now and the light not as good. He had to use the torch beam to pick his way across the rock to the pool. The heat struck up through his boot soles and he could hear the great abcesses of sulphur swelling and bursting in the dark. Now he was here, Mal's fears seemed daft. It would take somebody madder than poor Simon to drown himself in this black stink. Then his torch beam fell on the boot.

One boot, then another, splayed out at an angle, both toes up. Knees and thighs splayed too, then stomach and lower chest arched up, covered with camouflage cloth, moving up and down with the seethings of the water so that at first they seemed to be breathing. But nothing and nobody, not the Devil himself, could breathe with its head under the hot sulphurous water as this thing was pretending to do. He took a leg by the knee and pulled. It was hot, sticky and dampish with the moisture already travelling up from the submerged half. He got it under both knees and pulled harder, till the sunken chest came clear and the head emerged like a diabolic birth, trailing sulphurous water. He left it there, wondering how he was going to break it to Ellie, and went for his torch which he'd left lying on the rocks. Reluctantly, to confirm his certainty that the thing couldn't be living, he swept the beam over the face.

'Bloody hell!'

A bright pink face, boiled pink like a prawn and swollen already from the water, with cheeks plumper than they'd been in life. Eyes closed and mouth open, as if surprised. And that, as far as Birdie was concerned, was mutual. He was so surprised he practically dropped the torch. As far as he was concerned, the man he'd been pulling out of the Devil's Bath Tub was Simon, but here, gaping up at him in the torch beam, quite unmistakable in spite of its parboiling, was a face, sharp-nosed and yellow-toothed – the face of Morton.

His decision to get down as soon as possible to Morton's hut was because the only radio set on Diabola was there and Birdie's first reaction, in spite of what happened later, was to report the accident to the authorities on St Lucia. What complexities of officialdom would begin once he'd reported that the island's only resident had fallen, dead drunk, into the island's only tourist attraction, he couldn't bear to think about. The thing was to get a report out to somebody. He stayed just long enough to carry Morton's body well clear of the pool, then began picking his way downhill along the maze of paths Morton and the peccaries had made. By the time he got to the road it was four o'clock and the dark was turning to transparency, with trees visible as black shapes against a pale sky. He could hurry from here, and ran down the road until he saw the roof of Morton's bungalow. A few strides further and he could see that there was a light on, a square of bright yellow lamplight coming through the window and across the verandah. He stopped, puzzled, until he remembered that Toby and Peter had gone to the bungalow, and possibly Simon too. They might have decided to spend the rest of the night there. He paused at the gate and called to them. There was no answer, just a scratching sound from the back of the bungalow which he thought must come from Hamilcar, the peccary.

He rapped hard on the door with his knuckles and, getting no reply, pushed it open.

His first thought was that Morton must have been much more drunk the night before than any of them had realised. The last time he'd seen this room it was as tidy as a barracks; a table with writing things, books in orderly rows. Now it looked as if a hurricane had hit it. Morton's room wasn't just untidy, it was wrecked. Maps and charts had been torn off the walls and scattered haphazardly over the floor; books were piled on the floor in disorderly heaps as if somebody had simply upended the bookcases; the smell of rum was so strong that somebody must have opened a bottle and scattered the stuff. As for the radio, that wouldn't be sending any messages ever again. When Birdie picked it up off the floor he saw the damage was worse than could have been caused by the fall itself. Somebody had been battering it with a heavy object, probably the spade that was lying beside it on the floor.

It was this that told Birdie he was dealing with worse than a case of accident and drunkenness. It was conceivable, just, that a man in a drunken frenzy might have flung his books and papers around, but not, surely, that he'd have destroyed the radio that in an emergency was his only lifeline to other islands. Then he noticed a piece of paper on the top of Morton's desk, very orderly and square among the devastation. Red felt-tip letters on a sheet of lined paper torn off a spiral-bound pad. 'To the Bargain Basement Hit Man. One of us isn't going to get off this island alive – and it isn't me.'

'The little . . .'

Birdie crumpled the message in his hand and smoothed it out again. Evidence. Evidence of what? That Justin, in his drug-addled mind, really believed the nonsense he'd been talking about Birdie being his father's hit man and Morton his accomplice, believed it enough to wreck Morton's home then, finding him drunk and wandering by the sulphur pool, take the thing a stage further. The little sod had really done it this time, and not all his father's money and influence could save him from the consequences.

There was another worry though that came creeping up on Birdie as he stood holding the crumpled message in the middle of the wrecked room. What had Debbie been doing at the time? It was inconceivable to him that she'd helped in the attack on Morton, but had Justin for some twisted reason of his own dragged her into this vandalism, even into the leaving of the message? He knew Debbie carried a spiral-bound notebook with her because she'd used it for their provision lists, but he hadn't seen that sort of notebook in Justin's hands. The logic was that he'd stolen or borrowed it from her to write his message, but it bothered him enough to make him sure of one thing: before he handed Justin over to the nearest available authorities he had to find Debbie and discover how much she knew. And if, in the slightest possible way, the little sod had involved her in this, then he'd have to get her uninvolved before anybody started asking questions, even if it meant lying to the others for a while.

As he stood there thinking he heard the scrabbling noise again, coming from the back of the hut. Mechanically, he thought he'd better feed and water the bloody peccary. It could hardly be left there to fry in the sun. He took a last look at the disorder of the room, turned off the lamp and walked out, closing the door firmly behind him. It was quite light by now, with a cool breeze blowing from the hills behind the lodge. He stood for a while looking up the road, then strolled round the back towards the peccary pen and collected a bucket of water and a bowlful of dried pellets he hoped might be peccary food.

'Hamilcar, breakfast time.'

The door of the pen was wide open and though he called and rattled the buckets, no moustached snout appeared at the doorway of the little hut inside. It looked as if the pig had flown. Justin, in his thorough-going vandalism, must have opened the pen deliberately, and the scrabbling Birdie had heard could have been Hamilcar waking up and taking advantage of it. Well, that was one problem less. Morton had talked about letting the animal go. It might have been a satisfaction to him to think of it doing its duty for the propagation of the species.

While he'd been fiddling with the buckets it occurred to him that he couldn't leave Morton's body sprawled where he'd left it in the dark, on the plateau by the Devil's Bath Tub. He struck off the road into the forest again and, after nearly an hour's climbing, came to the plateau as the sun was rising clear of the ridge and the tree frogs were winding down for the day. The body was where he'd left it, flopped on its back with water leaking out over the rocks. He did a quick examination of it and found no obvious injuries except a soft and bruised patch behind the right ear, but that might have been caused by Morton's head striking the pool bottom when he went in. His guess was that Justin, finding Morton standing on the edge of the pool or perhaps decoying him there, had simply taken advantage of his drunkenness and pushed. A spoilt child's murder. He turned his back on the body and walked towards the pool, trying to see exactly how it had happened.

Something squashed under his boot sole, like a dog turd only firmer. Automatically he looked first at the sole of his boot, then down at the rock, and couldn't believe what he was seeing. Pink, with a nail on it, lying there on the warm rocks, a little flattened from his boot, but unmistakable. What he'd trodden on was the top two joints of a human finger. He crouched down and picked it up. It had been cut clean across at the joint, the blood on it hardened and congealed from the heat of the rocks. A few feet away from it he found another, but this one was just the tip of a finger, the nail and a little ledge of flesh. He told himself his powers of observation were going. There he was, examining Morton's body and not even noticing it was missing two bits of finger. It had been more than an impulsive push into the Bath Tub. Justin must have come at Morton with the stolen machete and he'd put up a hand to try to stop him, the sort of useless gesture a drunken man would make. He walked back to the body and lifted up the swollen hands. Left hand: all fingers present and correct. The right hand was tucked in against the rock and he had to prise it loose. It lay, heavy and confiding in his hand, complete with thumb and four fingers, not a scratch on any of them. Whoever the finger belonged to, it wasn't Morton.

The logic was that they were Justin's. Morton had done more to defend himself than putting a hand up. He'd managed to draw his machete and make at least one chop with it, and a fairly effective chop at that. He'd made sure, if nothing else, that his murderer would be marked as surely as if he'd branded him, but then Justin, maddened with the pain of it, had got near enough to push, and that was that. With a bit of luck, in this climate, Justin would have blood poisoning to add to his troubles. He wrapped the fingers in a plastic bag and stowed them in his haversack, then carried Morton's body along the path to where the square roots of the chataignier tree made a natural wooden tomb and stowed him tidily away. He noticed as he carried him that the machete had gone from his belt.

On the way back to the lodge there was something that bothered him because it seemed to be a symptom that his nerves weren't as much under control as he thought. Half way along the path he had a feeling of being watched. It was so intense that it brought the hairs rising on the back of his neck and forced him to stop and look round. He could see nothing but trees and tree shadows, hear nothing that wasn't accounted for by the ordinary sounds of the forest, but when he walked on the feeling was still there, keeping pace with him. At the lodge he went straight up the side steps to the kitchen, raspingly thirsty, and had the place to himself, although he could hear depressed voices on the balcony. He found a mug and gulped chlorinated water, staring at the every-day objects that belonged in another world, the enamel plates, the rubbish sack, the kitchen machete hanging from its nail.

He was staring at it for long seconds before he remembered that it shouldn't be there at all; that it had disappeared at the same time as Justin. Now it was hanging there quite clean and innocent, blade shining, neat white band around its wooden handle. But the handle had never had a white band and when he grabbed the machete off its hook it turned out to be a page from a spiral-bound notebook, folded up and tied round the handle with plant fibre. He unfolded it and, for the second time that morning, saw scrawled letters in red felt-tip. This time they read: 'Birdie Linnet. This is to let you know that if you follow me it's at your own risk. I reserve the right to retalliate.'

He put it in his pack, along with the fingers.

CHAPTER SEVEN

Round the corner on the balcony something like a protest meeting was going on. Faces turned to him, Ellie's strained and questioning, Henry's with the portentous look of a man who knows he should be saying something important but doesn't know what. Helena, paper-white with tiredness, rings under her eyes the colour of African violets, was flopped against Mal's shoulder. Only Annabel had a satisfied, far-away look in her eyes, but she was probably working out her wedding present list. Birdie noticed that Toby had returned and was sitting at the table with the others, but there was no sign of Peter.

Ellie asked, 'Have you found Simon?'

He shook his head. Henry appointed himself spokesman for the protest group.

'Some of us . . . er . . . don't think we're having much of a holiday, Birdie.'

You can say that again, Birdie thought. Mal was whittering something about going down to the sea for a swim. The thing couldn't be put off. Birdie cleared his throat.

'I'm afraid there's been a bad accident. Morton's dead.'

Helena gave a little scream, as if she'd just split her nail varnish. Henry's mouth dropped open and Mal's face was red and resentful. Even Toby paid attention.

'What happened?' Ellie asked, in a high, tense voice.

'I found him in the Devil's Bath Tub. I think he must have fallen and hit his head last night.'

'How did he do that?'

Russ's voice was as level as ever, but it seemed to Birdie that there was a hint of disbelief in his face. There was nothing to do but attack.

'You said he seemed pretty drunk, Russ, when you lost him.'

Ellie leaped to the defence. 'He was drunk, rolling drunk, he could hardly stand up.'

Which wasn't strictly true. As Birdie remembered it, Morton, although he'd definitely had a drink too many, was perfectly capable of walking straight. Still, if Ellie had her own reasons to exaggerate his drunkenness, that was all to the good.

'I didn't lose him,' Russ said. His eyes were still on Birdie's face and he was clearly trying to puzzle something out. 'I told you, he just buggered off and left us to it.'

'He didn't say anything about going to the Devil's Bath Tub?'

'Nothing.'

Birdie glanced around the table. Helena inevitably had broken down in tears and was being comforted by Mal. Henry had moved close to Annabel, obviously expecting her to do the same, but she was looking no worse than worried. It seemed to be Ellie who was most distressed, twisting her thin hands together, glancing from Russ to Birdie and back again.

'I suppose we've got to report it to somebody,' Russ said.

'I've done that.' Birdie at least had thought this far in advance. 'I used his radio to get a message to St Lucia.'

He hoped that was just surprise on Russ's face, not suspicion. Now, among other complications, he'd have to make sure that neither Russ nor anybody else got into Morton's bungalow to discover the broken radio transmitter and his lie. It wouldn't be for long, though – just long enough to get his hands on Justin and make sure Debbie wasn't involved when officialdom arrived. Twelve hours or so should do it. He couldn't stay hidden for long.

'Did they acknowledge?'

Birdie nodded. 'It might take them a while to get somebody over.'

Russ said, 'I could get down there and stay with the radio if you like. I know a fair bit about signals.'

He bloody would.

'No, we'll need you up here. We've still got someone missing, remember?' He was worried now about Simon. If Justin had got it into his head that Morton was a paid assassin, he might be quite capable of transferring his obsession to anyone else he met.

Mal said suddenly, 'And I suppose we'll have to bury Morton.'

God knew how many generations of colonising ancestors had

taught him that bodies shouldn't be left lying around in the tropics. He sounded almost enthusiastic about it.

Birdie said hastily, 'We'll talk about that later.' He looked in what he hoped was a meaningful way at Helena, trying to convey to Mal that it was a matter better not discussed with ladies present. Judging by Mal's gulping and embarrassed look, he'd hit the right button.

'Oh, right. Yes, Birdie, right.'

Morton's body would have to take its chance in the tomb of roots until other things got sorted out. He wondered whether peccaries were carnivores, but only Toby was likely to know that and it was hardly a question to ask in the circumstances. There were other questions for Toby, though.

'You and Peter got down to Morton's bungalow last night?'

'Oh, yes.' Toby seemed startled to be noticed.

'What time?'

'About half an hour after we left you.'

Around half-past midnight, that made it.

'And you didn't find anybody there?'

'No.'

'Did you look inside?'

'Yes. Nobody was there.'

Now he had to tread carefully.

'Everything quite normal in the bungalow?'

'Yes. Why shouldn't it be?'

The general jumpiness even seemed to have got to Toby. Anyway, he knew now that Morton's bungalow had been vandalised well after midnight.

'Where's Peter?'

He'd assumed he was probably still asleep in the men's dormitory and was alarmed at Toby's reply, although it was given casually enough.

'Peter didn't come back with me. He decided to stay out for a while.'

'Stay out?'

Toby took his glasses off and polished them.

'We knew the peccaries would be going to the watering place for a drink around sunrise. We wanted some pictures.'

'So you let your brother go wandering off on his own to

photograph peccaries, after all I've told you?'

'Peter's used to looking after himself. He stays out for days sometimes to get the pictures we want.'

'Well, he's not going to stay out for days this time. I don't want anyone wandering off alone for whatever reason from now on. Is that understood?'

Russ said, 'So what are we going to do? He was clearly longing to declare Birdie incompetent and take charge himself. The problem was to find something that would divert his itch for leadership without doing any serious harm. Birdie unrolled a map of the island on the table and borrowed Toby's pencil as a pointer, trying to sound more decisive than he felt.

'Search parties. It's an extension of what we've been doing anyway, but this is the real thing. Russ, I want you and Ellie to take the area behind the lodge here.' His pencil circled the area to the north, where the contour lines rumpled like a disorderly duvet and clumps of rock broke through. 'Simon might have wandered up there, but for goodness sake go carefully because you can see there's not much in the way of paths.'

Russ thought, as he was intended to think, that Birdie had given him the mountainous sector because it was the most dangerous. From Birdie's point of view it was just the reverse, taking him well away from Morton's corpse, Morton's bungalow and the chance of running across Justin and Debbie before Birdie did.

'Toby, I want you, Henry and Annabel to find your brother. Keep close to the freshwater stream here. I suppose that's where he's most likely to be.' His pencil traced the blue line from below the lodge to the harbour, passing well behind Morton's bungalow.

'Mal and Helena, I want you two to stay here in case Simon comes back.' He got a grateful look from Helena for that. She'd recovered a bit and was possibly calculating that a few hours alone with Mal would give her a chance to draw level in the engagement stakes.

'What are you going to do then, Birdie?'

Russ, of course.

'I'll take the sulphur side.'

Somebody had watched him as he came along the path from the

Devil's Bath Tub, he was sure of that. Sure, too, even before he found the note on the machete that the person was Justin. Justin was out there, waiting for him as he'd waited for Morton. But, if Justin was out there, where was Debbie?

'I thought we weren't supposed to go in the rain forest on our own,' Russ said.

Birdie ignored that and handed out firm instructions to the two search parties. They were to take water and food with them. They were to come back as soon as they started getting tired or, even if not tired, come back and report by early afternoon and take a rest. If they hadn't found Simon and Peter by then, they'd discuss what to do next.

The one he had most compunction for in all this was Ellie. She was on her feet already, wanting to be off, and he knew there wasn't much chance of finding her husband in the direction he was sending her. He hardened his heart, telling himself that if she hadn't been so occupied with Russ she wouldn't have lost him in the first place. If Simon had got tired of being humiliated, and taken himself off to worry her, he might have been gratified to see how haggard she was looking. But she and Russ got themselves together efficiently and left, up a narrow path that Birdie knew would soon peter out in rock and scrub. The other search party took longer to get going, mainly because of Henry's fussing, but at last he, Annabel and Toby were on their way.

'Keep to the stream,' he yelled after them.

He wished now he'd taken some time to tidy up Morton's bungalow and put the books straight. He said a few words to Mal and Helena, warning them not to leave the lodge, then picked up his pack and plunged down the side ladder into the forest.

He hadn't gone far before the feeling of being watched started again, on the path between the lodge and the Devil's Bath Tub, not far from the tree roots where he'd left Morton's body. There was no sound to account for the feeling, or none he'd consciously heard; no movement other than the swaying of branches as birds flew away from him. It came from something deeper than hearing or seeing, from an instinct he'd first been aware of a quarter of a century ago, on patrol for the first time alone in a tangle of rainy terraced streets at two o'clock in the morning, with nothing but skulking cats to see. He'd been ashamed of the instinct then and it had taken him months to admit to it and find with relief that other people had it too. Since then he'd learned to trust it, although not understand it or how it came or went. One minute he was on his own with nothing but green leathery leaves around him and the heat beating down, the next minute, without any conscious transition, he knew there was another human being not far away. He took a few steps, thinking it over, then stopped to listen, but there was no sound louder than his own breathing. It could have been anywhere, left or right of the path, in front of him or out of sight behind him.

The note was still in his pocket. 'Birdie Linnet. This is to let you know that if you follow me it's at your own risk. I reserve the right to retalliate.' That didn't bother him, not from the likes of Justin. It did surprise him, though, that Justin, after what should have been an anxious night in the open, should still have enough left of his wits and energy to make a good job of tracking him. He hadn't underestimated his madness, not from the time he'd found Morton's body, but he might be underestimating his intelligence and physical strength. Justin was probably armed with the machete he'd taken from Morton, otherwise he'd hardly have abandoned the other at the lodge with his threatening message. Was it some kind of challenge, even? Fair fight, one machete for himself, the other for Birdie? But that seemed far too full-blooded a notion for the Justin he thought he knew.

The idea of it worked in his mind though, so that by the time he got to the plateau round the Devil's Bath Tub he had to test it. He walked a few steps and turned with his back to the bubbling pool.

'Hello, Justin. What do you want?'

He called it quite loudly and listened. Nothing. Another sulphur-loaded bubble rose and burst, spilling its cargo of fresh stink.

'I'm waiting, Justin.'

He turned towards the pool with his back to the path and counted in his head to fifty. When he looked round, the plateau was still empty. It wasn't a fight in the open that Justin wanted then, just to skulk in the bushes waiting his chance, as he'd waited for poor, drunk Morton. Birdie wasted some time after that going back along the path for a few hundred yards, searching the rain forest on either side, pulling down swathes of creeper till his hands were torn raw, getting salt rivers of sweat down his face and insects that resented it and stung down the back of his shirt. At last, when his head was throbbing from the sun and his throat raw with thirst, he realised the folly of tearing the rain forest apart with his bare hands to try and find Justin. He could be perched twenty yards away in a tree or under a bush, laughing to see Birdie waste his strength. He went back to the rock plateau, drank three gulps from his water bottle and considered.

Justin wouldn't come when he expected him, he'd try to wear him down, wait till he was exhausted or asleep, then, with Morton's machete, despatch the second of his father's paid assassins. If he wanted to get his hands on Justin he'd have to go along with the game, pretend to be more exhausted than he was and, when the time came, tempt him out of hiding and into the attack. One more thing, and he wasn't sure whether that made things better or worse: if Justin was playing that game, then Debbie couldn't be with him. She'd run off with him, that couldn't be denied. She might just, for reasons he couldn't understand, have got involved in that senseless vandalism down in Morton's bungalow. But she wouldn't help Justin track her own father with murderous intent, any more than she'd have been involved in Morton's killing. They'd got a camp somewhere, that was the only thing that made sense, and Justin had left her there while he went off to kill Morton, then hunt for Birdie.

From his high perch on the plateau he looked out over the forest, imagining her down there somewhere, lonely and scared, waiting for Justin to come back with whatever story he was spinning her. When he thought of that, the urgency of finding her became far stronger than any thought of catching Justin. Behind him the rock wall reared up, steep and waterless. He couldn't believe that Debbie and Justin had gone that way. Below him, the long rock spur split the forest into two, the left-hand side running steeply down to the sea, right-hand less steeply to the interior of the island, rucked up in lines of approximately parallel ridges as if something had taken a giant handful of the land and crumpled it, the whole thing covered with an impenetrable pelt of vegetable life.

He opted for the inland side, guessing they wouldn't have

pitched camp too far away from the lodge and, for the next few hours, searched methodically through the heat of midday and early afternoon, sometimes on paths so thin they were no more than veins through the green stuff, more often forcing a way through the forest on no better evidence than a torn branch or a few crumpled leaves suggesting somebody might have gone that way before. It was an effort to remember his own survival lessons, to rest now and then, to drink regularly but never more than a few mouthfuls because his two litres had to last until he could find Debbie, with a little to spare in case she needed it when he found her. This kept thirst at a permanent nagging level at the back of his mind and he kept hoping that he'd find, over the next ridge, pools and waterfalls as there were on the other side of the island. When he judged, as far as he could make out with map and compass, that he was no more than half a mile from the road, he turned back towards the rock ridge, not wanting to meet Henry's search party and get distracted. It was by then about four o'clock and the sun was not far from the tops of the trees on its way to the sea. Two clear hours of daylight left.

Soon after that he heard the noise. He was on his way down the slope to the bottom of a gulley in a controlled slide, clutching at trees with his hands to slow himself down. He'd stopped to pick a few more thorns out when he heard a crashing, rustling sound from below, no more than fifty yards or so away. The watcher, he was sure, was still behind him, so it couldn't be Justin. He wondered whether to call out, but decided against it and slithered on down the slope as carefully and quietly as he could, towards the source of the noise.

There was a heap of boulders, more than man-sized, probably trundled down there red hot when the volcano had split open, now covered with dry grey lichen. Bushes grew out of the middle of them, creepers tangled round them and, on one of the smaller rocks, a figure in a camouflage suit was standing, arms stretched up into the bushes. It took Birdie some time to realise that the figure was picking handfuls of leaves, plucking them and throwing them down, like somebody playing she-loves-me, she-loves-me-not. His first thought was that Debbie had gone mad with the strain; his second, with a lurch of disappointment when he saw the hair, that it wasn't Debbie after all.

'Simon, what the hell are you doing here?'

Simon turned, mouth gaping. His face was red with sunburn, his lips were cracked and his mouth plastered round with dry mucus. He gave a little croaking sound and, mouth still open, slithered off the rock and lay in a heap on the trampled earth at the foot of it, bright eyes fixed on Birdie. He had the air of a particularly large, particularly inept fledgling fallen from its nest. He kept trying to croak something, but Birdie couldn't understand what it was.

'Easy. Take it easy.'

He held Simon's head up and fed him water, one gulp at a time. He used a little more of the water sparingly to swab his inflamed face. The skin was so hot he was surprised it didn't steam and sizzle. After minutes of this, the croak became intelligible.

'Some holiday,' was what Simon was saying.

'Why did you go and wander off like that?'

'It doesn't work, either. Not leaves.'

He remembered mentioning in one of his survival talks that, when really up against it, it was worth looking into the leaves of certain plants for the water that gathered at the base of them.

'Wrong leaves, Simon.'

'How was I to know? I want my money back.'

That, at least, was hopeful, showing a return to normal health by tourist standards.

'You should have stayed with the rest of them. I told you.'

'I'd had enough of them, her and bloody Tarzan.'

He demanded more water. Birdie, seeing his precious supply diminishing, let him finish off the first bottle.

'I didn't want to come on this holiday in the first place,' he said. Now there was more moisture in his body the tears had started flowing slowly down his cheeks. 'I wanted to spend the money on a caravan. We could have got a nice little caravan for that money. A nice little caravan.'

He stared at Birdie with imploring eyes, inviting him to share his grief for the lost caravan.

Birdie said, 'Have you been wandering round like this all day?'

'I've been looking for her.'

Birdie, head full of his own search, didn't understand what he meant at first.

'Looking for my wife, looking for my lawful wedded wife, whether she likes it or not. She says there's not enough excitement in her life, do you know that? Not enough excitement. I wonder if she's had enough now.'

'But, Simon, she's back at the lodge. Ellie got back with the rest of them last night. She's worried sick about you.' He thought it best not to add that since then he'd sent her off on a wild goose chase with bloody Tarzan.

Simon shook his head, and his mouth set in a stubborn line. 'Oh, no. Everybody takes her side. I'm used to it now. I can see through that now. I heard her, crashing around looking for him. I thought, let her look, let her get on with it. Then I thought I'd find her after all, but I couldn't.'

Birdie, thinking he was talking about the night walk, said, 'I thought you'd gone off and left them.'

'No, not last night. That wasn't last night. That was this morning.'

'This morning? Where?'

'Over there.' He made a vague gesture in the direction of the road. 'Just after it got light I heard somebody crashing around. I guessed it was her. I tried to follow, but I lost her, then I got lost.'

He knew it couldn't have been Ellie. When it got light, she'd been on the balcony at the lodge worrying about her missing husband. So whom had Simon heard? Justin, possibly, on his way back from vandalising Morton's bungalow?

'Are you sure it was one person, not two?'

'Oh, it was only one.'

Birdie would have liked to believe him, but didn't see how Simon in his confused state could have been so certain. With the evening coming on, though, there was no time for long discussion.

'We've got to get you back to the lodge.'

Simon looked pinkly determined. 'No, I'm staying out here. I'm going to find her. She's not going to lose me that easily.'

Birdie sighed. This was the last thing he needed. He spoke slowly and as reassuringly as he could. 'She's back at the lodge. You've only got to get there then you'll find her and you can tell her whatever you like.'

Ellie and Russ would surely have had the sense to give up their search and come down well before dark.

'You're not lying to me? You're not trying to shield her?'

Birdie sighed. 'Why should I? It's not my problem.'

Simon gave in reluctantly but at last allowed Birdie to persuade him up the steep slope to the path that ran from the lodge to the sulphur pool. It was weary work because Simon was unsteady on his feet and several times Birdie had to prop him against trees and go ahead to tear a gap for them. By the time they got to the path a golden light was coming horizontally through the trees and they were less than an hour from sunset.

Birdie knew he should see Simon all the way back, but explanations would waste the last precious hour of light and half light he needed to find Debbie. The idea of leaving her to spend another night in some makeshift camp with Justin was more than he could stand. He took Simon by the shoulders and pointed him in the right direction.

'It's only about half a mile along there. Can you make it?'

But Simon couldn't or wouldn't understand, stupid with heat and exhaustion. Birdie had to spend another precious twenty minutes supporting him along the path until they could see a light from the oil lamp on the balcony.

He shouted, 'I've found Simon. Can somebody come and look after him?' He gave Simon a gentle push in the direction of the light, then took off as fast as he could back along the path to the sulphur pool before the rest of them could come and ask questions.

The light was going fast now. To plunge off into the forest again would be worse than useless and the pool drew him like a magnet. That was where Morton had been killed, where Toby had seen a couple embracing the evening before. If he could do nothing else he could wait there until first light and, if nothing happened, start the search again in the morning. He got to the deserted plateau in time to see the sea to the west turning to bronze as the sun went down. With luck the afterglow would give him just enough time for another search of the scrub and small trees that grew just below the plateau. He left his pack on the open rocks and scrambled down.

What concerned him was that he didn't know any more whether the watcher was with him or not. The keen sense of something present had got scrambled while he was having to fuss about with Simon. Since he'd left him near the lodge, his ears and eyes had been straining for any sign but the rain forest at sunset was as noisy as an infant school, with daylight things going to their resting places and night things waking up and announcing their presence. There were clacks and clatters, chirpings and croakings and a whole percussion section of crashings from every part of the undergrowth that could have been anything in the human or animal kingdom. This went on as he pushed his way through the bushes under the plateau, searching unsuccessfully for any sign that somebody had made camp there. When he'd fallen a couple of times, wrenching his knee badly, he decided it was time to give it up until daylight, and climbed back up to the plateau.

His pack was exactly where he'd left it, half way between the sulphur pool and the rock face, but the second he saw it he knew something had happened. The shape was different. He stopped, looked all round him, then limped over to it, staring at something that was lying on top of it. Not one thing: four things. He picked them up, one by one, feeling more puzzled with each: one tin of sardines, unopened and with key attached of the sort they kept back in the kitchen at the lodge, one water bottle, also like the ones back in the kitchen, about one-third full, one small hard tangerine of the kind that grew sparsely on trees around the lodge. The fourth thing he didn't notice at first because it was so small. It was only when he was putting down the tangerine that he saw something else lying on top of his pack: an ordinary picture transparency in a plastic mount. With so little light, he had to carry it to the edge of the plateau and squint at it against the last glow in the sky before he could see what the picture was.

'Well I'll be . . .'

For a second or two, amusement cast out puzzlement. In spite of the excellent manners of Justin's father, or because of them, he'd felt pretty much the hick at their meeting and picking up that cheque, welcome as it was, had placed him as the hired retainer. It was some satisfaction to know that even Justin's father wasn't always the picture of dignity. Birdie had even had to help raid a place like that once in his early days on the force. Less classy than this one, though. What he chiefly remembered of the raid was a fat, white thigh bulging through holes in fishnet tights. The girl in this picture, though, had a nice pair of tights and a nice pair of long legs to go in them. When the rich looked ridiculous, at least they did it in style.

But the smile didn't stay on his face long. Justin, bloody Justin. He'd lost track of the watcher, but the watcher had been there all the time and, now dark was coming on, wanted him to know it. What else was meant by the transparency? So my father's paying you to kill me, Birdie Linnet. You see the kind of man you're working for? It was as clear as the message left on the machete handle. But what was he to make of the other things – the water, the tangerine, the tin of sardines? Looked at in one way, it was all of a piece with the return of the kitchen machete: a challenge to a fair fight. Justin intended to fight and kill him, as he'd killed Morton at the same place, but was too chivalrous to take on a hungry and thirsty opponent. It might have made sense if he'd never met the little sod, but nobody who'd known Justin for as much as five minutes would accuse him of being so scrupulous. It would be more in character to drug him and drown him sleeping, as he'd killed Morton drunk.

Which, come to think of it, was exactly what the little sod intended to do. Forget the sardines and tangerine, they were no more than bait. What mattered was the water. If Justin had seen him emptying his water bottle into Simon, he'd have guessed he'd be thirsty, calculated that the water would be irresistible. How he'd managed to get his hands on whatever he'd put into it, goodness knows, but the likes of Justin could probably conjure it up when they needed it, even on remote islands. Perhaps he always carried an emergency supply with him. One things was sure: if he'd been close enough to see Birdie leaving the pack and take his chance, he wouldn't be far away now, just back along the path perhaps, where the trees grew thickly. He could have gone to look for him, but there was an easier way. He straightened up, the bottle in his hand, and pretended to pull the cap off. In this light, the watcher couldn't see clearly.

'Thanks, Justin. Here's to a fair fight.'

He tilted his head back. Making convincing swallowing sounds with a dry mouth was harder than he expected, but he managed it.

'Ready when you are, Justin.'

He walked about for a while. Making himself look sleepy was no problem, after the day he'd had. When he thought the performance had gone on long enough he took his pack to the edge of the plateau under the rock wall. The rocks were cooler there and it was possible to stretch out on them. There, too, he could lie along the rock wall with his back defended. He yawned noisily and lay down, his eyes on the opening of the path, a darker patch in the gathering darkness, wondering how long Justin would wait.

CHAPTER EIGHT

The moon rose. Around midnight the rain poured down for a while, sluicing off the rock plateau and hissing into the sulphur pool. Birdie wondered what to do about that. Was whatever Justin had put in the water bottle strong enough to make him sleep on through a rain storm? He decided not to take any chances and stayed where he was, turning sidways towards the rock as if rolling over in his sleep until the storm was over. From then on he lay there in clammy dampness, flexing shoulders and knees now and again so that they shouldn't stiffen up when he needed them, but trying to do it in the way a sleeper might move. It was harder listening after the rain, too. The big drops pattered off the leaves along the path and below the plateau, sounding like footsteps coming from all directions. If he relied on hearing, Justin could be two steps away from him before he knew it but it was a struggle to keep his eyes open all the time. At some point, against his will, he slept and woke to find the moon down and the darkness total. Even the forest was quiet. The luminous face of his watch said twenty-past three and he was angry with Justin for making him wait so long. Didn't the little sod realise it would be getting light soon? By half-past four when the sky to the east was pale and the first cheeps and screeches from the day shift were rising from the trees he accepted that he wasn't going to come after all.

He gave it another twenty minutes to make sure, until the sky had turned from pale to apricot, then sat up, damp shirt clinging to him. He couldn't understand what had happened; why Justin should go to the trouble of tracking him, trying to drug him, then not closing in for the kill? Had he lost his nerve at the last moment or even guessed Birdie was only pretending to be asleep? If he'd guessed, then he was sharper, much sharper, than Birdie had allowed. He wondered if he'd been wrong, if the water hadn't been drugged after all. But, if not, how could he explain the out-of-character gifts left for him? He opened the suspect bottle and sniffed, but the smell from the water purifying tablets they used at the lodge was strong enough to mask anything else. The water would have to wait for proper analysis. He opened his own, safe bottle and drank a few gulps, longing for a mug of coffee to warm him and smooth the sulphur rasp from the back of his throat. The knee he'd damaged the night before was aching and he didn't look forward to plunging around in the forest again. No choice, though. Justin was out there somewhere and Debbie was out there somewhere, apart or together. Perhaps he was just joining her at their camp, wherever it was, with some story about what he'd been doing through the night. Birdie had no idea at the moment whether he was being watched or not. The hours of waiting with senses alert for any noise had scrambled the radar again. Justin might have been yards or miles away. He stood up and put his pack on. The night chorus of the tree frogs had dwindled to a few isolated patches of croaking, giving some rare minutes of near silence. Until, that is, the screaming began.

It wasn't any normal rain forest sound. No parrot would screech like that. The Devil himself, lowering his haunches into his own bath tub, might scream like that if the water was too hot. But nothing, animal or human, would make that noise except in the last stages of distress and fear. On and on the scream went with no pause for breath and, while it went on, all the other sounds of the island were frozen. Even after it stopped everything seemed to be in a state of shock. Not a frog croaked or a bird twittered for the first long second of silence that followed the scream, waiting in case it started again. But it didn't start again. One terrible, drawn-out scream of protest and that was it. After the silence an exploratory frog croaked, then another; the birds started up again and the normal life of the forest closed in, like scar tissue over a raw wound.

Birdie had felt his heart stop when the scream started. Now it lurched and thumped twice as fast as usual and, for the first few seconds, he couldn't think or move, frozen with fear and a sense of something being broken. When he did move, it was in a run to the edge of the plateau, looking out over the tops of the trees. The scream had come from down there somewhere, to the left or right of the long rock rib where the iguanas sunbathed, but there was nothing to see, no sound or movement out of the ordinary to show the source of it. Trees waved in the dawn breeze coming off the sea, but that was all. He had to fight a temptation to dive off the plateau and into the trees, to tear away at them until he found what had been screaming.

'It's all right, I'm coming,' he called to the forest.

He scrambled off the pleateau and down on the right-hand side of the rock ridge, the trees closing over him as he went. He knew there was a narrow path on that side that would give him the quickest route down. Down where he didn't know, but down there somewhere, was where the scream had come from. There was no time or need to worry about the watcher now, no time even to think about anything but the urgency of getting there. He fell over tree roots, got up again and blundered on, tangled in creepers and tore himself free, setting trees swaying for yards around. An outraged trail of birds, butterflies and insects rose behind him as he went, like a maddened giant peccary from Morton's herd.

The track, he knew, led to the end of the rock ridge a mile or so below the sulphur pool. There was a waterfall there where the stream came out and a pond that was warm and sulphur smelling like all the water courses on the east side of the island. When he picked himself up after another fall he could hear the water trickling over the fall and smell sulphur, not as strong as at the Devil's Bath Tub, only a hint of it. He went towards it not because he expected to find anything there, but because that was where the path was going. The ground turned first damp, then muddy. There was a great patch of lilies on his right, with dark green leaves and flowers so white they seemed fluorescent. They reminded him of lilies in old-fashioned funeral parlours, and it might have been the associations of that, rather than mud and tiredness, that made him slow down. Cautiously, as if tracking a shy animal, he went round the end of the ridge towards the waterfall.

It was, at normal times, one of the sights of the island. The rock ended in a face about forty feet high. In the middle of it was a black hole with a stream of light brown water spurting from it then turning silver in the light as it crashed down to a deep pool fringed with more of the white lilies. Ferns grew on the rock face, quivering all the time as drops of water hit them and petals from flowering creepers swirled in the currents of the pool or went with the stream down towards the sea.

Only one thing spoiled it, though; the thing that floated in the middle of the pool along with the whirling petals: a sodden, patchy thing that moved reluctantly with the water, like a cheap toy flung away. A life-size toy it was, but not lively. It was floating, head down in the water, because one of its canvas boots and one patchy leg were lodged in the mud by a clump of lilies. If it had tried to dive headlong in, then changed its mind at the last moment, it might have ended up in that position, sprawled and ludicrous. For a moment he even thought that it might be alive.

'It's all right. We'll get you out,' he told it.

But when he grabbed the leg, even through the thick cloth of the camouflage overalls, the feel of it told him that there was no hurry, not as far as the thing in the water was concerned. The echoes of the scream – ten minutes, half an hour ago, he had no way of telling – dinned in his head although the only sound around him was the crash of the waterfall into the pool.

The fabric of the trousers ripped in his hand and the leg escaped from him, falling with a plop into the mud. If he'd taken hold of it and pulled, the body would have come to him but he couldn't face that. He splashed waist-deep into the warm water of the pool and got his arms around its shoulders, dragged it into the muddy shallows with the head still hanging down. There was no excuse any more. He slid his arm under its armpits, hearing fabric rip again, then slowly, with his free hand, took it by the chin and raised the head.

The gash sank deep into the right side of the neck, gaping like a fish's mouth. One part of his mind couldn't understand why it wasn't pouring blood or why there was no stain on the water. But that was only a small part of his mind because the rest of it was stunned with relief, concentrating not on what was there but what wasn't. The neck had a machete gash but it didn't have the pink arrowhead of hair on the nape he'd been expecting and dreading to see ever since he fished it out of the water. It was a man's neck, pink with sunburn, with pale soaked hair straggling across it. If poor innocent Peter, interested only in bugs and peccaries, had looked to Justin like one of his father's hired assassins, then nobody on the island was safe. As Birdie stood in the shallows with the body drooping, face down, in his arms, he was aware that Justin couldn't be far away. He dragged the body out and laid it on its side to get a better look at the machete gash, but kept half his attention on the path and the bushes round it. He thought he'd heard a noise there that might not be an animal. The wound was deep and gaping and there was a shallower gash just under the ear. He still couldn't understand why there was no bleeding, but perhaps the sulphur in the water had something to do with it. There was certainly a strong smell of it around the body, stronger than he'd have expected from the comparatively mild concentration of it in the pool.

He took the body by the shoulders and turned it over. Two of the fingers were missing from the right hand or, at least, half the index finger and the tip of the one next to it, cut off clean as on a butcher's slab. The hand he took in his to examine it was still warm from its sulphur bath, pale and hairless, as slim as a woman's. But Peter's hands, he remembered, had been red and square, the backs covered with black hairs. He'd noticed them scribbling away in the lamplight. It wasn't Peter's mutilated hand he was holding. For the first time he looked up at the face.

'No.'

His mind, unable to make sense of it, refused to take it in at all. Then there was a cold superstitious feeling that ran down his spine like a lizard. A man couldn't be in two places at once. A man couldn't be lying dead beside a waterfall with a machete gash in his neck and still be watching from the bushes up there, waiting for his chance. And yet the face he was staring at, yellowish from the sulphur with a spongey look about it that wiped out the sharp bone structure, was still beyond question the face of Justin.

'But who . . .?'

Justin was the watcher, wasn't he? Justin had left that threatening message. Justin had tried to drug him. Justin was at this moment up there in the bushes, watching and waiting for him. And if it wasn't Justin, then who the hell was it coming down the path towards him, swaying the bushes without any pretence at secrecy, no more than a hundred yards away? He jumped up, facing across Justin's body to the bushes. An arm in camouflage overalls pushed the creepers aside.

'Who is it?'

A figure stepped out of the shadows on long camouflaged legs and stood there looking down at him and the body.

'Hello, Dad,' it said.

CHAPTER NINE

'I didn't kill him,' he said.
He hadn't intended to say that. She stood looking down at him. The face was turned towards him but she must have seen at first glance the gaping wound on the neck.

'It's Justin,' he said.

'Yes.'

She came slowly across to him. He took her elbow gently and tried to turn her away from looking at the body but she shook him off and crouched down beside it, sitting on her heels.

'I heard a scream,' she said.

'So did I. I was up at the Devil's Bath Tub when I heard it. I came down here and found him floating in the pool.'

He was talking too fast and explaining too much. He didn't have to give alibis to his own daughter, for goodness sake, but he couldn't have stopped doing it any more than he could have held back those first few disastrous words.

'You're wet,' she said, turning her eyes from Justin's face to him. Her voice and expression were quite blank.

'I had to go into the pool to get him out. I could have just pulled him, but I couldn't . . .'

Couldn't face the idea of taking the leg and pulling when he thought it was her leg, but how could he say that to her? His voice died away while she stared at him. With Justin dead by the pool, her father, who hated him, soaking wet and standing over the body, could he blame her for thinking what she must be thinking? But he did blame her, and was bitterly angry, with the helpless feeling that the more he explained the deeper he sank and the more remote she was from him.

'It was an awful scream. It sounded . . .'

Her voice trailed away, too. She stared up at him, the body in between them.

'When did you last see him?' he asked.

God knows, he hadn't wanted to cross-question her, especially not like this, but if she was going to blame him he had to start fighting.

'Wednesday night, just before it got dark.'

She didn't seem to resent the question but her voice was mechanical and so flat that it took a while for the significance of it to sink in.

'Last night, you mean?'

'No, Wednesday; the first night.'

'But it was Wednesday morning when you went off with him. You're telling me you split up on Wednesday evening?'

There was a spark of anger in her eyes at last, but at him for his question, not at Justin.

'He had other things to do,' she said.

It infuriated him that she should still be defending the man.

'He had, had he? So he goes off and leaves you alone for the night?'

'He said he'd come back.'

'But he didn't?'

'No.'

She made a gesture to sweep the hair back out of her eyes. She'd always done that when she was trying to concentrate on something from the time she was quite a small kid, but now her hair was upright and spikey there was nothing to sweep back. It disconcerted her and she turned her head away, staring at the waterfall.

'And did he tell you what those other things were that he had to do?'

She shook her head, still not looking at him.

'He didn't tell you he was going to break up Morton's bungalow and leave a threatening message for him?'

'No, of course not.'

She was looking at him again, and the eyes were angry, refusing to accept what he said. She'd still believe Justin rather than her own father, even when he was dead and lying beside her like a sulphurous sponge.

'And he didn't say anything about drowning Morton in the Devil's Bath Tub? He didn't mention he was going off to do that?'

She was on her feet, staring at him wide-eyed and scared.

'What are you talking about, Dad?'

'Morton's dead, too. He was killed on Wednesday night.'

She just stared. He spoke slowly, not sure he was getting through to her. 'So two things happened between sunset and sunrise on Wednesday night. Morton's bungalow was broken up and the radio was wrecked, and Morton was drowned. And sonny boy went off and left you because he had other things to do.'

'Why would somebody break up his bungalow if they were going to kill him anyway?'

It was no more than a murmur. He disregarded it. He saw her looking at the hand with its missing fingers.

'Morton was drunk, but not so drunk he didn't have a try at defending himself.' He didn't tell her about finding the missing fingers up by the sulphur pool. 'Another thing, just after I got back to the lodge after finding Morton's body, I found a message from him threatening me. He's been following me ever since.'

'Can I see it?'

It was still in his pocket, but had turned to a soaking wad of pulp.

'It was in red felt-tip. It said he reserved the right to retaliate, except he'd spelt it wrong.'

She nodded. 'I was with him when he wrote it.'

'Oh, were you? Sitting cosily together under a tree writing threats to your father? You must have enjoyed that.'

Or had they done it, giggling, up at the sulphur pool?

'If you must know, I told him it was childish. He put them away in his pack. I thought he'd forget about them.'

'You seem to have had a lot of influence over him.' He'd meant it sarcastically but she took it seriously.

'I listened to him, you see. I wanted to help him.'

He'd have liked to kick the sopping body lying at their feet, could even hear in his mind the squelch as the toe of his boot went in. To get himself away from the temptation he suggested they should go and sit down under a tree. She looked down at the body.

'What are we . . . ?'

'Never mind that for the moment. Nothing will happen to him while we're here.'

It was the first time she'd seen a dead body. He had Justin to blame for that as well. She let him take her elbow and guide her over to the tree, but she moved like a puppet.

'Now, you say he went off and left you on Wednesday evening. Do you know what time?'

'About half-past five. Before it got dark, but not long before.'

'And what did he tell you about why he was going off?'

'He . . . he didn't say much. He'd been asleep, and when he woke up he . . . was angry because it was later than he thought. He said he'd got to go and he . . . went.'

'And he didn't tell you why?'

'He didn't say much at all. He was in a hurry. He said he had to see somebody.'

'Where were you then?'

'Not very far from here. By the rock ridge, further up.'

'And what direction did he go?'

'Back up the path.'

'Towards the Devil's Bath Tub, then?'

She nodded.

'And you didn't go with him – you're sure of that?' The embracing couple Toby had seen were still on his mind.

'Of course I'm sure. He didn't want me to go with him so I stayed where I was.'

'And you expected him to come back?'

'He said he'd come back.'

'But he didn't. You didn't see anything of him after that, or hear anything?'

She shook her head. 'Not until that scream just now.'

She looked at Justin's body and Birdie, following her eyes, saw that flies were gathering around the wounds in the neck. Even that, he felt, was Justin's fault. He spoke sharply, to drag her attention back. 'So you decided to stay out there all night on your own? Where?'

'On top of the ridge. I heard you all, on your exercise.'

'Why didn't you shout out to us?'

'I didn't want to. First it was Ellie and Simon and Russ, bickering at each other, then you and the Helibels. I heard you unwrapping her ankle from something.' The voice was accusing.

'She'd got it caught in a creeper.'

There he was, on the defensive again, and this time with a less than watertight case.

'And what was she talking about, saying you took them to that sulphur place because you thought you'd find me and Justin there?'

'That was just Annabel.' He didn't want then, or perhaps ever, to open the question of whether Debbie and Justin had been making love by the pool, but she wouldn't let it go.

'No, it wasn't. You asked Toby if he was sure it was us. You must have meant something.'

He said bitterly, 'Toby and Peter thought they saw the two of you there.'

'Us? When?'

'About an hour before sunset.'

She stared. 'It couldn't have been. He'd left me by then. I was down here.'

'Toby was sure it was Justin.'

When he saw the expression on her face, he hated himself for saying it, and even more for the relief he felt. Justin leaves her in a hurry to keep an appointment. Not long afterwards Justin is seen not far away with a woman. Justin doesn't return. The sudden hurt in her eyes as that sank in was proof to him that she'd been speaking the truth when she said she hadn't gone with Justin.

He said, 'Toby probably got it wrong. He's not reliable about anything except bugs or peccaries.'

'It doesn't matter.'

They sat in silence. As the sun got to Justin's body, trails of sulphurous steam began to rise from the soaking fabric of his overalls. Birdie hoped she hadn't noticed. When he said Toby might have got it wrong it had been no more than a half-hearted attempt to console her for the damage he'd done. Now he wondered whether he believed it or not. The idea that Justin had hurried away from Debbie to keep an appointment with Helena or Annabel or Ellie struck him as unlikely. All three of the women seemed more or less happily involved elsewhere. Of course, given Justin's life-style, it might equally well have been a man he was meeting, except that Henry, Russ or Mal seemed even less likely erotic partners. He was inclined to doubt Toby's evidence, if only on the grounds that Justin must have been busy enough elsewhere.

Which had he done first? The killing, or the vandalism at the bungalow? Probably the killing first, if Toby had been telling the truth about finding the bungalow unvandalised after midnight. But, in that case, he must have waited hours by the Devil's Bath Tub to keep an appointment with Morton. Why Morton should have agreed to break away from the party and meet him there, Birdie couldn't imagine, unless, just possibly, there was something in the cannabis business after all. Suppose his indignation with Justin had been for public consumption only and he'd agreed in private to meet him later and hand over some at a price? He'd clearly not taken seriously Justin's outburst accusing him of being in an assassination plot with Birdie; probably hadn't even known what Justin was talking about.

'He never intended to come back,' he said. 'He killed Morton, then he left that warning message and started trying to do the same for me.'

'No.' She said it quite flatly.

'I'm afraid so, love. He left that message for me, first thing Thursday morning, and he's been following me around since then, waiting for a chance. He even tried to drug me last night, so he could get at me while I was asleep.'

'No.'

'Oh, yes. I'd put my pack down near the Devil's Bath Tub. When I came back there was a photo of Justin's father and some water in a bottle. If I'd drunk that I'd probably have woken up with my neck in two pieces.'

'Did you keep it?'

He opened his pack and passed the water bottle over to her.

'The smell of the purifying tablet would hide anything else he put in there. We'll have to wait and get it analysed.'

She pulled the top off and sniffed it. Then, before he could stop her, she put it to her mouth and drank greedily. He grabbed it away from her and threw it on the ground, spattering both of them with water. She stared at him and there was a smile on her face, although not the sort of smile he liked to see.

'It's all right, Dad. There's nothing wrong with it. I put it there.'

He couldn't say anything, just stared at her, but his expression made the smile fade.

'I thought you'd guessed. I was worried you were running out of water after you'd given most of yours to Simon, so I left it there for you.'

'Simon? How did you know I was giving water to Simon?'

'Because I was watching you, of course. I've been watching you for ages, since yesterday morning.'

'But it was Justin watching me. He left that message on the machete, then he was following me.'

She shook her head, smiling again. 'You've got an obsession with Justin, Dad. That's what I was worried about.'

'Worried? You were worried? You told me you hadn't seen Justin since Wednesday evening. Now you tell me the two of you were trailing me around from Thursday morning onwards. What am I supposed to believe?'

She spoke calmly and slowly, as if to an infant. 'Dad, forget about Justin for once. It wasn't Justin and me following you, it was just me. I was following you because I knew you were looking for Justin and I was worried about you.' Then she added, in a softer voice, with her eyes on the tree roots, 'And worried about what you'd do to him when you found him.'

The steam was rising from the body steadily now. She must have noticed too.

'But the message? The message on the machete in the kitchen. Was it you who left that?'

She shook her head. 'Of course not.'

'He did then. And you're telling me you didn't see him, you had nothing to do with it?'

'Yes.' Her eyes stared back at him, calm and level.

'But the photo. That was left with the water bottle.'

She nodded. 'Justin's father in the brothel. Yes, I left that. I thought you should see it.'

'Why, for heaven's sake?'

'I thought you should see what Justin's father was really like. I thought you'd stop harassing Justin when you knew.'

'It's bloody disgusting, carrying a photo of his own father around like that, showing it to you. Where did he get it? What did he want with it?'

'He was going to have it published in the papers. He wanted me to look after it because he thought somebody was trying to take it away from him.'

'Meaning me or Morton, I suppose.'

She didn't answer.

'So you agreed to look after it, did you? You were going to help him get it splashed all over the gutter press?'

He couldn't keep the anger out of his voice. He wished Justin were alive again so that he could get at him.

Her voice was still calm. 'It was the hypocrisy that got Justin. His father telling other people what to do, then going off and doing things like that. He wanted people to see what he was like.'

'Oh, yes. Justin the crusader now, is it? Justin the upholder of public morals? Did he tell you how much he expected to get for that photo?'

'What's that got to do with it?'

But he could tell from her voice that he'd scored a hit, and he pressed the point. 'Ten thousand? Twenty thousand? Or were they supposed to pay him in cocaine?'

She was angry at last. 'What's Justin's father paying you, then?'

Five hundred quid, over and above his pay, plus half an hour of man to man conversation and two glasses of good malt. In the circumstances, he'd have to give the money back.

'That's got nothing to do with it. I was just supposed to be keeping an eye on him.'

Involuntarily both of them looked at the steaming body and the flies gathering round the wound on the neck.

'I'll get him into the shade,' Birdie said. 'Then I'll go up to the lodge and get some of the others to help carry him back.'

He accepted the polythene sheet from her pack to wrap Justin in, but wouldn't let her help as he carried him with difficulty to the shade of the tree where they'd been sitting. He was used to this. All the time she was standing by the fluorescent lilies, looking up at the waterfall. When he'd finished he went over to her and risked putting a hand on her shoulder.

'Ready, love?'

She nodded, without turning round. Although he knew it was a bad idea, he couldn't stop himself asking, 'You don't think I killed him, do you?'

Silence, except for the sound of the waterfall.

'Do you?'

'Dad, don't ask me that.'

He was too hurt to be angry. He took his hand off her shoulder and walked towards the path. 'We'd better be getting back.'

He was several yards into the trees before he heard her following him.

For the first half mile he walked slowly, wondering what to do. Several times he had to turn round to stop branches whipping back across her face, or to see she negotiated a rough patch safely. Every time, he avoided looking at her face. When they were about half way up the path beside the rock spur he made up his mind and turned to face her. With the sun still well down in the east they were in shadow there.

'I don't need a rest,' she said.

'It's not for a rest. We've got to talk.'

Her shoulders rose and fell in what looked like a sigh.

'We're going to be back with the others before long. For a start, we've got to decide what we tell them.'

'Why?'

'I haven't told them Morton was murdered. I said he'd had an accident. It seemed best that way.'

He thought it was a scornful look she gave him, but he couldn't tell her that he'd decided to hide Morton's murder until he knew for sure she had nothing to do with the events surrounding it.

'The thing is, I want to tell them the same about Justin.'

He'd even considered going back and telling them simply that Justin was still missing, but that would put too hard a burden on Debbie.

'Won't they think it's a bit funny – two accidents in two days?'

'They can think what they like. The point is, at least one of them will know Justin wasn't an accident.'

He watched her face, but the point was slow in registering.

'What I mean is, whoever killed Justin will know it wasn't an accident.'

'Yes, I see.'

Her tone wasn't convincing. He reminded himself that he couldn't afford to get angry again.

'Look, love, let's leave aside for now whether you think I killed him or not. I know I didn't. The point is, proving to you I didn't, and if I'm going to do that I've got to have your help. That's fair enough, isn't it?'

She considered it and, so slightly it was hardly a movement at all, nodded. That would have to do.

'Right. And that means finding out who did kill him. They should all have been back at the lodge when we heard that scream, in the dormitories. It'll be easy enough to check that if they don't know it's a murder investigation.'

'But the person who did it will know, and he'll know we know.'

'Yes, but don't you see, that'll unsettle him, or her, wondering what game we're playing. They'll be more likely to make a mistake that way.'

'There'd have been footprints,' she said, 'in the mud.'

On the face of it, that was encouraging. If she was in the business of hunting for clues, at least it showed some part of her mind was still open.

'There would have been, except I trampled all over them with my size tens when I was pulling him out. I didn't notice any.'

'I thought they taught police not to do things like that.'

He'd closed his eyes and counted up to six before he decided he could let himself be annoyed.

'Yes, they do teach police not to do things like that. Only, when you think it might be your own daughter there, you don't stand around taking casts of footprints, do you? You get in there and pull her out.'

She stared. 'You thought it was me in there?'

'Of course I did. You missing; knowing he was wandering round the island with a machete, then that scream. Of course I thought it was you.'

'You mean . . . you thought Justin had killed me? Me?'

'Yes.'

'But why would he want to do that? I was helping him.'

'He wasn't sane, love. You can't help the likes of him. He'd turn against anyone. He turned against his own father, didn't he?'

'But you were wrong, weren't you? He didn't kill me. Somebody killed him.'

'Yes, I was wrong. But you can't blame me for thinking that, not when I knew he'd killed Morton.'

'I don't believe Justin did kill Morton. I don't think he killed anybody.'

'Well, who did then? Or do you think I killed Morton as well?'

'No. No, of course not.'

He saw the distress on her face and made himself calm down. 'Love, I know how you feel, but look at the facts. Justin goes off at sunset, telling you he's got an appointment with somebody. The last anybody sees of Morton alive is on that damned night walk, not so far from the Devil's Bath Tub. Come morning, he's floating about in it dead and there's a message in his bungalow from Justin about one of them not getting off the island alive. Then you say he didn't do it.'

'Perhaps somebody framed him.'

He nearly howled with exasperation. 'I wish to God you were as eager to find me not guilty.'

'I am. Of course I am.'

He thought she added, under her breath, 'Even more,' but didn't ask her to repeat it in case he'd been wrong.

'Well, then, if somebody framed Justin for killing Morton, you tell me why?'

'Perhaps his father suggested it.'

'You mean somebody else here's supposed to be in his father's pay – beside me, that is?'

'Yes.'

'What would be the point of framing Justin for a murder? He wanted Justin kept out of trouble, not dropped in it.'

'That's what he told you. That could have been a blind.'

'A blind for what?'

'You've seen the picture.'

'You're telling me Justin's father was so worried about some smutty picture of him being published in the *Sun*, he'd not only have Justin murdered, he'd frame him for murder as well?'

'Justin said he was ruthless.'

'He did, did he? Coming from Justin, that was pretty good.'

Impasse. They stared at each other. The shadow of the rock was sharpening as the sun came nearer the ridge.

She spoke first. 'His pack wasn't there. He had it with him when he went off on Wednesday night.'

'He must have dumped it somewhere.'

'Not near the waterfall. I looked. And he wouldn't leave it anywhere else because it would have his water bottle in it.'

'Perhaps it got thrown in the pool.'

She shook her head. 'I looked there too.'

So that was why it had taken her some time to follow him. He marvelled that she'd kept her wits about her but felt threatened by it too. This was a Debbie he hadn't met before.

'So whoever killed him,' she said, 'must have taken his pack. And that must have been because they thought the photographs were in it. They'd have just found the messages in there instead.'

He shook his head.

'Well, why do you think he was murdered, then? Why should anybody have wanted to kill Justin if it wasn't that?'

Practically anyone who'd met him, he thought.

'I don't know. That's what we've got to find out.'

He decided not to argue about it any more. He didn't accept a scenario that cast Justin's father as a ruthless assassin of his own son, but if that was her starting point for helping him find Justin's killer, so be it.

'We'd better get up there and start work then. You leave the talking to me. Just listen as much as you can.'

They'd swung their packs to the ground when they stopped to talk and, as he was bending to pick them up, something caught his eye that he hadn't seen while the rock rib was more deeply in shadow. An angle of rock stuck out and inside the angle was a dark slit that looked as if it led somewhere.

'Hang on a bit. It looks as if there might be a cave in here.'

She didn't want to stop and look at caves, he could tell that. She wanted to be back at the lodge, tearing the group apart with bare hands until she found Justin's killer.

'Can't we come back for that, Dad?'

The slit was about three feet high and two feet wide. He had to crouch sideways to get through and, while he wriggled, his body blocked the light so that it was total darkness inside. When he was through the opening and kneeling on the rock floor he could see a little more, but not much. The smell was the main thing that hit him, a rank animal smell suggesting goats or peccaries. He shuffled forward on his knees, squelching on some kind of droppings. There was a distant rushing sound that bothered him until he decided it must be the sulphur river running under the rock, to emerge at the waterfall. After a few minutes he could make out the outlines of the cave and see it was high enough to let him stand, as long as he kept his head bent. He took a step forward, one hand on the cave wall, eyes straining into the dark. One step forward, two steps, then he saw something that didn't belong in the cave or have anything to do with any possible animal's lair, something angular and pale in the dim light. He got his hands on it and carried it to the cave mouth to see it in the light.

An ice box. A blue and white plastic ice box of the sort you took on picnics. The exact ice box, or the twin of it, that Toby and Peter had been fussing over. He undid the clips and took the lid off. From outside, Debbie shouted to ask if he was all right and he told her he'd be out in a minute. It was still quite cold inside from the refrigerated pad, and more than half full of leaves. Quite ordinary leaves they looked to him, leaves of rubber plants and crotons of the kind that grew in their millions all over the island, nothing special at all. He sifted through them and found nothing else in the ice box, not even the smallest frog. He left it and, by the back wall of the cave, found something else – a haversack like the ones all his party had been given. It contained standard kit: map, compass, mint cake, water-purifying tablets. Then, at the bottom, he found a rubbery mass that puzzled him. He unrolled it and found seven condoms, vastly stretched out, and two pairs of thin surgical rubber gloves, one set used, one unused.

The condoms were no puzzle. He'd distributed one each on the first day of the survival class, much to the delight of Mal and Henry, explaining that they made a very good way of transporting water if you hadn't got a bottle with you. By the look of these, somebody had used them to bring water to the cave. But he couldn't make sense of the rubber gloves. Nobody in his right senses would use them to carry water. The only explanation seemed to be that they'd been used for their most obvious purposes – to avoid leaving finger prints. Anybody that careful would have wiped the machete handle after use. As the ice box would have been a nuisance to carry with them, he put it back where he'd found it in the cave. A search on hands and knees revealed no other clues.

'Dad, what are you doing in there?'

'Just coming.'

He squeezed back to the sunlight, dragging the pack with him.

'Is this Justin's?'

'No. His was newer, not so faded. Did you find it in the cave?'

'There was an ice box too, with a lot of leaves in it.'

'Toby and Peter had an ice box.'

'Yes, and Peter's been missing since Thursday morning.'

'But why would Peter . . . ?'

He could see her problem. If you had to nominate somebody from the party as a paid assassin, then Peter wouldn't be high on the list. But it was his problem too, because what could Peter have been doing in a cave with rubber gloves and an ice box full of inedible leaves?

But, then, the presence of the ice box didn't prove it had been Peter in the cave. Whoever had killed Justin might simply have come across Peter, butterfly-chasing in the forest, and taken the ice box off him, perhaps thinking there was food inside. But, if so, what had happened to Peter?

'We'll have to see what Toby says about it.'

He shouldered two packs, Debbie one, and they went on their way up the path. The sense of being watched by Justin had grown to be so much of a habit with him that now he had to remind himself that he wasn't out there somewhere in the trees.

CHAPTER TEN

There was tension at the lodge that reached out at them as soon as they came up the ladder to the balcony. Ellie, Russ and Annabel were sitting in a huddle round the table, surrounded by unwashed plates and cups. They all looked as if they'd slept badly. Ellie was on her feet as soon as she saw them.

'Where've you been? Have you found him?'

Dumping the two packs, Birdie shook his head.

'I'd better tell Toby. Where is he?'

'In the dormitory. But why do you have to tell Toby about my husband?'

Her voice was shrill and her fists clenched. She looked ready to hit somebody, probably Birdie, although he couldn't see what he'd done wrong.

'Simon got back all right, didn't he?'

'No, Simon did not get back all right. We haven't seen him since that bloody walk. I thought you'd have found him by now.'

His head was spinning. After two nights with very little sleep he had to fight to keep a grasp on events.

'But I did find him, yesterday evening. I sent him back here. He was no more than a hundred yards away from where you're standing when I last saw him.'

Russ said, 'He didn't get here, Birdie.'

His voice was solemn. He was clearly having a bad attack of born leaderdom.

'How can he have not got here? I mean, all he had to do was walk straight along the path for a hundred yards. He could see the light.'

Ellie said, 'You're telling us you brought him to within a hundred yards of here and went off and left him? You didn't even have the sense to see him safely back?'

'What sort of state was he in?' Russ demanded.

'Tired, a bit dehydrated. Nothing worse than that.'

'That's it, then, isn't it? If he was dehydrated he probably got giddy and lost his sense of direction. After you left him, he could have wandered off goodness knows where.'

Birdie had had enough. 'If you must know, the main thing wrong with Simon was that he was half out of his mind with jealousy about the way you two are carrying on. If he didn't come back here after I left him, it was probably because he couldn't stand any more of it.'

That stunned them into silence for a while.

Annabel said, 'What about the others? At least you've found Debbie.'

Debbie had slumped into her favourite place on the edge of the balcony, one leg dangling over. Her eyes were half closed and the way she kept her hand to her forehead showed she had a headache as thumping as his own.

'I didn't find Peter, though. Did any of you see any trace of him yesterday?'

Annabel shook her head.

Russ said, 'Ellie and I spent all day up there in the hills. I can tell you for sure, Birdie, nobody's been up there. I know something about tracking and there wasn't a sign.'

The implication was that Birdie didn't know about tracking or anything else. He wasn't looking forward to breaking the news about Justin, although it couldn't be put off much longer.

'Where are all the rest of us? We've got things to discuss.'

Russ snorted. 'We certainly have.'

Annabel was more helpful. 'Still asleep. It was a long day yesterday. Do you want me to go and get Helena?'

'If you think it's all right to wake her. Did you get enough sleep?'

Annabel ran a hand through her blonde, sweat-streaked hair. 'All sorts of funny dreams. What about you, Ellie?'

'I didn't sleep much,' Ellie said.

From the look she gave Birdie, she blamed him for that as well, but at least he'd got part of his answer. The three women had apparently spent the night together in the dormitory. He decided to wake Toby and the two Hoorays himself. Henry, flat on his back, was giving out great gurgling snores, dressed only in a sweaty tee-shirt reading 'Brompton piss artists do it in lifts'. Mal was curled up in a foetal position, hugging his pillow. Toby was the only one awake, sitting on his bed and rummaging through his pack.

'I'm sorry, we haven't found your brother.'

Toby blinked. He looked as if he was having trouble remembering what Birdie was talking about. 'I told you, you shouldn't worry too much about Peter. He often goes off on his own. Does it for weeks sometimes when he gets interested.'

'Recognise this pack?' He swung it on the bed beside him.

Toby stared at Birdie, then at the pack.

'Have a look inside.'

Carefully Toby laid its contents on the bed beside him, including the condoms and rubber gloves.

'Yes, it's Peter's. Where did you find it?'

'In a cave. What would he be wanting with rubber gloves?'

Toby seemed, for once, at a loss. His shiny forehead creased and his eyes darted round the room.

'Snakes.' The word exploded out of him. 'You never know when you'll need to handle a snake.'

Birdie stared at him. He wasn't much of a naturalist, but it was obvious even to him that surgically thin rubber gloves would be poor protection against snake-bite.

'You sure you don't mean porcupines?'

Toby didn't seem to notice the sarcasm. 'No. No, they're for snakes.'

Birdie began to put the things back in the pack.

'There was your ice box in the cave, too, with a lot of leaves inside. Any idea what he'd want with that?'

'You can live a long time on leaves, if you know what you're doing.'

'Like rubber plant leaves?'

Again, Toby seemed to take him quite seriously, although the answer was ludicrous.

'Oh, yes. Almost any kind of leaves.'

He seemed preoccupied. Sweat was forming in the folds of his forehead. What interested Birdie almost as much as his crazy answers was the thing he didn't ask. He'd been told his missing brother's pack had been found in a cave but had shown no curiosity about where the cave was. This, along with his lack of worry about Peter's whereabouts, suggested he'd known where he was all the time. He was beginning to think he'd taken the ecological brothers too much at their face value. He jerked his chin towards the Hoorays.

'Have those two been sleeping like this all night?'

'Yes. Yes, I suppose so.'

Birdie suspected he wouldn't have noticed if they'd grown wings and flown through the roof.

He went over to Henry and shook him by the shoulder. 'Wake up. We're having a conference out on the balcony.'

It took a lot more shaking to tear him away from his sleep. By then, Mal was awake too, hair tousled, and blinking.

'Found the wanderers, Birdie?'

'That's what we're having the conference about.'

It took a while to organise them all around the table. Annabel made the coffee, taking pity on Debbie's exhaustion. When they were assembled he looked around. There were Mal and Helena, mopingly intertwined on one side of the table, Annabel perched astride the end of the bench, emanating mosquito repellent and musky sweat. Ellie sat bolt upright, staring ahead of her, deliberately not looking at Russ, who'd perched himself on the far end of the table, opposite Birdie, in a posture that was all too clearly adversarial. Henry, between loud yawns and stomach rumblings, kept making inane remarks about manhunts and bring on the bloodhounds, but only Annabel giggled. Then there was Toby, still with creased forehead and a general sense of not being in the same world as the rest of them. Debbie had stayed where she was on the edge of the balcony, but her eyes were wide open now. He could feel them on him when he dropped his bombshell, or rather his half-bombshell.

'I thought you should all know this as soon as possible. Justin's had an accident.'

The first thing to break the silence was a little scream from Helena. Then Russ's voice, 'What sort of accident, Birdie?'

'I found him in the pool under the waterfall. He'd drowned.'

He'd have liked to have seen Toby's face when he said it, but the arrangement of the group meant he was staring at Russ, and what he saw there was disapproval, mixed with a kind of triumph.

It was Henry, though, who broke the silence. 'I say, this is getting a bit much, isn't it?'

Nobody else said anything, and he bleated on, sounding much as if he were complaining about a flat bottle of champagne at a charity ball. 'I mean, I know we're paying through the nose for a survival holiday, but one did expect that one would, well, survive, so to speak.'

'That's right. That's two in five days.'

Russ provided the plebeian baritone line to Henry's upper class tenor, but seemed content to let him lead the protest for a while: 'I mean, first there's poor old Morton, though one couldn't be too surprised about that, seeing he was as drunk as an alligator's aunt most of the time. But when it comes to the likes of Justin, well I mean . . . there's something wrong somewhere.'

His voice trailed away. Even Henry was capable of seeing that it might not be in the best of taste to imply that while accidents to the likes of Morton were acceptable, it was a different matter when they happened to a chap of one's own social class.

Helena, meanwhile, was well launched on a course of hysterics. She had her arms clamped round Mal's neck and was sobbing the same thing over and over again into his chest. Being used to Helena by now, it wouldn't have occurred to any of them to be interested in what she was saying if Russ hadn't taken it on himself to notice.

'What's that she's saying, Mal?'

Mal, distressed and embarrassed, shook his head. He couldn't hear what she was saying either.

Annabel went over and knelt beside her. The coolness caused by her victory in the engagement stakes had vanished with the crisis.

'It's all right darling. It's all right.'

She stroked Helena's dusty hair.

'I want to know what she's saying,' Russ insisted.

'Don't keep on at her. You can see she's upset.'

All the attention of the group was on Helena, and Russ, now leaning over the table at her. Birdie had a sense of events going out of control.

Russ spoke directly to Helena, 'What are you saying?'

The roughness of his voice among all the sympathy had the effect of a slap on the face. She surfaced, gulping from a sea of tears, and said with the clarity that opens garden fetes, 'I don't think it was an accident.'

Birdie stopped breathing. He heard a sharp movement from Debbie behind him. Once Helena had delivered her line she took refuge in Mal's chest again, but Russ's voice dragged her out of it.

'Why do you say it wasn't an accident?'

'They were all against him. Everybody was against him.'

'Darling, you didn't even like him.'

That was Annabel's calming voice.

'I know. That makes it worse.'

'I don't think anybody liked Justin very much.' Henry had found his voice again.

Mal shushed him. 'Yes, but *de mortuis* whatever it is.'

Russ said, 'Are you implying that somebody killed him?'

A shock ran round the table. Helena's mouth dropped open.

'No. No, why should anybody kill Justin?'

Russ said, patiently, 'You said everybody was against him.'

'But that doesn't mean they'd want to kill him. I mean, you can not like somebody without wanting to kill them, can't you?'

'What did you mean then?'

Tears were streaming down her face, dripping off her chin. 'I think he killed himself. I think he came here knowing he was going to kill himself.'

Birdie breathed again.

'Oh, come on.' That was Henry. 'Why would he want to kill himself? I mean, he had everything ahead of him. He'd have had plenty of money when his old man died.'

'Who inherits now?'

It was a technical question from Mal, and Henry treated it that way.

'There're a couple of sisters. But the point is, people like old Justin don't go and kill themselves.'

'They do if everybody hates them,' Helena insisted, but more weakly.

'Oh, come off it. Justin loved people hating him.'

And that seemed to settle it. Helena subsided against Mal's shoulder and Russ did what he'd clearly been intending to do all along and turned the attack on Birdie.

'All right, it was an accident. But accidents don't just happen.' He said it as if he'd just invented the idea. 'Accidents happen when people aren't properly organised, and this thing hasn't been properly organised from the start.'

There were several murmurs of agreement at that. Birdie thought they came from Ellie, the Hoorays and possibly Toby.

'We've had people running off into the forest and getting lost. We've had to spend practically the whole holiday running search parties and now we've got two people dead. We don't want any more accidents.'

'I don't want any more accidents, either,' Birdie protested.

'I'm sure we're all glad to hear that. So, priorities.' He looked round the table. Nobody spoke. 'Priority one: get the bodies decently buried. Priority two: find Simon and Peter. Priority three: get ourselves off this damned island. Priority four: when we get back to England, get our money back.'

'Plus damages,' Henry said. 'Mental strain and so forth.'

Russ ignored him. 'Does everybody agree with that?'

This time the murmurs of agreement sounded unanimous. Birdie, with the prospect of perpetual bankruptcy added to his problems if the firm tried to make him pay, cleared his throat and wished his head would stop thumping.

'You're moving too fast, Russ. For a start, about the bodies. It's no good burying them. They'll have to go to St Lucia for a post mortem.'

'They can dig them up again.'

Mal sounded quite cheerful about that. Jungle funerals seemed to have quite a hold on his limited imagination.

'We can't just leave Justin out there rotting,' Henry said, then added, 'or poor Morton.'

Birdie realised he might have to give in on this, but how to get the bodies buried without somebody noticing Justin's neck had been sliced with a machete was more than he could work out in his present state. Russ was dealing with his second and third points.

'Then we've got to get ourselves properly organised and find Peter and Simon.' A glance up the table at Birdie, convicting him of being improperly organised. 'Then we need a boat to get us off.

Have you been in touch with St Lucia again, Birdie?'

With his other troubles, Birdie had forgotten he was supposed to have put out a call for help on Morton's broken radio. 'No. I'm sure they'll send somebody as soon as they can.'

'Then where are they? You're sure they got your message in the first place? Did they acknowledge?'

'Yes, they acknowledged,' he lied.

'Well, where are they? That was yesterday morning. They could have been here and back several times over by now.'

'Perhaps the boat's broken down.'

Birdie didn't expect Russ to be impressed by this, and he wasn't. 'Then, they'll just have to get another boat. We can't stay here till Monday, not after all this.'

Monday, three days away, was when their own boat was scheduled to arrive and carry them for rest and recuperation on the beaches of Barbados. Birdie knew he'd need all of those three days, uninterrupted.

'We'll have to contact them again,' Russ said. 'I'll come down with you next time.'

Something in the way he said it made Birdie wonder if Russ guessed he'd lied. He tried a diversion. 'We should find Peter and Simon first. They've been away thirty-six hours now. They can't have any food left.'

'Unless they've managed to trap a monkey,' Henry sniggered.

Russ rounded on him. 'If you can't be helpful, you can at least stop making stupid comments.'

'Aye aye, sweetie.' Henry sketched a salute that turned into a two-fingered gesture on the way down.

Ellie said hastily, 'If we didn't find them yesterday, how are we going to find them today?'

'Water,' Russ said. 'They've got to have water. Instead of running ourselves exhausted looking for them, what we've got to do is keep an eye on the freshwater stream from here down to the sea. They've got to come there at some time.'

'That's good sense.' It was Toby's first contribution to the discussion and it surprised Birdie because he seemed full of eagerness now to find his brother. It struck him that keeping attention on the freshwater side of the island would divert it from the cave where Peter's pack and the ice box had been found. He was more sure than ever that Toby knew about the cave and, he wouldn't be surprised, knew where Peter was as well.

Russ was planning his campaign, scorning maps as usual and demonstrating his memory for terrain.

'We'll have someone at the water hole, and where the path cuts across, and down a bit further behind Morton's bungalow. If we set up a cordon, we're bound to find them sooner or later. They'll have to come to where the water is.'

Birdie knew he was being demoted, but it suited him very well that Russ should be exerting his powers of leadership somewhere comparatively harmless. He tried to signal tactfully to Mal and Henry that he wanted to talk to them. It took a while to get the message over, but eventually they ambled across to him in the corner of the balcony.

'Funeral party,' he said.

He collected two sheet sleeping bags from the beds, his own and Justin's, and the shovel from under the balcony they used to dig pits for the Elsan waste. When they were ready, he got Russ on his own and told him to go ahead and mount his cordon by the river. The three of them would meet him near the stream when the job was done. He could see Russ would have liked to be part of the burying party as well but, as he pointed out, he'd got the search party so well in hand it would be a pity to waste his energy. To his relief, Russ accepted the flattery. He could handle Mal and Henry. Russ poking around the bodies would be a different matter. On his way down the steps, he saw Debbie was following them.

'You stay here, love. We won't be long.'

'I'm coming with you.'

And that was that. She stayed with them as he chose a piece of soft, comparatively flat ground in the bushes beneath the rock plateau, insisted on taking her turn with the Elsan shovel as they hacked a double grave out of the warm earth, and all the time he was cursing Justin in his mind for bringing this on her. At least he persuaded her to wait by the grave with Henry, who was being kind to her in his clumsy way, while he took Mal down the path to bring up Justin's body. His belief that Mal's enthusiasm for tropical funerals would stop short of viewing the body proved to be justified. Mal came over quite squeamish and left Birdie to shroud the body in the white sheet sleeping bag, then in a sheet of polythene for its journey uphill. After that it was Henry's turn to help with the removal of Morton's body from its temporary resting place in the tree roots, and he proved even more squeamish than Mal. Birdie had to speak to him quite sharply to get him to carry his share of the shrouded burden. Then it was simply a case of shovelling the earth back over them, an operation Birdie performed while Henry was noisily sick behind a tree. So far, so good.

'I don't envy the people who have to dig them up,' Mal said.

All this time Debbie had hardly uttered a word, but on the journey back she surprised Birdie by carrying on what amounted to a social inquisition of Mal and Henry. At first he thought it was a result of the strain, but as he listened he realised there was more to it than that.

'Had you known Justin long, Henry?'

'Well, sort of. He and my younger brother were in the same form at prep school till Justin got chucked out for poisoning the gerbils.'

'Did you see him after that?'

'Well, sort of. Parties, the odd wedding or funeral, that sort of thing. I mean, we were never what you could call close.'

'What about his father? Do you ever see him?'

'He's on some of the same boards as my stepmother's first husband. He comes to shoot with my father sometimes.'

'Do you like him?'

'Seems decent enough.'

'What about you, Mal? Did you know Justin long?'

'He was at the same school as I was for a couple of terms. Two forms lower down, though. That was after he had to leave Harrow.'

'And his father?'

'His bank does some business with our firm. I was at a meeting with him just a few days before I came away.'

'Did he say anything about Justin then?'

'Oh, no. You didn't talk about Justin to his father.'

That seemed as far as she was likely to get, but a few minutes later she started again on a different tack.

'What about Helena and Annabel? Did they know Justin well?'

Mal said, 'I think they'd met him at parties and so on.'

'Have you two known Helena and Annabel long?'

Here, for once, there was disagreement. Henry said, 'Oh, yes,' just as Mal said, 'Oh, not really.' Then they both fell over themselves to qualify what they'd said.

'Well, not all that awfully long, I suppose.'

'That's to say, we've known them, but not known them particularly well till now, if you see what I mean.'

'No, I don't.'

Birdie knew she was being deliberately obtuse, but with Henry at any rate it seemed to work.

'What Mal means is, you can be in the same sort of circuit as people, you know, same parties, some of the same friends and so on, but not really know them all that well. Then later you get to know them well and . . . well. That's it.'

'That's why you've got engaged to Annabel?'

'Yes, I mean, we really got on well so I thought . . . well.'

Henry's eloquence ran out and Debbie started on Mal again. 'Are you going to get engaged to Helena?'

'Well . . . ' Mal began awkwardly, and Birdie thought if either of them uttered the syllable again he'd brain him.

'Well, I . . . that's we, haven't decided. I mean, you have to be sure, don't you? It's not just a case of liking somebody on holiday, however much you like them. You have to be sure it's going to work.'

'Oh, stop shivering around on the edge. Jump in, man.' Henry sounded genuinely exasperated and Birdie had an idea there'd been arguments between them already on whether Henry was doing the right thing.

'It's all right for you, Henry,' Mal said stiffly. 'You're a younger son. You can do what you like.'

'I intend to do what I like. If my father or my stepmother don't like it, they'll just have to lump it.'

But there was a shade too much defiance in Henry's voice and Birdie thought Annabel still had some hard work ahead of her before she converted that band of creeper around her finger to a solitaire diamond. Henry's anger killed conversation for a while and he and Mal fell some way behind, leaving Birdie and Debbie together.

'Well, did you get what you wanted out of that?' he asked her.
'It's odd. Those two, the Helibels, Justin, Justin's father. They seem to know each other, but in a funny sort of way.'
'It's tribal.'
'Mal and Justin's father met just a few days ago, you heard that?'
'Yes, at a business meeting. Is Justin's father supposed to have pushed a note under the blotter?'
'It could have been a cover, that meeting.'
'If Justin's father was paying Mal to murder Justin, he'd have hardly have met him in public, would he?'
'Why not? It would make people less suspicious. Anyway, I don't think Justin's father necessarily wanted him murdered. What he wanted were the photos.'
'All that's beside the point. You heard the scream like I did, just after half-past five this morning. Mal was curled up asleep in the dormitory then. So was Henry and so were the Helibels.'
'We don't know that. Mal might have slipped out and Henry protected him.'
'There's still Toby to deal with. He was there as well. As a matter of fact, Toby's a lot more interesting.'
It was his first chance to tell her about Toby's reaction to his brother's pack, and his suspicions that he'd known about the cave all along.
'And, remember, the only people we know were away from the lodge when we heard that scream were Peter and Simon. They're the two we've got to concentrate on, when we find them.'
'But Justin's father could easily have met Mal and Henry or the Helibels. Where would he meet Peter or Toby?'
He opened his mouth to tell her she wouldn't solve it through this obsession with Justin's father and the pictures, but a gnat flew in and by the time he'd choked it up he'd thought better of it. He could only dislodge that idea from her mind by producing Justin's murderer. Until then, argument was a waste of energy.
When they got to the lodge, he suggested that Henry should stay behind to look after Annabel and Helena, while he and Mal went to join Russ's party at the stream. He wanted Debbie to stay at the lodge too, but expected opposition and was surprised when she agreed without argument. When he and Mal were well on

their way down the road it occurred to him that she'd stayed because she wanted a chance to cross-question Helena and Annabel. He'd always known Debbie could be stubborn, but he was only just beginning to appreciate her skill in getting her own way.

CHAPTER ELEVEN

Birdie and Mal caught up with Russ's party near the freshwater stream, on the path to the place where the peccaries came to drink. Russ was on his knees, with Ellie and Toby standing over him, and for an optimistic moment Birdie thought the born leader had a rebellion on his hands. It turned out that what he was seeing was the revelation of Russ the expert native tracker. He was poring over two footprints in the muddy path, one new one just planted by Toby and another less clear example to one side of the path.

'You can see they're not the same, can't you? Yours is a KSB. The other one's a straight Vibram.'

He was too absorbed in his role to pay much attention to the arrival of Birdie and Mal, beyond a raised hand warning them not to step on the tracks. Birdie, looking over Ellie's shoulder, saw the fainter track was pointing towards the watering place. It had been dried by the sun but had probably been made since the overnight rain.

'Your brother's got KSBs like yours,' Russ said, 'so it isn't him. What sort of boots has Simon got, Ellie?'

'Ordinary old hiking boots.'

'Standard Vibram sole pattern, then. I think this is Simon's footprint, probably made a few hours ago.'

He looked up at them for approval.

'If we had one of his socks,' Birdie said, 'we could give it to you to sniff.'

'All Simon's socks smell of athlete's foot powder,' Ellie said. There was a note of regret in her voice that hadn't been there two days before.

Baulked of his applause, Russ got to his feet. 'I want you all to stay behind me. We don't want anybody's big feet spoiling the trail.'

Birdie, whose feet were by far the biggest, fell resentfully into place behind Ellie. He had a mental picture of Russ ten years younger as a scout, stiff with badges from wrist to shoulder. Putting Russ in his place was a luxury he couldn't afford in the circumstances. It was at least some relief that after that first scuffed step the track of the Vibram soles was so clear that even Russ couldn't pretend there was any great art in following it. It looked as if Simon – if it was Simon – had taken some care to keep to the edge of the path when he was near the road, then abandoned caution either out of haste or boredom. As they got nearer the watering place the ground became softer and the prints overlaid lines of animal tracks, mainly peccaries.

'That shows he came along here after sunrise,' Russ said. 'The peccaries had gone by then.'

It was just past eleven o'clock. The wanderer with the Vibram boot soles might have passed that way as much as six hours before.

Birdie, less obtrusively than Russ, was trying to do his own deciphering of the tracks, looking for an answer he could hardly expect them to give. What he wanted to know was whether they could be the tracks of a man who, not long before making them, had done Justin to death with a couple of blows from a machete. So far, all he'd been able to gather was that the person who made them was in a fair state of exhaustion. The prints were close together, little steps rather than strides. They meandered from side to side of the path and in places in the soft mud there'd be a deeper print, suggesting he'd stood for a while to get his strength back before going on. If Simon, in the state that Birdie had left him at sunset the night before, had wandered down to the waterfall by dawn, killed Justin, then dragged himself half way across the island for fresh water, he'd have been in the last stages of exhaustion.

'What's that?'

Russ stopped suddenly and bent over, and the whole line concertinaed behind him. He was looking at a long smooth mark in the mud that, for a yard or so, replaced the footprints.

Birdie guessed the answer but said nothing. It was Ellie who spoke, her voice tight and angry.

'It's a knee. He was crawling along. Look, there's a handprint.'

Whether she was angry with Simon, Russ or all of them, Birdie didn't know. There was the clear print of a left hand to the side of the track, driven in deep as if he'd fallen spreadeagled. After a few yards or so, the footprints began again, closer together than before and more wavering.

'He must have been in a bad way,' Russ said.

Birdie thought it was just beginning to dawn on the pair of them that they'd driven Simon nearly mad with their affair. If his suspicions were right, they still didn't know the half of it.

'We'd better go carefully from now on,' he said.

Russ glared at him. He'd been put out when Ellie had scored a tracking point of her own and was in no mood for advice.

'Why have we got to be careful about Simon, for goodness sake?'

It was on the tip of Birdie's tongue to say, 'Because Simon killed a man this morning on the off-chance it might be you.' That would have to wait until they'd found Simon and, besides, something still puzzled him. Russ was several inches taller than Justin and much broader across the back and shoulders. It would be hard to mistake one for the other, even from behind. But Simon would be ill with anger and exhaustion by then and, with the sun just coming up, the light would have been dim down by the waterfall. It might have happened that way and, if Simon was hiding somewhere up ahead of them, his reaction when the man he thought he'd murdered walked in at the head of a posse would be explosive.

'Say what you like, Russ. I'm going first.'

Russ shrugged but gave in, and Birdie led the party the last few hundred yards along the path to the watering place. The freshwater stream tipped itself over a few feet of rock and spread into a deep pool, overhung with bushes and creepers. The mud round it was pitted with animal tracks. When he knew they were near the place, Birdie ran on ahead. It had occurred to him that pools on Diabola had a habit of producing floating bodies, and if this one was going to make it a hat trick he wanted to get there before Ellie. For once, though, there was nothing there but water, flowing down the rock and pushing itself in a gentle current through the pool and on down to the sea. The tracks ended at the water's edge and there were toe prints, showing where the person had knelt down to drink. Russ marched up beside him.

'Don't trample all over them, Birdie.'

He cast around for a while, sniffing the air and falling dramatically to his knees while the rest of them refilled water bottles. Birdie watched him closely and saw the great tracker was baffled. The path from the watering place turned at right angles to follow the stream down towards the sea and was muddy enough to show good footprints, but there wasn't a sign that anything had used it except peccaries. There was a fainter path leading upwards towards the lodge, but no prints on that either. On the far side, the watering place was closed in by a steep bank of trees.

'He must be in there somewhere,' Ellie said.

From where they were standing, the forest looked too dense to let in anything bigger than a mongoose.

'Ellie, wait.'

The shout came from Russ. Without consulting any of them, Ellie, as neatly as a cat, had jumped the stream and was standing on a rock on the far side. The race to join her there was won narrowly by Russ, with Birdie splashing through on his heels, both of them telling her to wait.

'Somebody's been through here. I can see.'

Her voice sounded scared. Russ pushed her aside and plunged head first into the trees. Birdie followed, dislodging fern plants, feet slipping on a bank of wet earth. He had a sense that disaster was up there a few trees ahead and he could do nothing to prevent it.

'Russ, for goodness sake, wait a minute'

Whether Russ was still following a trail he didn't know. The man's own bulk would obliterate any signs of it. What stopped them, after some minutes of burrowing, was a huge trunk that had staked out a space for itself among the other trees like the pole at the centre of a bell tent. Nothing grew for ten feet or so around it except some discouraged trails of spikey grass.

Russ straightened up. 'He's somewhere around here.'

He spoke with complete certainty and Birdie agreed with him. A man as exhausted as Simon must be would go no further than this for a hiding place. Both Birdie and Russ jumped round when

the bushes behind them rustled, but it was only Ellie.
'Have you found him?'
'He can't be far away,' Russ said.
She called his name several times. It was a pity, Birdie thought, that anxiety for him gave a shrill edge to her voice, so that it sounded as if she was calling him in to do some neglected job around the house. Hurry up, Simon, and bring your Black and Decker. If he'd been Simon, he'd have stayed under a bush. And that, apparently, was just what Simon was doing.
'Simon, do stop playing about.'
If Simon had been tempted to answer his wife's call, Russ's voice would have sent him back under again.
Birdie tried a more conciliatory tone. 'It's all right, Simon. You can come out now.'
Come out and tell us if you killed Justin, he thought. And, don't worry, I don't blame you. It was as ineffective as the other two.
Russ gave an exasperated sigh. 'We'll just have to come and get you, then.'
He moved round to the other side of the giant tree trunk, Birdie following.
'Here, what's this?'
There was something blue and rectangular lying beside the trunk. Russ bent to pick it up.
'It's a book. What would he be . . . ?'
'Look out!'
Birdie didn't see what happened. All he heard was a movement in the bushes on their right, and by then the thing was launched, coming straight at Russ as he bent over to pick up the book. Instinctively he flung himself at Russ with all his weight, catching him by surprise so that he fell sideways. And even then the fool didn't know what was happening. It was Birdie he cursed, kicking and elbowing at him like the losing side in a bar-room brawl. It was some satisfaction to Birdie to do what he'd been itching to do for days and pin him down in a shoulder hold that left him nothing to do but curse.
'Russ, you bloody idiot. Simon was out there with a machete. If I hadn't knocked you over, he'd have got you.'

It took Russ some time to understand. He was still inclined to blame Birdie and only the sight of Ellie standing there frozen and white faced began to bring home to him what had happened. That, and the machete lying on the ground beside the book he'd dropped, and the wedge of wood it had gouged out of the tree when it struck.

'That could have been your neck,' Birdie said, holding out the wedge of wood.

'Simon.'

Ellie's voice was a long wail addressed to the forest at large and this time it worked. A bush quivered no more than ten feet away from them and a battered figure in a camouflage suit crawled out from under it, hair matted with twigs and leaves. He straightened up and brushed at the knees of his trousers like any suburban gardener.

'Hello, dear. I'm sorry about that.'

He might have been apologising for stepping on the lobelias, except lobelias would have caused more emotion.

Russ goggled at him, face sweating and red from the fight with Birdie.

'What did you want to go and do that for? You fucking nearly killed me!'

'I'm sorry, but you shouldn't read other people's books. It's very rude.'

'Of course I wasn't reading your bloody book. What would I want with your book?' He looked ready to twist Simon's neck.

Ellie stepped between them. 'I don't think he meant to hurt you, Russ.'

That seemed to strike Russ dumb and Birdie, who'd picked up the machete, could sympathise with him for once. He said to Simon, as calmly as he could manage, 'Why didn't you go back to the lodge last night?'

Simon seemed to be aware of him for the first time. He stared and blinked, as if last night was a long time ago.

'I was going to,' he said, 'but they were out there on the balcony.' He looked first at Ellie, then Russ, then back at Birdie. 'Would you go in, if your wife was messing about with some muscle-bound moron right over your head?'

'You little . . .'

Russ made a movement towards him, but was restrained by Ellie. Birdie, still trying to sound calm, said, 'So what did you do, then?'

A sidelong glance from Simon suggested he knew where the questioning was heading.

'I . . . I wandered.'

'Wandered where?'

'Does it matter?' Ellie asked.

She was standing slightly closer to her husband than to Russ, but there was no more than a couple of feet in it.

Birdie persisted, 'Where did you go?'

'I . . . I don't know. I went down to the road and I . . . I walked up and down a bit until it got light. I'd thought of going down to the harbour and trying to signal a boat. I thought I'd go off and leave them to it, but . . .'

'But what?'

'I remembered what you said about not many boats coming here. Then I thought it was a long way to the harbour and I was thirsty again, so I came here instead.'

There was a total simplicity about the way he spoke, like a man too exhausted physically and emotionally to tell anything but the truth. Birdie wondered if he could simply have blanked out the killing of Justin. He showed him the machete.

'Where did you get this?'

'I found it in a ditch.'

Russ made a disbelieving sound. Birdie held up a hand to shush him.

'In a ditch by the road this morning. The books were there, too.'

Birdie had been holding the book without taking too much account of it. Now he glanced at it and saw it was not a printed book but a typescript bound in a floppy blue cover. A label on the front identified it as a doctoral thesis presented by one D D Schwartz to the Sociology Department of the University of Hawaii: 'Developmental aspects of Obeah in the Eastern Caribbean 1952-1986'. He remembered the row of books like it that had sat neatly on Morton's desk, until they'd been vandalised.

'It isn't your book, is it? Wasn't it one of Morton's?'

'Whoever's it was didn't want it. They'd left a lot of them in the ditch.'

'What does it matter about the bloody book?' Ellie said. 'Can't you see he's ill?'

It was true enough. Simon was making a pathetic effort to keep upright and deal with Birdie's questions, but he was swaying on his feet and his face was yellow-grey. They managed with difficulty to get him back down the steep tunnel of bushes to the watering place, where Mal and Toby were waiting. Once there he collapsed on them and it was clear they'd have to give him some rest before they took him any further. They made him comfortable under a shelter of branches cut from the forest with the machete and Russ's Swiss Army knife and Ellie sat beside him, sponging his face from a water bottle. After a few minutes he seemed to go to sleep. Birdie, when he saw there was nothing to be done, took the book and machete and went to sit on a rock apart from the others.

He hadn't intended to read the thesis. As far as he was concerned the significance was that it was one of Morton's books. Apart from that, it's subject matter was of no consequence, although he dimly remembered Morton telling them that Obeah was a sort of local voodoo and had been strong on Diabola when there was a slave plantation there. He riffled through the pages, noting that they and the cover were damp and a little misshapen, as if the book had been left out in at least one rain storm. But his interest in the subject was only aroused when he found a leaf acting as a bookmark. He opened it and nearly fell off the rock when he realised what he was reading.

'*A spell to get your woman back (St Lucia, St Kitts, Diabola, pre C20)*'
Adapted survival of early formula, collected by the author verbally on St Lucia from subject D. Said to have been practised up to grandmother's time. Involved invariably possession of some object personal to the woman, eg nail clippings, hair etc (See Appendix B). In some cases also of man believed to have taken 'his' woman. As in other curse spells (Chapts 2 to 4) in extreme cases Obeah man might require parts of human body, eg fingers. (See reported court case St Kitts Appendix D.) Obeah formulae vary from island to

island, but generally believed to be most effective on night of full moon.

After that effort D D Schwartz went into a long chapter about the changing position of women in the Eastern Caribbean, but Birdie let him get on with it. It was the bit about fingers that bothered him. He'd assumed Justin's fingers had been lopped off by Morton, trying to defend himself, but was there another explanation? Had Simon, dragged unwillingly from suburbia to rain forest, subjected to Russ, put somehow in possession of Morton's voodoo book, been planning a little Black Magic? He looked down at Simon lying open-mouthed under his shade of branches, wife beside him, and wondered. A less likely voodoo man he'd never encountered.

As he watched, he saw Simon's eyes open and Ellie bend over to say something to him. He slithered down the rock.

'How're you feeling, Simon?'

'Better.'

His voice was a weak croak but his colour had improved. In an hour or so, when the sun was past its worst, he'd be fit enough to travel. Meanwhile, there was something that Birdie needed to check.

'You said you found the machete and some books in a ditch by the road. Can you remember exactly where?'

'Why do you keep bothering him about them?' Ellie demanded.

Birdie ignored her. 'Was it near here? Near Morton's bungalow?'

'Near here, I think.'

That was the best Birdie could get out of him. He walked over to where the others were sitting in the shade of some bushes and told them to keep an eye on Simon, he'd be back in an hour or so.

Russ was on his feet at once. 'Where are you going, Birdie?'

'Just down as far as the road.'

'I'll come with you.'

It was the first time he'd spoken to Birdie since they'd been wrestling together on the ground. He sounded subdued and, although his presence would be a nuisance, Birdie felt he couldn't refuse. He even thought Russ might be intending to offer a few words of gratitude. An embarrassed, 'Thanks, Birdie, you saved my life,' might just about have met the case adequately. Instead, what he got when they were out of earshot of the others was more blame.

'Why did you let a madman like Simon get his hands on a machete, Birdie?'

'He bloody well wouldn't have been a madman if you hadn't started messing around with his wife.'

'That isn't the point. None of the rest of us was issued with a machete, so how come Simon got his hands on one?'

Birdie, wishing he'd done some damage to Russ when he had the chance, said, as patiently as he could, 'That's what I'm trying to find out. He says he found it in a ditch with some books. I'm going to see if I can find the rest of the books.'

'Oh, yes, and what's that supposed to prove?'

Birdie didn't like this talk about proof. As far as Russ was concerned, the two deaths were accidents and Simon's potentially murderous assault on him no more than a mental aberration. The time might come to tell him that it was linked with Justin's death, but not yet, not until he knew more.

'I'd just like to know if Simon's telling the truth or not. If we don't find any more books, he probably isn't.'

If the tale about finding the machete and the Obeah book in a ditch was untrue, then the likelihood was that Simon had simply stolen them from Morton's cottage. In that case, had Simon, and not Justin, been the vandal? He didn't believe it, and told himself it wasn't just a case of wanting to believe Justin was guilty. Justin, in his own weird terms, had a motive for wanting to harm Morton, but Simon had none.

'One of these days,' Russ said, 'you'll tell me what's going on here.'

Birdie didn't like the sound of that either. He decided not to answer and ignored that and various other pointed remarks on the way to the road.

Once there, he made Russ useful.

'You take the left-hand side, I'll take this one. We'll work our way from here down as far as Morton's cottage. Remember, we're looking for books like the one Simon had.'

It was Birdie who found them, before they'd gone more than a few hundred yards down the road. Rain had beaten down some of the grass and weeds in the drainage ditch and a flash of white caught his eye. It turned out to be a white page dimpled with rain and sun, small black beetles crawling over it. He picked it up, shaking off the beetles, and found he was holding another typewritten thesis, this time on varying speeds of photosynthesis, bristling with graphs and mathematical formulae. Rooting around in the weeds he found, in quick succession, three works on geology and something to do with speech rhythms that made his head ache just to look at it. Beyond doubt, it was part of the library of books that Morton had kept so proudly on his desk, claiming to have done more of the research for them than the authors themselves. By this time Russ was standing beside him and, with his help, they found a couple more works of much the same kind.

'What's all this about?' Russ said, flipping open one of the geology books.

Birdie read the title. '"Underground water courses and outlets on the island of Diabola. Some volcanic comparisons."'

'Christ, what would anybody want with that stuff?'

'Somebody didn't,' Birdie pointed out. 'They got thrown away.'

Simon had claimed to have picked up the machete and his book on Obeah that morning. From the look of the books they might have been lying there since Wednesday night or early Thursday morning, when Morton's bungalow was attacked, and there was nothing on the face of it that disproved Simon's claim that he'd simply come across them. If he was speaking the truth about that, he'd probably have come into possession of the machete after daylight, so he couldn't have got all the way to the other side of the island and killed Justin with it at the time Birdie had heard the scream, just about sunrise. It was a big 'if', though. He'd only Simon's word for it about the time when he'd found them. It could have been before dark the night before. In that case, though, where had he hidden them when Birdie had met him?

'Satisfied?' Russ asked.

'I suppose so.'

'Well, I'm not, Birdie. Do you recognise this lot?'

'Yes, they're Morton's.'

'That's right. So what are they doing in a ditch?'

Birdie tried to get his brain to move fast, and failed. 'Morton was pretty drunk that night. He was a peculiar character.'

'Balls. You remember his bungalow – neat as a nun's knickers. He wouldn't change that much when he was drunk.'

'So, what's your theory, Russ?' He knew it was a mistake to ask. Russ the tracker was bad enough. Russ the detective was a genie that should have been kept in the bottle at all costs.

'I'm glad you asked me that, Birdie. I think somebody was trying to get at Morton. I mean, you could tell he liked books. He had such a lot of them.'

'Perhaps somebody thought they'd go in and have a look at them after he was dead.'

'Funny thing to do, though, wouldn't it be, for one of us?'

'One of us just threw a machete at you.'

'Look at it another way, Birdie. Suppose somebody got in there and took them and threw them away before he was dead. What would that say to you?'

'That somebody didn't like Morton.'

It was inescapable. Even Birdie couldn't pretend to be that dim.

'Right, Birdie. Bit of a coincidence, isn't it?'

'Coincidence?'

It was like being under a landslide. You could see it coming, but there wasn't time to get away.

'Yes, coincidence, Birdie. I mean, somebody hating Morton enough to throw his books away, then he goes and has this accident.'

'I don't see why . . .'

'You're sure it was an accident, Birdie? You wouldn't have missed anything?'

'I didn't miss anything.'

Russ stood staring down at the cover of a geology book, then added it to the untidy pile Birdie was holding.

'I think we should go down and have a look at his bungalow, Birdie. See if we can find out a bit more.'

'No.'

It came out as a yelp. If Russ saw the wreckage in Morton's bungalow he'd ask himself, among other things, how Birdie had been able to summon help from St Lucia on a radio set with a gaping hole in it.

'We've got to get Simon back. We can't leave him lying about in the hot sun.'

'There're plenty of people to take him back: Mal and Toby and Ellie. It's probably just as well if I keep out of his way for a bit in any case.'

'I wish you'd thought of that before.'

'Anyway,' Russ said, 'I'm going down for a look at that bungalow. You can come if you like.'

Birdie knew, after the morning's little episode, that he could pin Russ to the ground again if he wanted to, but he couldn't keep him that way for the rest of their time on the island. The best he could manage, now it had come to this, was to go along with him and try to control him.

'All right, Russ, I'll come with you. But we've got to go back and see to Simon first.'

Russ grumbled a bit at that but fell in with it. Birdie had a suspicion that, for all his bravado, he wasn't so enthusiastic about going anywhere on the island on his own. The attack from Simon had shaken him but, from Birdie's point of view, not enough. They trailed back along the path to find the patient sitting up eating Kendal mint cake and the rest of the party bored and ready to travel. There was no opposition to the idea that they should all walk back as far as the road together, then Ellie, Mal and Toby should escort him the rest of the way to the lodge. Nobody seemed curious about what Birdie and Russ would be doing in the meantime and it seemed to be generally assumed that they'd continue the search for Peter. As far as Birdie had any attention left to spare for it, Toby's attitude to this was beginning to puzzle him more and more. He'd shown no inclination to search around the watering place, no curiosity when Birdie and Russ came back to know if they'd seen any sign of his brother. Now, here he was, preparing to return to the lodge with the others, when surely he should have been agitating to go on with the search. It was all of a piece with his attitude to the discovery of the pack and the ice box, too laid-back by half.

On the way to the road Simon walked slowly, leaning heavily

on Birdie's arm. He seemed to be in a state of shock or reaction, said nothing, and Birdie asked him no questions. The books had been cached under a rock by the road but the machete was stuck in Birdie's belt. He caught Simon's eyes straying towards it now and again, but could see no reaction from him. Once they'd reached the road, he unhooked Simon from his arm and passed him to Mal and Ellie.

'Let him take it easy. When you get there, put him to bed and tell Debbie to make sure he gets plenty of water.'

It only occurred to him later that the man he was handing over to Debbie for nursing was a prime suspect for killing Justin. Something else he'd get blamed for in due course.

Meanwhile, the immediate problem was Russ. Once they'd seen the hospital party on its way he swung down the road with all the enthusiasm of a patrol leader out for another badge. His spirits seemed to be rising again, which was bad news, and he was inclined to conversation.

'What do you think they'll do with Simon?'

It took Birdie a second to realise that he was talking about the attempted attack on him and not the possible murder of Justin.

'I don't know. Depends whether you report it, I suppose.'

'I mean, they'll have to put him away or something, won't they? They can't leave him wandering around like that.'

'I don't know.'

'I wonder what she'd do. I mean, she's still quite young, really.'

About eight years older than Russ. Birdie, irritated by this patronage of the elderly, said, 'I dare say she'd visit him every Saturday with bunches of grapes and be the leading light of Friends of the Funny Farm. It takes them that way sometimes.'

'What do you mean?' Russ looked quite alarmed.

'I mean that's how some wives behave when they've driven their poor wretched husbands into prison or the mental hospital.'

'Do you think so?'

At least it kept him quiet for a while. Birdie wondered whether he really had been planning a life of trailer tents and karate classes with a disencumbered Ellie. Trees weren't the only things that grew fast on Diabola. He was still thinking about it when the roof of Morton's bungalow came in sight.

He'd already decided that he'd let Russ go in first because he didn't trust himself to act horror and surprise convincingly. It was irritating when Russ paused at the door, his hand on the latch.

'Seems wrong, just walking in like this.'

Russ the tough was bad, but Russ the nervous could be even more of a pest.

'Morton's dead,' Birdie said brutally. 'He can't object.'

Russ gave him a hurt look, pressed down the latch and opened the door. Birdie saw him walk two steps into the room, pause and freeze.

'Birdie, someone's been in here.'

There was shock, even fear, in his voice, which was fine by Birdie. He followed, looking over Russ's shoulder, and gave what he hoped was a convincing gasp.

'Bloody hell.'

Russ still hadn't said anything. He seemed dazed as he took a few more steps towards the middle of the room, in a litter of scattered books and papers.

'Somebody hated him,' he said.

He still hadn't noticed the wrecked radio and Birdie knew that would be the hardest part, crystallising suspicions that were already floating around in his mind. There was even the possibility that, in his state of shock, he might be persuaded outside without registering it. Birdie tried to distract him.

'It's the books they went for mainly. What I can't understand is, why take one lot away and dump them in a ditch?'

Russ was wandering around the room, poking at the books with his boot. Birdie suggested, 'We ought to have a look round outside. They might have . . .'

Too late. The radio had been lying in a shadowed corner but Russ in his wandering had stubbed his toe on it.

'Birdie, come and look at this.'

It was just the same as when Birdie had last seen it, except that cockroaches had eaten away some of the plastic casing round the torn wires.

'Why would anybody do that?' he said.

'It's obvious, isn't it? To stop us calling for help.'

He'd given Russ too long to recover. He was already snapping back to the role of Russ the hard-eyed investigator, and those eyes were hardening more every moment as they swivelled from the wrecked radio to Birdie.

'You said you put out a call on it on Thursday morning after you found Morton's body.'

'Yes, I did.'

'And it was all right then?'

'Of course it was. I couldn't have put out a call on it like that, could I?'

'You're quite sure you did put out that call, Birdie?'

'Yes.'

'And everything else was all right then, the books and so on?'

'Yes.'

Russ closed his eyes and massaged his forehead while Birdie asked himself whether there'd been any alternative to a string of straight lies. He came to the conclusion that there hadn't. To explain to Russ his fears that Debbie had been mixed up in the sabotage, and the later, fiercer, necessity of convincing her that he had nothing to do with the death of Justin would put himself entirely in the man's hands, and he neither liked nor trusted Russ.

He'd opened his eyes now and had walked over to Morton's disordered desk, planting his fists on it and staring up at Birdie.

'So on Thursday morning this place was quite normal, you say.' There was an emphasis on the 'you say' but he let it pass. 'Then this morning, Friday morning, Simon reckons he found some of Morton's books and a machete in a ditch up the road. When we find the books, they look as if they've been out in the rain, right? So what does that suggest?'

Birdie, a reluctant Watson, did his best. 'It means somebody got in here and broke up the place between Thursday morning and early Friday.'

'Very early Friday, to give them time to get rained on. Late Thursday night, more like. The question is, who do we know was wandering around then?'

'Simon and Peter.'

A silence.

'And you,' Russ said. 'And you, don't forget.'

Birdie decided it was time to get angry.

'Are you suggesting I did all this? What reason would I have, for Christ's sake?'

'I don't know, Birdie. But then there's a lot I don't know about you. I think you're keeping something from us. I suppose Morton and Justin really are dead?'

'Of course they're dead. Why would I make up a thing like that?'

'Some warped idea of an initiative test?'

'That would be bloody warped. You can ask Mal and Henry. They helped bury them.'

Russ gave him the sort of stare that suggested he'd got a badge for that as well.

'That's another thing. You took good care I didn't see the bodies, didn't you?'

'Look, Russ, I don't know what sort of fantasy you're making, but lay off. First you reckon Morton's death isn't an accident, then you're as good as accusing me of breaking up his bungalow. Then you say I'm inventing the whole bloody thing. Make up your mind.'

'I'm trying to, Birdie. I'm trying to.'

He did a bit more brooding with closed eyes.

'See you outside,' Birdie said.

After a few minutes, Russ joined him by the empty peccary pen.

'And that's another thing. Who let the pig go?'

'I think Morton let it go himself before he came up to the lodge. It could be why he got drunk.'

Russ shook his head. 'He wouldn't have let it go. He was crazy about that pig.'

'He was always talking about letting it loose to join the rest of them.'

'That's the point. He talked about it but you could tell he didn't want to do it. I reckon whoever took his books away let his pig out as well.'

That at least was something Birdie could laugh at.

'Am I supposed to be a peccary-napper on top of everything else? Anyway, there wouldn't be much point in doing it to annoy Morton if I knew he was dead, would there?'

That was something that had bothered him from the start about

141

Justin. Why do malicious damage to the house of a man you'd already killed? He'd explained it to himself by arguing that Justin wasn't rational, but the question still nagged. He found it hard, as well, to imagine Justin carrying armfuls of books away with him.

To humour Russ, he helped in a search of the yard that revealed nothing of interest except that Russ pretended to find great significance in a pail with traces of pig swill, scattered with rat droppings and seething with cockroaches. He claimed Morton must have prepared it for the peccary and that showed he hadn't planned to let it go. Birdie pointed out that the peccary might have eaten from the pail before the rats got to it. He couldn't see why Russ was so interested in the animal. They trekked back together to the lodge in bad humour and silence, stopping to pick up the books Birdie had cached. Just before they climbed the steps to the balcony Russ said, 'I'm not telling the others about Morton's bungalow, Birdie. Not yet.'

'That's right. We don't want to worry them.'

'That wasn't what I was thinking about,' Russ said, in a tone that left Birdie in no doubt he was being warned. Every word and movement now would be subject to the scrutiny of Russ, private investigator. It struck him that, alone among the group, the bloody man was even enjoying his holiday.

CHAPTER TWELVE

At the top of the steps, four pairs of eyes turned towards them. The Helibels and the Hoorays were spread around the table in listless and resentful attitudes. A smell of sweat hit Birdie's nostrils and seemed to be coming mainly from the damp patches under the arms of Henry's designer jungle shirt and Annabel's elegant bare feet. He thought there was a smell of sex in the air, too, but a nervy, sweaty sex, not much enjoyed. Helena had put on fresh copper-tinted mascara, but she looked as if she'd been crying.

'Anything happening?' Henry demanded.

Birdie shook his head, leaving Russ to make conversation, and found Debbie round the corner in the kitchen. Her look of relief at seeing him made him happy for a moment, until he remembered she'd been cooped up for hours with adults who were more or less strangers to her and a secret on her mind. Grief, too. That was the only word for the shadow on her face, although he hated to admit it in connection with Justin.

'Hello, love.'

He dumped his armful of books on top of the cupboard.

'Where did you get those?'

'Simon found them dumped in a ditch, or says he did. How is he?'

'Asleep. Ellie's with him.'

'How did he seem?'

'Confused. Is it sunstroke, Dad?'

He'd thought about this moment a lot on his way up from Morton's bungalow, but there wasn't any soft way to tell her.

'I think it might be worse than that, love. I think Simon might have killed Justin.'

He'd expected a gasp from her, tears, even anger. What he

hadn't expected was this puzzled look, biting her bottom lip and, all the time, shaking her head slowly as if wondering how to point out to him that he'd got it wrong.

'Simon's not the sort of man who kills people,' she said. 'He's too scared.'

'A lot of people who kill do it because they're scared. Anyway, he had a good try at killing Russ. I saw it myself.'

At least that changed her expression to surprise. Toby and Mal, who'd brought Simon back, hadn't seen the attack themselves and obviously Simon hadn't talked about it. He gave her the details and even found himself defending Simon to her.

'He didn't know what he was doing. Some women just like playing games with people. I'm afraid Ellie's like that and she eventually drove him too far. It was just bad luck he came across Justin when he did.'

That was a lie. It struck him as the only piece of good luck in the whole scenario, but he could hardly say that to her.

'What about Morton?' she said. 'Is he supposed to have killed Morton as well?'

'It's possible.'

He still thought Justin had killed Morton, but wasn't going to break this truce. He needn't have bothered, though, because she broke it herself seconds later. 'It's no good Dad. I just don't see it. Not Simon. Anyway, where would he have met Justin's father?'

'Justin's father? What's Justin's father got to do with Simon going mad?'

'That's just it, Dad. Nothing.'

They stared at each other. The forest was turning bronze again as the sun went down.

'It's too much of a coincidence. Justin comes here with photos that would ruin his father if they get out, and somebody kills him. I'm sorry if poor Simon's ill, but I just don't see what that's got to do with it.'

'All right then, it's Peter you think was getting paid to kill him, is it?'

He said it bitterly, knowing he was driving back to the question she wouldn't answer: whether, in one part of her mind at least, she was convinced of his own guilt. If she heard that bitterness, she didn't react to it.

'Oh, no. Why should it be Peter?'

'Because,' he said, not able to keep away from the dangerous brink, 'there's nobody else on this damned island who could have killed Justin except Peter.'

She shook her head. He took another step towards the brink. 'Work it out for yourself. We both heard that scream. It was about half-past five this morning. We get back here an hour later and find most of them still in bed and asleep.'

'Not all of them. Russ and Ellie were out on the balcony. And Annabel.'

'Right, but did any of them look as if they'd gone over a mile through this forest in the dark, killed somebody and then run back again to get here before us?'

'No.'

'Well then, the only other person loose was Peter, and we know he couldn't have been far away because we found the things in the cave. If you're looking for a hired assassin, why not Peter?'

'He's not the type.'

'Oh, who is the type, then?'

He just stopped himself from adding, Me?

'What about Mal and Henry?' she said.

He'd been ready for the drop, but this stopped him short with surprise on the brink. There was relief, too, that she was still trying to get him off, even against the evidence as she saw it. But she'd have to do better than that. He pointed it out regretfully.

'They were asleep, love. Sleeping like babies. I went to wake them up myself.'

'They could have crept out and back again. Or one of them could and the other one covered for him.'

She was a trier, he appreciated that.

'But Russ and Toby were in the same dormitory, about four feet away. They'd have noticed.'

'I'm not sure Russ was there. I think he and Ellie were up together most of the night. You remember she said she hadn't slept well.'

He hadn't remembered, and was amazed and half scared about how much she was noticing.

'She did say something like that, but that doesn't mean . . .'

'You could tell.' Her voice was impatient, as when she'd blamed him for not noticing footprints. 'Annabel had just got up.

She was all sleepy-eyed and bedroomy. They weren't.'

'You might as well say Russ and Ellie did it, then.'

She considered this seriously. 'Yes. But the thing is, we don't know they'd ever met Justin's father. We know Henry and Mal did.'

There was no arguing with her over the motive, so he didn't try. 'But if they'd been paid by Justin's father to kill Justin, they wouldn't have admitted they knew him.'

'Everybody knows everybody in their sort of life.'

That struck him as true, but he couldn't adjust to the picture of the Hoorays as paid assassins, or disregard Toby's presence in the dormitory as Debbie was doing in her enthusiasm. Half her mind was doing a spirited job as counsel for her father's defence, but it wasn't good enough. A case of – what's her name? – Portia wondering if she might be on the wrong side. Fatal. Still, he was grateful.

'Another thing. It would explain why they're making such a big thing with Helena and Annabel.'

'I wouldn't have thought that needed much explaining.'

He wondered again, but wouldn't ask, if she knew about his own night with Annabel.

'I mean, things like Henry getting engaged to Annabel. He as good as said this morning that his family wouldn't like it. Did you get the impression that the Helibels aren't quite in the same bit of the social set-up as Mal and Henry?'

'I suppose so.'

It had struck him that the two women were enthusiastically husband hunting, and perhaps that came to the same thing.

'It would be good cover, you see. Getting all romantic with the Helibels to distract attention from what they were really here for. I'll bet they'll drop both of them like . . . like two pairs of old tights when they get back.'

'But what about Toby?'

She frowned, not getting the point.

'In the dormitory. How could one or both of them have crept out with Toby there?'

She gave it a moment's thought. 'Perhaps he's a sound sleeper?'

And, God help her, she even tried that out over the lamplit dinner an hour or so later, when she'd organised the plates of tinned fish, Russian salad and biscuits, with lemon barley water made strong to disguise the taste of the water purifier. Came straight out with it in a silence that had been broken only by the sounds of people gloomily chewing, like some old-fashioned hostess across a breakfast table.

'Do you sleep well, Toby?'

And Toby, who'd been carefully dissecting a sardine and posing the fragments on quarters of broken biscuit, replied in kind, with simple politeness.

'I'm a very light sleeper. My brother says a gecko crossing the ceiling is enough to wake me up.'

Birdie didn't try to catch Debbie's eye. So much for Mal or Henry creeping out unnoticed. But when it seemed everybody was going to relapse into silent munching, Annabel took up the social chat, or seemed to. As it happened, she was sitting next to Toby, so her voice needn't have been quite so loud when she asked him, 'Was it a gecko that woke you up this morning, then?'

Toby simply ignored the remark, although that must have been hard to do with Annabel's ringing tones a few feet away from his ear, and broke another biscuit in half. Birdie saw Debbie opening her mouth to ask a question, but Russ the super-sleuth got in first.

'What are you talking about, Annabel?'

She gave him a sideways look, then, with all of them watching her, calmly picked up a half biscuit from Toby's plate and munched it. He stared, but didn't try and stop her.

'There are plenty more biscuits,' Ellie said, coldly.

Annabel swallowed and smiled. 'Are there really? I wouldn't have thought so, not with Toby getting up at night and stealing them.'

Now all eyes were on Toby but still he said nothing and just stared into space, apparently not taking any notice of them. Annabel, assured now that she'd got their interest, made a performance of it.

'I was dreaming about Henry. We were having our engagement party at his family's place and drinking gallons of champagne.'

Henry, who seemed embarrassed by the performance so far, looked decidedly glum at this.

'Anyway, I woke up and I was feeling so terribly thirsty after not drinking all that champagne, if you see what I mean, so I knew I just had to have a drink. So I switched on my little torch and padded out to the kitchen on my little bare feet . . . '

'Size six and a half, actually,' Helena informed the party. She didn't seem to be enjoying the performance much either.

'. . . on my little bare feet. And what should I find there?'

Dramatic pause, spoilt by Russ.

'You just told us. Toby getting at the biscuits. Is it true, Toby?'

Still Toby said nothing. He was staring at a moth fluttering its wings against the lamp, but even Birdie knew it was quite a common sort of moth so it couldn't be of such absorbing interest to him.

Debbie said, 'We are getting low on biscuits.' Then she added, fair-mindedly, 'But, then, Justin and I took two packets of them.'

It was the first time anybody had mentioned Justin during the meal and Birdie sensed a coldness in the air, as if the rest of them thought it bad taste. He was quite sure Debbie had done it deliberately and worried about what she was going to say next. Although she was trying to sound calm, he could tell she was tense to the point of explosion.

Mal took it on himself to be peace-maker. 'I don't know what the fuss is about. I mean, Toby and Peter paid a lot of money like all the rest of us. If Toby wants to take Peter a few packets of biscuits, I can't see anything wrong in that. They're revolting biscuits anyway.'

Birdie asked, 'Is that it, Toby? Have you been taking food to Peter in that cave?'

'He went off on his own this afternoon,' Annabel said. 'After they brought Simon back.'

Birdie tried to make Toby look at him and failed. 'Look, Toby, if your brother wants to go off and live in a cave, that's all right with us, but you should tell us about it. I'm supposed to be responsible for you all.'

'And you're doing a grand job, aren't you, Birdie?'

That came from Russ, who seemed determined that there should be a quarrel, whatever direction it came from. 'Two dead, one missing, one mad and seven to go.'

There was a protesting noise from Ellie at 'one mad' but apart from that they all stared at Birdie waiting for his reply. If Russ had intended to take the heat off Toby he could hardly have done a better job. Birdie was about to protest that Russ's list was unfair but, when he considered it, it seemed a reasonable summary of events.

'I don't think it's quite as bad as that, Russ,' was the best he could do.

'Oh, isn't it? I'm beginning to wonder how many of us there will be when the boat gets here.'

'Yes, what about the boat? You said you'd told them to send a boat.'

That was Mal, backed up by Helena. 'Yes, when's the boat coming? I want to get off this awful place.'

'There's been a bit of a delay,' Birdie said, not looking at Russ. 'They'll send one as soon as they can.'

That would have been the moment for Russ to challenge with his suspicions about the message but, to Birdie's relief, he said nothing. Russ's policy seemed to be giving Birdie enough rope to hang himself.

'Anyway, our own boat will be coming for us the day after tomorrow.'

The boat that was to take a tired but satisfied survival party for a few days' recuperation in the fleshpots of Barbados before the flight home. Now it was the deadline boat. Before it appeared down in the jagged harbour he must convince Debbie that somebody other than himself had killed Justin. As far as he was concerned, it could be as late as it liked.

'I don't want to wait that long,' Helena said. As usual with her, tears were not far away and neither was Mal's arm.

'Be a bit awkward when the boat does get here, won't it?' Henry said.

'Why?'

'I mean . . . ' Henry, who had started so confidently, became fidgety and ill at ease. 'I mean, well, we'll have to do something about Justin.'

'What about Justin?' Russ demanded.

'Well, I suppose his family will, um, want him back and so on. I mean, we can't just leave him planted here. It might be all right for poor old Morton but, well, you see what I mean.'

'You mean,' Russ said, 'we'll have to dig him up again.'

He sounded quite cheerful at the prospect, but then he hadn't been part of the original burial party.

'Your turn next time,' Henry said.

By this time Helena had started crying in earnest and Debbie was biting her lower lip so hard that Birdie expected to see blood flow.

'We'll discuss this later,' he said firmly, but Henry's clumsiness couldn't be diverted.

'After all, he was the heir and so on. I mean, it's no secret his father might not be exactly inconsolable, but you can't just leave him rotting away under the foreign banyan tree, or whatever it is.'

'Henry, that's an awful thing to say,' Helena sobbed, 'about his father.'

Henry looked genuinely puzzled. 'I don't see why. I mean, it's very sad and so on, but it's no use pretending that Justin was anybody's favourite person.'

'Justin wasn't as bad as everybody said. Not all the time.'

This glowing epitaph came from Mal and Birdie felt grateful to him, not for defending the little sod but because he, alone of all the party, seemed to have some idea of what this was doing to Debbie. Birdie had noticed him glancing across the table at her several times and he could hardly have missed the message on that strained white face. But any good he might have done was immediately undone by Annabel.

'Oh, come off it, Mal. Justin had done some awful things. Everybody knows that.'

'That's right,' Henry said. 'Complete disaster from conception up. I mean, look at it, spoiling everybody's holiday by going and drowning himself like that.'

Somebody might have objected that Morton's death had already cast a blight, but the response to Henry's remark was much much worse than that. Debbie, as Birdie had been dreading all evening, finally broke under the strain. As Henry went burbling on with various half-remembered examples of Justin's shortcomings she stood up, planted her fists on the table and leaned across at him. Her shadow, wavering in the light from the paraffin lamp, loomed over the wall of the lodge and alarmed moths scattered back into the dark. Henry, taken up with his stories, was the last person to notice what was happening. The

150

others sat and watched like people who know two cars are going to collide but can't do anything about it. Birdie, in his haste to get to her, to put his arms around her and make her sit down, knocked a glass of barley water all over Annabel, but still didn't make it in time.

'The only thing wrong with Justin,' said Debbie to Henry, very loudly and clearly, 'was that he just couldn't live with the hypocrisy of fat maggots like you and his father.'

'Debbie!'

'She's a what-do-you-call it . . . you know, plants bombs and begins with T . . . '

'She's had a bad time, poor kid. She . . . '

'Don't you dare talk to Henry like that.'

'What's all the noise out here? I'm trying to get some sleep.'

The last reaction came in an aggrieved croak from Simon, appearing at the doorway to the dormitories, with a towel around his creased waist. Ellie went to him.

'Don't worry. Henry's only being tactless as usual. You go back to bed and I'll bring you some water.'

'I was not being bloody tactless. I was simply pointing out what everybody in London knows and she goes and attacks me.'

'You shouldn't have said it.' Mal tried to calm him down. 'You know she liked him.'

'I know she went off with him, but plenty of girls have gone off with Justin and come back pretty damn quick.'

'Oh do shut up, everybody,' Helena sobbed.

Birdie had his arm around Debbie by now, but she shrugged it off and stayed where she was, leaning across the table. He could see her thin arms trembling with the strain.

'Debbie, love, come and sit down and we'll . . . '

He might as well have saved his breath. She didn't even seem to notice he was there.

'All right, Justin wasn't perfect, but at least he didn't just sit there and take all the privileges he could get his hands on. At least he wasn't a hypocrite.'

Henry by now had his fists on the table too, and was shouting back at her.

'Justin the social reformer? Don't make me laugh. Justin took everything he could get his hands on, including you, my girl.'

At this point Russ hit Henry, a sideways blow to the well padded jaw that sent him sprawling off the bench and onto the floor, several plates and glasses going with him. Birdie had mixed feelings about that. When he'd heard what Henry said he'd wanted to hit him too, and he'd have made a better job of it, but Russ had been on the right side of the table to be in on the action. Unfortunately for Russ, so was Annabel. She picked up a big enamel jug of barley water, poured the contents over Russ, then hit him so hard with the jug that he joined Henry on the floor.

Ellie screamed, 'You bitch!' at Annabel and fell to her knees beside Russ, asking if he was hurt. Up to that point Simon had remained standing in the doorway, looking aggrieved. But when he saw his wife kneeling beside Russ, he moved with surprising speed for an invalid.

'I thought you promised me you weren't going to have any more to do with him.'

In his hurry the towel round his waist unhitched itself so he joined the tableau in a state of aggrieved nudity. Ellie, caught between the felled lover and a pink and quivering husband, tried reason. 'But he's hurt. That great fat tart tried to kill him.'

'I am not fat!' Annabel yelled back. 'I'm only nine and a half stone.'

'Ladies, ladies.'

Toby, who seemed to have found his voice at last, issued an antique protest, but might as well not have bothered. Meanwhile Henry was bawling at everybody to let him get his hands on Russ, although Mal seemed to be restraining him without too much difficulty.

Debbie seemed to be the calmest person present, if you didn't look too closely. Birdie got her to sit down again and went to sort out the confusion on the other side of the table. By persuading Russ that he wasn't seriously hurt, so allowing Ellie to take Simon back to his bed, he managed to break up the female half of the fight. Annabel plumped herself down, elbows on the table, and fumed quietly. As for Henry and Russ, he simply offered his services as referee the following morning if they wanted to fight it out properly, but got the impression they might not be required. After a while he had most of them sitting down again and seemed to have achieved a return to order. As it turned out, though, he'd only, paved the way for something that, from his point of view, was considerably worse than what had gone before.

It began calmly enough. Ellie came back from the dormitory. Henry, prompted by Mal, apologised to Debbie if he'd said anything to offend her. The heat, the strain and this damned island all figured in the apology and, even if it couldn't have been called handsome, it was at least adequate. Debbie was still as tense as a spring but she heard him out quietly enough. The opening of her reply, 'I've got nothing against you personally, Henry . . . ' was no more gracious than the apology itself, but at least it was conventional enough not to ring any alarm bells in Birdie's mind. So, when she went on as she did, he wasn't alert enough to stop her.

' . . . it's just that you've been over-privileged all your life and you accept it. Justin didn't. That's why he was murdered.'

Her tone sounded so flat, so reasonable, that even after the word was out, Birdie wasn't sure she'd actually said it. The effect on the others must have been the same, because it was a second before anybody reacted.

Then Ellie said, in a tight little voice, 'Murdered? Justin murdered?'

Henry started telling them that Debbie was suffering from sunstroke, lots of cases like it, look at poor old Simon. But Russ, of course, took it seriously. He gave Birdie a quick, suspicious glance, then said to Debbie, 'What makes you say that?'

His hair was still dripping lemon barley water.

Birdie, at this point, could either have dragged Debbie protesting off to bed, assuring the others that Henry's sunstroke diagnosis was right, or he could have sat there and let her get on with it. If he'd thought the first course had any chance of working he'd have tried it, but dragging Debbie off in this mood would be like dealing with unstable explosive. Besides, the damage had already been done. If Russ had been suspicious before, he wouldn't leave her alone now.

'He didn't drown,' she said. 'Somebody killed him, with a machete. It was because he knew something about his father and his father didn't want anybody else to know about it.'

Everybody around the table had gone very quiet and still.

Russ said, gently, 'Are you telling us that Justin's father had him killed?'

'Yes.'

There was a flutter of sounds; sighs of exasperation from Henry and Annabel, and a little indrawn sobbing gasp from Helena.

Russ ignored them and concentrated only on Debbie, speaking slowly and clearly as if to a child. 'You're not saying Justin's father was actually on the island?'

'No.'

'So you think somebody . . . ?'

Birdie broke in, 'Don't keep on at her, Russ. What she needs is to get some sleep.'

Debbie rounded on him. 'You keep out of this, Dad. I haven't got sunstroke. I'm quite sane and I know what I'm doing, thank you very much.' She turned back to Russ. 'You were asking?'

Russ repeated, 'So you think somebody killed Justin on his father's behalf. Have you any idea who it was?'

'No.'

'Do you think it was somebody in this party?'

'Oh, for heaven's sake!' Annabel said. 'You're only encouraging her.'

'It must have been, mustn't it?' Debbie said. 'I mean, there's nobody here but us, is there?'

She was still speaking in that unnaturally clear, wrought voice, determined that nobody round the table should miss a syllable of it.

Helena sobbed, 'I want to go home. Please let me go home.' But nobody took any notice of her, not even Mal.

'Did you see him being killed?'

'Russ, if you don't stop this, I'm going to make you.'

Birdie was already on his feet and advancing round the table when a look from Debbie stopped him in his tracks.

'Dad, I can't help you if you won't let me.'

So this was supposed to be helping him, was it? This was her idea of getting him off a murder charge, in her own mind if nowhere else. And if he did what he'd been planning to do, which was lay Russ out and carry Debbie off by force if necessary, he'd only be confirming her worst suspicions. He sat down again, but closer to Russ.

'No, I didn't see him being killed,' Debbie said. 'I heard him, though. He screamed. Dad heard it, too.'

'When was this?'

'Soon after it got light.'

'Is that true, Birdie?'

He nodded, reluctantly. 'About half-past five.'

Mal said at once, 'At least that puts all of us in the clear. We were all tucked up in our dormitories, then.'

'Some of us weren't,' Annabel said. She was staring straight at Ellie.

'Some of us were up and about.'

'If you mean me,' Ellie said, 'I was worried about my husband.'

'And Russ was helping you worry, I suppose.'

Ellie turned her back on Annabel, refusing to answer.

Russ said, 'Ellie and I were out on the balcony here at sunrise. We didn't hear a scream.'

'You wouldn't, not up here. It happened down by the waterfall.'

'And you and your father were near there?'

Debbie nodded. Birdie realised that Russ had assumed, reasonably enough, that the two of them were together when they heard the scream, and that Debbie had chosen not to contradict him. It showed how quickly her mind must be working; quicker than his own.

'And you found him at the waterfall, and he'd been attacked with a machete?'

She nodded again.

Russ said, 'Why didn't you tell us this, Birdie?'

'I didn't want to alarm you.'

A chorus of derisive sounds around the table.

Henry said, voice high and indignant, 'Well, we bloody well should be alarmed. I mean, if people are going around hacking at people with machetes well . . .'

'You mean there was nothing about that in the brochure?' Birdie said.

'It's no good getting sarcastic about it. I mean, if there's this maniac going around hacking people to death with a machete, there's no telling who he'll go for next.'

There was a long wail from Helena.

Debbie said, 'I don't think it's like that. It was Justin who had to be killed.'

Russ was ready with another question, but it was Mal who got in first. 'Look, I know you're shocked and all that, but it's nonsense about Justin's father, you know. I mean, he wouldn't do a thing like that.' His tone was quiet and reasonable, but it obviously exasperated Debbie.

'You say that because he's an MP and a director of things and you all went to the same sort of schools. That's what Justin meant about hypocrisy. He wanted to show his father up for what he was. That's why he had the photographs.'

'What photographs?'

For once, though, Russ didn't get the answer he wanted. Debbie became evasive.

'Just photographs.'

'Of Justin's father?' Mal demanded.

Henry said, 'It would be just like Justin to try blackmailing his father. He tried something like it with his sister once. They hushed it up and she went off and married somebody in Brisbane or somewhere.'

'Blackmail his own father?' Toby was giving his first sign of waking up to the conversation. 'You're saying Justin was blackmailing his father.'

'It wasn't blackmail,' Debbie said. The unnatural control over her voice was slipping and she sounded near to tears. 'He just thought his father should be shown up for the kind of person he was.'

Russ asked, 'Have you seen these photos?'

She nodded.

'And you think Justin's father wouldn't want them to come out?'

'Yes.'

It was no more than a gasp. Above anything else now, above anger or fear, Birdie felt pity for her. He wanted to take her away from them, not to stop anything else coming out, because almost everything that could be damaging had already been said, but to protect her, make her rest. The idea that she was, in her wrong-headed and stubborn way, campaigning for him against her own better judgement made it worse.

'Debbie, love. Bed.'

To his surprise she responded, getting up and moving like a sleepwalker towards the dormitories.

'You can have my bed out here tonight.'

He wasn't going to let her stay in the dormitory to be bitched at by Annabel and Ellie, or kept awake by Helena's sobbing. Conscious that everybody was pretending not to watch them, he made her comfortable on his own bed on the corner of the balcony and rigged up a tent of mosquito netting.

'My pack, Dad. It's in the dormitory.'

He fetched it for her. On the way back he looked into the men's dormitory and saw that Simon was apparently sleeping soundly. All the time, he'd been conscious that a whispered council of war was going on around the table. He joined them reluctantly to find that Mal had been appointed spokesman, although Russ was sitting glowering in a way that warned of more trouble to come from that quarter.

'Is it true, Birdie? Was Justin killed?'

He nodded.

'And this stuff about Justin's father?'

He said, in all honesty, 'I don't think Justin's father had anything to do with it.'

There was a loud sigh of relief from Henry.

Mal said, 'All that was just Debbie, then?'

'I'm afraid so. She's very upset. She was . . . she'd got quite fond of him.'

Annabel said, 'Poor kid, you can make some horrendous mistakes at her age. I mean, she's still very young, isn't she?'

'Seventeen.'

'We've been a bit unfair to her. Like me to go over and have a few womanly words?'

Birdie said hastily that he thought she'd be better left to sleep. Annabel's robust sympathy would hardly be what she needed. But the unexpected ministering angel act reminded Ellie of her duties.

'I'd better go and see to Simon.'

'I looked in on him a moment or two ago,' Birdie said. 'He was tossing and turning a bit.'

That was untrue, but he knew what would be coming next and needed Ellie out of the way.

Sure enough, as soon as she'd gone through to the dormitories, it came.

'But the fact is,' Mal said, 'Justin was killed.'

'Yes.'

'And the way she said it happened? I mean, the scream, then the body with the machete cuts?'

'Oh, don't.' Helena shuddered.

'Yes.'

'And there's nobody else on this island but us?'

'I don't see how there could be. We'd have seen a boat.'

'So what it adds up to is that one of us killed poor old Justin.'

'It looks like that, yes.'

Henry exploded, 'What do you mean "looks like that"? I mean, unless you're saying Justin cut his own throat with a machete, which would be bloody difficult, I should think' – Henry mimed an enthusiastic chopping motion – 'somebody killed him. Right?'

'Right.'

'So the question is who? We were all tucked up in our dormitories, you and Debbie were out on a nature ramble or something, so who does that leave?'

Birdie said, 'Simon and Peter were out all night.'

He watched Toby, but he didn't react at all.

Mal said, 'What about it, Toby? Was your brother being paid huge sums to kill poor old Justin?'

Toby simply shook his head. It looked like a gesture of irritation rather than a negation, as if he simply couldn't be bothered to answer. Mal and the others stared at him, waiting for more, but he said nothing.

'Well, that's it then. Peter's brother says Peter's not guilty, though God knows where he's got to. So who does that leave us with? Enter Simon, the mad machete man from suburbia.'

The others shushed him hastily. His voice was getting louder, threatening to carry through the thin walls to where Ellie was, presumably, tending her sick husband.

Birdie said, 'I think you'd better tell them what happened to you today, Russ.'

It was partly a determination to draw Russ into the conversation. He looked more dangerous when he was sitting still and brooding. He seemed none too pleased at the invitation and scowled round the table before saying, 'Simon threw a machete at me. He just missed.'

As Birdie had expected, that shut them up for a second or two. He thought Russ might have mentioned that Birdie had saved his life, but perhaps that was too much to expect.

'Why did he do that?' Annabel asked.

'I'd picked up a book.'

'On witchcraft,' Birdie added, watching their faces.

Annabel, her voice very low, whispered, 'But why would he want to kill Justin? I mean, I could have understood him killing Russ, but why Justin?'

Birdie said, 'He was in a pretty bad state by then. He might not even have known who it was.'

More silence around the table while they took that in. Toby took off his glasses and polished them on his shirt front. Helena, who'd been hanging on every word from Mal, looked so interested that she'd forgotten to cry.

'But . . . but what are we going to do about him?' Henry said.

'We can't do much except wait till the boat arrives on Sunday. After that, he'll be somebody else's problem.'

'Poor Ellie,' Annabel sighed.

'Her own bloody fault if you ask me,' said Henry.

Russ ignored them.

'Are we going to just leave him walking around free?' Mal said.

'I don't think he'll be doing much walking around. He really is ill.'

Henry said, 'But we've got to sleep in the same dormitory as him. Suppose he wakes up and runs amok in the night?'

'He won't,' Birdie assured them. 'It's all over as far as he's concerned. Anyway, there were only two machetes on the island that I know of, and I've got both of them now.'

There was a silence while they digested that. He didn't know whether they found it reassuring or not.

Then Henry said, 'What about Morton? Was that Simon as well?'

Birdie knew that there was no chance now of sticking to the fiction that Morton's death was accidental. The only question was, which version to give them. He remained convinced that Justin had killed Morton, but that would only complicate the picture and produce more questions. Better, for the moment, to push all the guilt towards Simon and adjust things later.

'We can't know for sure.'

He didn't mention the missing fingers.

It took a long time to get them off to bed. Henry and Mal insisted on drawing lots for taking it in turn to stay awake, in case, as Mal put it, Simon had a fit of the machetes coming over him again. Then Ellie came back in the middle of it and they had to pretend they were drawing lots for who got the last bit of processed cheese.

Annabel and Helena showed an instant sympathy towards Ellie that might have made her suspicious if everybody else hadn't been behaving so oddly, and hustled her off to bed with offers of night moisturiser and hop pillows and anything else a woman whose husband was liable to slay people with machetes might possibly want. She seemed puzzled but grateful. As they drifted away Birdie sat with his arms on the table, feeling like a thing washed over by several tides, longing only for a chance to be on his own and think. He wasn't going to get it, though. Russ was back, standing at his side.

'Birdie, can I have a word with you?'

CHAPTER THIRTEEN

Russ made no objection when Birdie led him down the ladder and a few steps into the forest, telling him, as far as he could in sign language, that Debbie under her mosquito net should be allowed to sleep in peace. Darkness and vegetation closed around them and, although Russ was only a few feet away from Birdie, the only things visible were his face and the pale patches on his camouflage overalls. When he spoke his voice reminded Birdie of the way a night club bouncer appeals to somebody to be reasonable, a split second before throwing him down the steps.

'You really expect me to believe that, Birdie?'

'I don't care what the hell you believe, Russ.'

He might be twenty years older than Russ, but he'd already demonstrated to his own satisfaction that day that his reflexes were quicker. He wasn't having any market stall big mouth come the heavy with him.

'It stinks,' Russ said. 'It stinks like a shit house in a heat wave.'

Birdie said nothing.

'I mean, you don't expect me to believe Simon killed Justin because he mistook him for me. There's no similarity, Birdie. No similarity at all. Justin was about six inches shorter. He'd got shoulders like the arse on a French poodle. A blind man on a dark night couldn't mistake Justin for me.'

Birdie said, 'Simon must have been half mad by then. He'd been wandering around the rain forest all night, brooding about you having it off with his wife.'

'I hope you're not blaming me for that, Birdie. She damn near raped me. Before they brought the first drink on the plane she was squeezing her thigh up against mine. Desperate for it. Why did she come on a holiday like this?'

With every word he spoke he was distancing himself from

Ellie. Russ, with all his assumed toughness, didn't want trouble. It occurred to Birdie that he might well have a police record at home.

'From what you say, Ellie enjoyed humiliating her husband in public. I don't suppose you were the first man she'd used for that. Sooner or later he was going to crack, and this place and you did it between you.'

Russ shook his head.

'It's no good, Birdie. You'll have to do better than that.'

His tone had changed from aggression to spurious sympathy.

'You're doing your best, Birdie, but we'll have to come up with something better than that pathetic little prick, Simon.'

'What are you talking about?'

Birdie's tone was too sharp. He realised from Russ's laugh that the man knew he'd got him off balance.

'Don't worry Birdie. I'm on your side. I'm not bothered about what happens to an overprivileged little pervert like Justin.'

'My side?'

'Yes, Birdie. Your side.'

Bloody hell. So here was somebody else who thought he'd killed Justin. And, given Russ's character and probable background, it was no consolation at all that he was apparently offering assistance in covering it up. For a price, naturally.

'Russ, I just don't know what you're talking about.'

A hand came out of the darkness and landed heavily on his shoulder.

'Don't worry, Birdie. I understand. I'd be doing the same if she was my daughter.'

'Your daughter?'

When it struck him what Russ was talking about he was at first too surprised to be angry. He let the man run on, pouring unwanted sympathy on him.

'I mean, God knows what he tried to do with her, out there for two days on their own. She's a good kid, you can tell. She's not from his sort of world. She's inexperienced and, when he tries something she doesn't want, she grabs the first thing handy and goes for him. I mean, if it came to court, she'd get off. No doubt about that.'

'Came to court?'

'Yeah, but I can see you wouldn't want that. And, happening in this devil's hole a long way from anywhere, you can see it doesn't happen. I'd do the same in your place, Birdie, honest, only you'll have to think up something better than Simon.'

He waited, having said his piece.

Birdie said, 'And who's supposed to have killed Morton?'

'Justin. He didn't like him.' But Russ sounded no more than casually interested in that. 'The thing is, Birdie, if Simon's not a runner, who did it?'

It sounded as if he were spreading out a pack of cards, inviting Birdie to choose. When there was no reply he said, in the same casual voice 'I fancy Peter myself. After all, he's the one beside Simon who hasn't got an alibi.'

'But why would Peter want to kill Justin?'

It was a question that Birdie had been turning over in his mind, but as soon as he said it he knew it was a mistake. All it did was signal to Russ that Birdie was joining his fantasy.

'I've been thinking about that, Birdie. The way I see it, Justin kills Morton, then he goes along to his bungalow, throws his books all over the place and releases his pet pig. For all we know, he even kills the pig as well.'

Russ's obsession with the peccary was still inexplicable to Birdie, but he let him run on, hoping against hope that there might even be a grain of sense somewhere in the fantasy, anything that would give him some foothold on this accelerating slide.

'Now, who out of our party got on best with Morton?'

He paused, and got no answer.

'Toby and Peter, that's who. Conservation nuts, all three of them. I mean, if they knew Justin had killed Morton and killed their precious peccary as well, they might decide to take the law into their own hands.'

Birdie couldn't stop himself making a disbelieving noise at the idea of Toby and Peter as ruthless avengers.

'All right, Birdie, but you tell me what Peter's been doing all this time. Toby knows what he's been doing, you can tell that. You heard what Annabel said about him raiding the food cupboard. You can bet he's taking food to him. So what are those two up to?'

Birdie could have added to the case against Toby by telling

Russ about the discovery of the pack and the ice box in the cave, but had no intention of doing it.

'And the point we come back to. Peter's got no alibi, if you go by the time you heard that scream. And when was that again, Birdie?'

'About five-thirty.'

Birdie answered automatically, before Russ's tone sank in. Russ didn't believe in the scream.

'It happened. We both heard it.'

Again, Russ had managed to get him off balance.

'Of course you did, Birdie. Of course you did.'

Debbie had killed Justin and Birdie was covering up for her, so of course they'd both say they heard it.

'We'd better go back.'

Russ showed no sign of moving.

'Then there's the blackmail line, about those photos. I think you should take that seriously, Birdie.'

'It's just an idea Debbie's got into her head.'

'You should listen to her. That's a bright girl you've got there, Birdie.'

Brighter than her father, was the unspoken implication.

'Does it exist, this photo?'

'It exists all right.' Birdie wasn't having him think that Debbie had made up the whole story.

'You've seen it?'

'Yes.'

'Hot stuff?'

'Justin's father dressed up as a schoolboy. Being caned by a woman in a mask.'

Russ whistled. 'That's enough for blackmail any day.'

'Probably quite normal with his class.'

'Not to the voters, Birdie. The man's an MP, isn't he? Power in the land and so on? Imagine having that all over the papers. That's worth a murder in anybody's book.'

'Russ, I'm not playing games.'

'Nor am I, Birdie. Nor am I. I'm just saying you should take this blackmail business seriously.'

'I'm going back.'

Birdie turned away and heard Russ fall into step behind him.

'Where is that photo, Birdie?'

'I've got it.'

'I should keep it safe.'

'I intend to.'

They were at the foot of the ladder by then and went up it in silence. Birdie glanced over at the shape under the mosquito net and found Russ was looking in the same direction.

'She's a good kid, Birdie. She's all right.'

A last squeeze of Birdie's shoulder and he tiptoed ostentatiously across to the dormitory, making more noise on the creaking boards than if he'd walked normally. Russ all over.

Birdie slept on the floor of the kitchen, too tired to care if cockroaches were marching over him on their way to the food cupboard. When he woke, still in darkness, a couple of them were gnawing at his hair. They rustled off when he flailed and cursed at them, but even when they'd gone his waking worries made him feel as if there were cockroaches inside his skull as well. He lit the oil lamp, deciding to brew himself some coffee.

While he was waiting for the water in the saucepan to boil he idly sorted out some of the books they'd picked up from the ditch. What bothered him was not so much the books themselves as the light they might throw on the question of the machete. It was nagging at his mind that there was something important there if only he could sort out what it was. He'd felt the stirrings of an idea, but Russ had distracted him before he could work it through.

The point was that, as far as he knew, there were only two machetes on the island, the one kept in the kitchen at the lodge and Morton's. The kitchen machete had disappeared, presumably taken by Justin, then reappeared the morning after Morton's murder, along with a threatening note in Justin's handwriting. That one, machete number one, had been in Birdie's possession ever since, so could hardly have been the one used to kill Justin at sunrise on Friday morning. That meant the murder weapon must be machete number two: Morton's. Undeniably, at some point on Friday it had been in the possession of Simon, until Simon had hurled it at Russ. Simon claimed to have picked it up in the ditch along with the Obeah book some time after sunrise that morning. If he was telling the truth about that, he found it only after Justin was killed. The whole case against Simon rested on the belief that he wasn't telling the truth about that and had come across the machete earlier.

If, on the other hand, Simon was telling the truth, it followed that somebody else had used machete number two to kill Justin, cleaned it and dumped it in the ditch where Simon found it. But, with a whole island to choose from, it would be an unthinkable coincidence that the murderer should happen to throw it away in exactly the same place as the books had been dumped two days earlier, when Morton's bungalow was vandalised. If Simon were telling the truth, the implication would be that the books and the machete had been dumped in the ditch at the same time, on Wednesday night. But that couldn't be the case, or machete number two would have been lying in the ditch all the time it was, theoretically, being used to kill Justin. Birdie had just got as far as working out that the state of the books was of some importance. It had rained heavily at least twice since Wednesday night. If the books looked as if they'd been out in two rain storms, that would at least dispose of the possibility that somebody else had dumped them later. With this in mind, he picked them up and riffled through their pages in the lamplight.

His first conclusion was that they did indeed bear the marks of books that had been left out in a tropical climate for some days. The pages were dimpled and pockmarked, as if they'd got soaked and dried again. A librarian's rubber stamp on the front of the one about photosynthesis had run in thin purple streams down the cover. One of the geological works had even been slimed and nibbled by slugs. He picked it up and flipped over the pages. 'Underground water courses and outlets on the island of Diabola. Some volcanic comparisons.' Nice to be an academic, with no worse problems than that to think about. But Morton had taken all of it very seriously, as justification for his hermit's life; oracular source of obscure theses at a dozen universities. God knows what satisfaction there could be, though, for him or anybody else, in corrugated graphs and flurries of footnotes: 'Comparative water penetration in non-igneous rock', 'Comparative seasonal acidity of precipitation'. Then, as far as he could make out, a whole chapter on how long it took if you fed a marker in somewhere and waited for it to come out somewhere else. He was flipping over it without much interest when the words 'Devil's Bath Tub' caught his eye, then, further down the page, 'waterfall'.

His heart started thumping and, for no reason he could yet understand, the feeling of being on the edge of something important expanded and burst out so that he was tearing through the pages with clumsy fingers, forcing a way through the geologist's language because he needed suddenly to know what these people were talking about. They'd put a lot of coloured paint down the Devil's Bath Tub, that much was clear. It had swirled around for a while, then run out with the rest of the water on its journey underground. There was even a rough map and now Birdie knew what they were talking about he could recognise it was the sulphurous side of the island with its watercourses. Just as he'd been told by Morton, the hot water ran underground from the Devil's Bath Tub, under the rock spur where the iguanas sunbathed, to emerge some time later at the waterfall where he'd found Justin's body. So far, there was nothing new, but it was the destination of that paint that was bothering him.

It was bothering the academics too; he could tell that through a maze of convoluted prose and footnotes. Apparently the problem was that the paint tipped into the Devil's Bath Tub had taken much longer than expected to emerge at the waterfall end. Twenty-six hours the poor devils had camped out at the waterfall, stop watch at the ready, waiting for the water to change colour. At twenty-six hours and thirty-five minutes, came the happy ending as far as they were concerned, as the falls began to belch blue water and the marker paint tipped in at the Devil's Bath Tub the day before came through. This suggested, the academics pointed out, the existence of an underground system of unexpected complexity, meriting further investigation when time and funds would allow.

Birdie was content to leave them to it. He'd got what he wanted, more than he wanted. In the last few minutes his entire view of what had happened to Justin had been turned upside down. He'd assumed when he found Justin's body in the pool under the waterfall that it had only just got there. Things he'd noticed at the time but pushed to the bottom of his mind because they didn't seem to make sense came back to him – the pulpiness of the face, as if the body had been in the water for some time, the smell of sulphur stronger than could be accounted for by the waterfall itself, the absence of bleeding. They all went with the theory that Justin's body, like the paint in the geologists' study, had been fed in at the Devil's Bath Tub and taken its time coming through whatever Devil's plumbing system was bubbling away there under the rock ridge. Then there were the footprints, or the absence of them. Debbie had been angry because he hadn't looked for footprints before trampling in, but if they'd been there, wouldn't he have noticed them, even subconsciously? Wasn't it possible at least that there'd been no footprints by the waterfall because it had needed no human agency to deliver Justin's body there?

'But the scream?'

He said it to himself out loud, but could make no sense of it. There'd been a scream, Debbie had heard it too; a scream of such misery and terror that the hairs rose on the back of his neck when he thought about it. Finding Justin's body half an hour or so afterwards had naturally seemed connected with that scream, even to the exclusion of clues that should have pointed the other way. But, if Justin had already been dead, perhaps twenty-four hours dead, and travelling down the Devil's plumbing at the time of the scream, who else had been screaming, and why?

The water in the pan had nearly boiled dry while he was trying to work this out. There was just enough left to make a cup of strong, syrupy coffee and he drained it in one scalding gulp, trying to shock his brain into activity. All he managed to do was burn his tongue. All right then, take it methodically. Trying to draw the separate problems out of the mass of them churning away in his head was like trapping single strands of spaghetti.

Strand one. Leave aside that scream and ask yourself when did Justin die. Remembering the state of the corpse, the verdict must be that Justin had been dead and in sulphurous water for some time before he found the body first thing on Friday morning. The question was, how long? The geologists' paint had taken twenty-six and a half hours to come through the system. Would a body of, say, eleven stone maximum, have gone through faster or slower than a trail of paint? Here Birdie found himself suddenly converted to the view of the academics that a lot more needed to be known about the underground watercourses on Diabola. Suppose there was another pool down there under the rock? A body could swirl around in it for days or hours before the current took it on its way. On the other hand, if it were a steady downward flow, wouldn't a heavy body travel faster than paint? After a lot of hard thought, he decided a body would be highly unlikely to travel faster than the academics' paint, so that meant Justin had taken at least twenty-six and a half hours to come through the system. If you discounted the scream there was no way of knowing how long he'd been in the pool under the waterfall before Birdie found him, but the same time limit applied. If Justin had been under the waterfall by six a.m. on Friday morning, the latest he could have been dumped in the Devil's Bath Tub was three-thirty a.m. on Thursday morning.

As for the earliest possible time, there was no way of knowing that. All he had to go on was Debbie's evidence that Justin had left her before it got dark on Wednesday evening, talking about having an appointment to keep. If that appointment had been at the Devil's Bath Tub, it was at least possible that he'd been killed then, as early as Wednesday evening. Birdie put an arbitrary time to it of around eight o'clock, not long after it got dark. That would give a picture of Justin being killed at the Devil's Bath Tub between eight p.m. on Wednesday evening and three-thirty a.m. on Thursday morning – the same night that Morton died and Morton's bungalow was vandalised.

If so, the reasonable conclusion would be that one person was responsible for both deaths, probably at the same time. Some trick of the currents in the Devil's Bath Tub that might interest the academics had sent Justin's body on its way while keeping Morton's washing around, to be found by Birdie on Thursday morning. It was logical, but a hard conclusion for Birdie to face. He couldn't get out of his mind that Justin was guilty. He even tried for a while to construct a scenario in which Morton and Justin, fighting with machetes, managed to kill each other more or less simultaneously, but abandoned it as impractical, if only because that should have left two machetes lying beside the Bath Tub.

Machetes. It kept coming back to that. As soon as the word came into his mind he knew that his revised time scale had one insuperable snag to it: how could Justin be on his way down the plug hole by three-thirty a.m. on Thursday morning at the latest when, some hours after that, in broad daylight, he'd replaced the kitchen machete with a threatening message to Birdie around the handle? You'd have to believe in zombies to believe that, and Birdie didn't believe in zombies yet. So, if you accepted, as Birdie was now coming to accept, that Justin had been killed late on Wednesday night or early on Thursday morning, you were left with two problems: who had replaced the machete in the kitchen and who had screamed at sunrise on Friday morning? Plus, of course, one problem overall, was it, or were they, responsible for a double killing?

There was another thing about the revised timing. When he thought Justin had been killed at the time of the scream there were only two possible candidates for the murder: Simon and Peter. On Wednesday night, though, the case was as wide open as it could be. On Wednesday night they'd been blundering around in the rain forest, following a man who was either drunk or dead by then and getting so comprehensively lost that it was hard to tell where anyone was from one minute to the next. If you'd tried to set up a scenario for a murder you could hardly have done better. His head was drooping with tiredness by then, but that idea jerked it upright. If you'd wanted to set up a scenario for a murder . . . And who was it who'd agitated for a night walk and got Ellie to back him? Who was it who'd been dogging Birdie's footsteps trying to find out how much he knew, putting daft ideas into his head?

He dozed and worried until the sun came up and the first birds were taking over from the tree frogs, made two more cups of coffee with milk powder and carried them out to the balcony. Debbie usually woke early. She was awake, sitting up in her tee-shirt, sleeping bag drawn up over her legs. She looked pale but smiled when she saw him.

'Hello, Dad. Is that for me?'

She took a cup, sipped and smiled.

'Very nice of you, Birdie,' said Russ, reaching up for the other cup.

He was sitting on the floor beside her camp bed, quite at ease, and it looked as if they'd been talking for some time. His hands closed around the mug. He drank and winked.

'I told you. Sensible girl, your daughter.'

CHAPTER FOURTEEN

'Dad, will you please stop telling me to be careful. I'm being a lot more careful than you are.'

The talk with Debbie had been delayed until the others were sitting around the table at breakfast, and he went with her to refill the kitchen water barrel at the stream. On the way back, carrying it approved style between two poles, he'd insisted that they park it under a tree and sit down to talk about Russ.

'You can't trust him, love.'

'I can't trust anybody.'

It was a statement of fact and, in the circumstances, fair enough. What hurt was that she made no exception for him.

'I think I've found out something about when Justin was killed.'

He hadn't been sure until that moment whether he should tell her or not.

'When? I thought . . .'

'The scream? I know, only I'm not so sure now.'

Crouching in the shade of a tree he told her about the dump of books from Morton's bungalow and the geologists' research, watching her face. He softened as far as he could his reasons for thinking that Justin had been a long time in the sulphur water, but she didn't miss anything.

'I thought at the time . . . his face was all sort of swollen, but I didn't know . . .'

Her voice trailed away.

'So you see, he could have been killed before it got light on Thursday morning or after it got dark on Wednesday night. Either way, he'd have been dead more than twenty-four hours before we found him.'

'Are you sure?'

At first he thought she meant about the timings and started explaining all over again.

'No, I mean, are you sure he was dead when he went in? If . . . well if he'd been unconscious when he was going under there and then he came round, he might have . . . he might have screamed then.'

This was said in a voice so quiet that he had to bend towards her to catch it.

'No, love, I promise you that couldn't have been it. Not with those cuts on his neck. He was dead when he went into the water, or very soon after, I'm sure of that much.'

Her head was bent and he didn't know if she believed him.

'If he was killed on Wednesday night,' she said, 'it might have been not long after he left me.'

'You said he told you he had to keep an appointment with somebody. You're sure he didn't give you any hint at all who it was?'

She shook her head. 'No. I wish he had.'

'Another thing, you realise this makes the question of that message on the machete more important? The one threatening me.'

'Yes.'

'Justin couldn't have put it in there after daylight on Thursday morning, not if he'd been dead by three o'clock at the latest. Somebody else must have done that.'

'Yes.'

'And you're quite sure it wasn't you? You see how important it is?'

'It wasn't me.'

He had to believe her. Which, unless you put it down to some coincidental and entirely unconnected practical joke, meant somebody had an interest in making it appear Justin was alive hours after he was dead. That person, too, must have had access to Justin's pack to find the warning messages he'd already prepared and stored away. The only thing that made sense was that the machete with the message had been planted by Justin's killer deliberately to confuse Birdie about the time of death. Suppose he or she knew that a body dumped in the Devil's Bath Tub would take twenty-six hours or more to work its way

through? That would be a ready-made alibi.'
'Russ says you still think Justin killed Morton.'
He dragged his mind back to what she was saying.
'He shouldn't have been talking to you about that.'
'Do you, though?'
He stared at her, ideas going round and round in his head. The alibi would work, but only as long as the murderer knew about the time lapse and nobody else did, as long as nobody else found the geologists' study. But there'd been one person on the island who claimed, probably rightly, to know more about it than any academics, and that person would certainly know about the Devil's plumbing system.

Birdie said, 'No, I don't think Justin did kill Morton after all.'
When he let the idea go, it left a space like an extracted molar. Equally reluctantly, he was re-examining the idea of Justin as the vandal in Morton's bungalow. Wasn't it at least as likely that the person who killed Morton because of the knowledge in his head had taken the precaution of losing the knowledge on the page too, taking the geology book and tearing apart the rest of Morton's things to hide the loss of it. It would have stayed there in the ditch until the slugs ate it all, if Simon hadn't happened to stumble across it.

Debbie said, 'Russ thinks the same person killed both of them.'
Which brought them back to where they started, but he couldn't leave it at that. It would be just like know-all Russ to be clued up on cave systems.

'You realise, Russ could have killed them?'
She nodded. 'Any of us could have.'
'That wasn't what I meant. Russ went to a lot of trouble to get everybody lost. I know Ellie was supposed to be sticking close to him all the time, but Ellie's besotted with him, so that doesn't mean much.'

'Oh, Dad, you'll have to stop this.'
'Stop what?'
'Assuming any man I talk to is a murderer. First Justin, now Russ. Why should it be Russ any more than the rest of them?'
'Because he's a roughneck, you can tell that. If you're looking for somebody who might be a hired killer, you don't have to look much further than Russ.'

'That's just snobbery because he doesn't talk like the Hoorays. Anyway, I thought you didn't believe in hired killers.'

'I'm getting so confused I'm ready to believe anything.'

'Russ thinks I'm right about those photos, about his father wanting him killed before he could publish them.'

'Was that what you two were talking about this morning?'

She nodded. 'Some of the time. He wanted to know more about them, about what Justin's father was like. He was interested in everything I could remember about what Justin said.'

If Russ had appeared then, Birdie would have attacked him. The cynical bastard had sat there beside Debbie's bed pumping her for evidence he thought could convict her of murder. He'd accused Birdie in so many words of covering up for Debbie, then he'd gone to her at the first opportunity and, in the pretence of being sympathetic and believing her story, dug out every detail he could find.

'He thinks it was Peter,' Debbie said.

He wanted to howl at her, 'No he doesn't. He wants people to think it was you,' and nearly choked with the effort of keeping it back. If he said it, she'd only think he was trying to keep her away from Russ for his own purposes and be twice as stubborn.

'So what else did you talk about?'

'All of them: the Hoorays, Simon – and Annabel.'

There was a slight pause before Annabel's name that froze his blood. He knew he was meant to notice it.

'Oh, yes, and what did you say to him about Annabel?'

'I didn't say anything. He told me.'

'Told you what?'

Pause. She folded a leaf in her fingers, folded it again.

'What did Russ tell you about Annabel?'

She looked him full in the face. 'Annabel's a tart.'

It wasn't so much the words themselves that hit him as the cool way she said them, analytical, no sign of anger or hurt allowed to show. If she'd come straight out and attacked him for the night of the mosquito repellent, accused him of disloyalty to her mother, to Nimue, to heaven knows what, he could have dealt with it, hugged her, made her see it didn't matter. His helplessness mixed with another great surge of anger against Russ. So it had been Russ private eye that night, padding around watching them, and he'd kept it to himself just until he needed it, to get under Debbie's defences. The anger must have got to his face because he saw Debbie's expression change from blankness to defiance.

'He shouldn't have said that, and nor should you.'

'Why not?'

'Going around spying on people, judging people. What's it got to do with Russ?'

'It's hypocrisy again, isn't it? It doesn't matter what people do as long as you don't talk about it.'

'Debbie, love, it doesn't matter that much.'

He wanted to explain to her that it had been light-hearted in its way, not meant to hurt anybody, but she shrugged and turned her face away.

'We'd better be getting the water back.'

She stood up and shouldered her end of the pole, still not looking at him, and he knew any attempt to explain would have to wait. He picked up the pole and trudged behind her with thoughts of Russ filling the gap that Justin's death had left.

Back at the lodge, people were packing. It was much too early because the boat wasn't due until the next day and none of them had much to pack, but haversacks and tote bags were lying all over the balcony in token of everybody's wish to be away. They looked up when Birdie and Debbie arrived back but said nothing. The atmosphere seemed full of hostility against him. It wasn't, he thought, a case of believing he'd killed Morton and Justin. They only knew that they were scared and miserable, and they held him responsible. They were conscious, too, that the boat was only twenty-four hours off and they were drawing apart from him, knowing that he'd be the one who had to make the explanations and deal with the questions, or worse. It was Birdie's fault and Birdie could cope. And yet one of them there on the balcony, or Peter out in the forest, must be as tense as wire in the knowledge that in twenty-four hours it would all be over and the evidence would be left behind on Diabola. However miserable they might look walking up the gangplank tomorrow, one of them would be doing it with a consciousness of having won, unless he did something to prevent it. The trouble was, he had no idea what. He walked over to Toby.

'You'd better make sure your brother's here when the boat arrives.'

Toby simply nodded.

'And don't go taking him any more food. We've got enough to last until tomorrow, but none to spare. If he wants to eat, he'll have to come and do it with the rest of us.'

This time Toby didn't even nod. He sat on the bench staring out over the forest and gave no indication that he'd heard.

'I wish I knew what you two think you're doing,' Birdie said.

Toby turned round to look at him and stared for a long time as if trying to get him into focus. The eyes behind the glasses were pale blue, cool areas in his sunburnt red face.

'You don't need to worry about us. We're doing no harm.'

'Well, what are you doing then?'

'Storing things,' Toby said. 'We store things, Peter and I. Some time the world will need the things we store.'

'Conservation, you mean?'

'That's the word that's put a lot more people behind a lot more desks. We go our own way.' He stood up. 'If you'll excuse me . . . ' He drifted off towards the dormitories. It was too vague to be an abrupt departure, but it signalled clearly enough that he'd said all he intended to say.

Birdie was on the point of following him and continuing the conversation whether he liked it or not when he heard a giggle behind him and Annabel's voice.

'Have you been trying to pump Toby, too?'

'Too?'

He turned round. Annabel, in her sweat-stained jungle overalls, still had an air of bounding health that had deserted the rest of them. Helena, though, standing just behind her, was another matter. It looked as if she'd been crying again.

'Russ was trying it at breakfast,' Annabel said. 'Kept on at him about where his brother was and what they were doing. In the end I told him to stop nagging the poor old man.'

'Did he get anything out of him?'

'No. Toby just kept quiet and kept on eating. He's got an appetite like a pregnant crocodile. So much for Russ the private eye.'

'You'd noticed, too?'

'Stands out like a virgin at a hunt ball.'

Birdie, still wanting to follow Toby, waited for them to move away and get on with their packing, but they didn't. He had the feeling that Helena wanted to go but was kept there by her friend.

'Could we have a word, Birdie? In private?'

Annabel rolled her eyes meaningly to the other side of the balcony where Ellie, Russ and the two Hoorays were in deep consultation. Birdie suspected they were composing a letter of complaint as the first stage in the campaign for their money back. Birdie suggested they should go down the path towards the road, but Annabel vetoed that.

'Helena can't walk and talk at the same time.'

In the end Annabel solved the problem by leading the way to the women's dormitory and sat herself down on a rush mat, legs crossed in a way that showed her long brown calves to advantage. Helena perched cautiously on the side of a camp bed, staring at Annabel.

'It's Russ,' Annabel said. 'We've noticed he's been paying a lot of attention to your Debbie.'

'So have I.' He took no trouble to disguise what he felt about that.

'Helena and I don't want to interfere, but she's only a kid and, after what happened with the other one, I mean, we wouldn't like to see her making the same mistake again, would we, Helena?'

Helena gave an underwater kind of nod.

'The point is, how much do you know about Russ?'

Birdie said feelingly, 'As little as I know about any of the rest of you.'

She nodded. 'I thought so, that's why I told Helena we should tell you. Only she doesn't like to talk about it. It's a long time ago.'

'Nearly four years,' Helena said. It was like hearing a sea anemone speak.

Birdie put on his official voice. 'If either of you know anything about him, you should tell me.'

'Don't scare her,' Annabel said. 'It's no use if you scare her. She'll tell you in her own time.'

Birdie, suppressing a groan, joined Annabel on the floor, then wished he hadn't when he remembered the last time he'd done it. The balls of her feet were as round as apples. She sat, patient as a Buddha, and he crouched less patiently as they waited for Helena to utter.

'I don't like remembering it,' were her first unpromising words, but after some persuasion and soothing from Annabel she got started.

'I was twenty, I didn't know London and I was supposed to be taking a secretarial course, only that fell through. I mean, all sorts of things; they said my nails were too long for typing, then I kept spilling coffee all over the word processor and, you know, all those sort of things.'

She fixed Birdie with a tragic stare.

'I can't stand word processors myself,' Annabel said sympathetically, 'only the accountant made us buy one.'

'Yes, but what's that got to do with . . . ?'

'Don't hurry her,' Annabel said. 'She won't tell you if you hurry her.'

Annabel put in a few minutes' more Buddha practice while Birdie seethed and waited.

'I didn't know anybody, you see,' Helena burst out. 'With my parents being abroad and so on. And the other girls in the flat were really horrible. I had to share a bedroom with one who picked her nose, and when I said, Couldn't I have the bedroom on my own, they were really horrible. Honestly, you wouldn't believe . . .'

'What Helena's trying to get over,' Annabel said helpfully, 'is that she was miserable and lonely, weren't you, darling?'

'I'd grasped that. The point is . . .'

'And I didn't have any money, and they always seemed to have lots, and they had this friend with a spare room in a flat in Knightsbridge just across the road from Harrods, so naturally I didn't think, I mean, would you?'

Again the tragic stare at Birdie.

'What Helena's trying to explain,' said Annabel, herself showing signs of impatience at last, 'is that when she first came to London she got in with a bad set.'

'And that bad set included Russ?'

Helena shook her head. 'It wasn't like that. He was the

doorman at the club where we used to go. He stopped people getting in they didn't want in.'

There was nothing that surprised Birdie in that. Given Russ's outlook and physique, a teenage bouncer was just what he'd have expected him to be.

'The point is,' Annabel said, 'what he did as well.' She looked at Helena.

'He fetched things.' Helena's voice was almost a whisper. 'He fetched things for people who went to the club.'

'I suppose you mean drugs.'

When Birdie said that she looked at him wide-eyed. He had a feeling he'd spoilt the scene for her.

'That's right,' Annabel said. 'The CC was what Helena's friends used to call young Russ, wasn't it, darling?'

Helena nodded.

'CC?'

'Cocaine Courier.'

'Why didn't you say something when you recognised him?'

'Well, she wouldn't, would she? You couldn't expect her to drag all that up when she hardly knew you. She's only doing it now because she doesn't want to see your Debbie make the same mistake twice.'

'Did he recognise you?'

Helena shook her head. 'I looked different then.'

'I should just think she did. You should have seen her, as thin as a crab stick with hair I wouldn't have fed to a retired seaside donkey. I had to literally drag her away from that set, then I started feeding her up and found her a job with my firm, didn't I, darling?'

Birdie could imagine it. There was a vitality about Annabel that had to overflow somewhere and pretty, passive Helena made as good a conduit as any.

'I suppose it comes of being at school together.'

Helena, once again, looked amazed at this mild insight but Annabel giggled, a conspiratorial dormitory giggle.

'That's right, Birdie, there's nothing like being at school together.'

She smiled at him, but he didn't return the smile. He was too busy wondering if Annabel grasped the significance of what they'd just told him. Four years ago, Russ had been the cocaine courier. Now here he was arriving on the island in the same party as one of London's most prominent druggies, now blamelessly pushing up whatever a tropical rain forest had instead of daisies. He didn't believe that was a coincidence and he didn't believe Annabel thought so either.

'So we thought we ought to tell you,' Annabel said.

'I'm glad you did.'

But his mind, instead of being on what he was saying, was wandering back to that last afternoon Debbie and Justin had spent together. He'd been restless, she said, then he'd left her abruptly to keep an appointment with somebody unknown. More than that, he'd left her in the middle of the rain forest with night coming on, although anybody could tell by looking at Justin that wandering through rain forests on his own wasn't his idea of a good time. Assume, though, the restlessness of a drug addict who knew where he could get his next fix, and the whole sequence was explained. With that bait, Russ would have had no problem in tempting him to the edge of the Devil's Bath Tub.

'But what about Ellie?'

Until the night walk started, Russ had been on the balcony with the rest of them. And, during the walk itself, the account given by both himself and Ellie was that they'd kept together, even after they'd lost the others. If Russ had met Justin that night, had quarrelled and murdered him, then Ellie must be lying to protect him.

He must have put the question out loud because Annabel answered it, although not in the way he'd meant.

'I shouldn't worry about Russ and Ellie. She's old enough to look after herself. It's Russ and Debbie you should be worrying about.'

'I am.'

'She's a funny kid, but I suppose we all were at that age. What's this idea she's got about Justin's father?'

'He'd got hold of some photographs that . . . um . . . didn't show his father in a very dignified light. Debbie said he was going to send them to the papers.'

'The little sod. For a fee, I suppose. Did you see the photos?'

He said no. A vestigial loyalty to Justin's father made him

decide the less said about them the better.

'And that's why she thinks his father had him murdered?'

He said yes, brusquely. He didn't want Annabel's practical sympathy flowing over onto Debbie.

'Poor kid,' she said.

He'd been wondering all through the conversation whether to tell her the latest about Debbie and decided she'd better know. The presence of Helena was a nuisance, but he suspected she'd probably heard all about it anyway.

'I, um . . . I wouldn't say too much to Debbie if I were you. The fact is, Russ has told her about us the other night.'

'Russ!'

Both of them were looking at him wide-eyed.

'Yes. You remember I thought I heard somebody prowling about. It must have been him, and now he's told Debbie. She's . . . she's taking it pretty badly.'

He didn't say Debbie had called her a tart. There was no sense in making things worse.

Helena was still gaping as if she hadn't taken it in, but there was concern on Annabel's face.

'I'm sorry, Birdie. Poor Debbie.'

He didn't want to talk about it any more.

'Debbie will be all right.'

He hadn't much confidence in it even as he said it, which as things turned out was just as well.

CHAPTER FIFTEEN

The day got worse as it went on, a time of sweaty edginess when nobody would stray far away from the lodge but resented each others' closeness. It seemed to Birdie that they were caught up in a giant spider's web of watching. Russ, ostentatiously, watched both him and Toby. Neither of them could stir to the other side of the balcony without Russ's eyes following him. If Birdie went into the dormitory or bathroom, he'd find Russ watching him when he came out. In turn, Birdie watched Russ, determined to give him no chance to get Debbie on her own again. He invented jobs for Debbie that kept her close to his side, packing up some of the kitchen things into a tea chest, going a little way into the forest to see if they could find tangerines or avocados to add to their diminishing food supplies. Russ, of course, volunteered to come with them but Birdie forestalled that.

'One of us should stay here and keep an eye on Toby.'

Russ looked disgruntled about that, but couldn't object.

In the forest they found an avocado tree with ripe fruits the size of Birdie's fists.

'Pity we didn't find them before,' Debbie said, picking conscientiously.

He'd been wondering all morning whether to tell her about the conversation with Annabel and Helena and had decided against it. At present, there was an uneasy truce between them, but he sensed it wouldn't take much to break it. Criticising Russ, let alone re-opening the subject of Russ as potential murderer, would be interpreted as either a hostile action or a sign of desperation. Even if he told her what Annabel and Helena had said she might flatly refuse to believe it. The conclusion he'd come to was that he shouldn't mention the matter to her any more until he had proof positive, one way or the other. How he was to do that in the shrinking number of hours before the boat arrived was still far from clear to him, but the outlines of a plan were forming.

'If the boat doesn't come tomorrow we'll be running out of food,' she said. 'We'll really have to do the survival bit.'

'It will come.'

When they got back with the fruit, there were a line of faces looking down at them over the balcony: Henry, Mal and Annabel beside the inevitable Russ.

'You've been gone long enough to pick a whole plantation,' Henry complained.

They'd been away no more than an hour, but it was a reminder to Birdie that not only Russ was watching him. Mal and Henry might be a shade less obvious about it, but they'd developed a close interest in where he was and what he was doing.

'Where are the others?'

Toby, it turned out, was at the table writing in his familiar nature diary. Birdie, glancing over his shoulder, saw the page was full of delicate sketches of moth wings, then nearly bumped his head on Russ who was moving in to look over the other shoulder.

'Just taking a look, Toby.'

'They're very good, Toby.'

He turned round and stared at them both from behind his glasses. 'You've never seemed very interested in moths before.'

Debbie, with the avocados and a few small tangerines, had disappeared into the kitchen and Russ showed signs of following her.

'She'll need somebody to help take the stones out.'

'Debbie's perfectly capable of taking a few stones out. You leave her alone.'

Russ sketched a resentful salute.

'If you want the others, Helena's in the dormitory having a headache and Ellie's in the other dormitory nursing Simon.'

By now Birdie was suspicious enough to check on everything he was told but, sure enough, when he opened the door of the women's dormitory a crack he saw Helena's hair spread over the pillow and, in the room next door, Ellie was keeping watch beside her husband.

'How is he?'

Ellie put a finger to her lips, but Simon opened his eyes at the whisper and sat up when he saw it was Birdie.

'I'm much better.'

He sounded better too. The fiery red of his face had faded to normal sunburn and his eyes had lost their glazed look. He seemed, for the first time since Birdie had met him, content.

'We've been talking,' Ellie said. 'About our marriage.'

'Oh, yes.'

More counselling, he supposed, more determination to make a go of things. He wondered what they'd try next time and had a mental picture of Simon in fur ear muffs behind a husky team, poor sod. Even prison might be kinder.

'It makes you see things in a new light,' Simon said. 'I mean, when I was lost out there in the forest I started thinking. It's surprising how it starts you thinking, something like that. Then with being so ill and so on.'

He sounded positively pleased with himself, as if getting lost and sunstruck were major achievements.

'And Ellie's been so marvellous about it.'

He beamed at her and she actually stroked his hand. If she'd nursed him night and day for months he could hardly have sounded more grateful.

'After all,' Ellie said, 'it's our decision in the end, isn't it? It's our lives.'

'Oh, quite.'

All Birdie wanted to do was get out of this scene of matrimonial bliss and make sure Russ wasn't helping with the avocados.

'So we've been talking it over, and we've decided.'

'Oh, good.'

'We've decided to get divorced,' Simon said, beaming all over his sunburn.

Birdie gulped back what he'd been going to say, then decided on reflection that it would be all right after all. 'I'm sure you'll both be very happy.'

'Oh, we will,' said Ellie. 'I'm sure we will.'

He took a step to the door, but they were determined to have their say.

Simon began. 'We want you to know, Birdie, that Ellie and I are very grateful to you.'

'Whatever the others say,' Ellie put in.

'You've helped us to know ourselves, discover things about ourselves we didn't know existed.'

Birdie miserably identified the quote from the Tooth and Claw Adventure Holidays brochure.

'And we shall always be very grateful to you and Diabola.'

As far as the island was concerned, that probably made them the first in history. As far as he was concerned, it was pretty rare as well. He thought if he stayed around long enough they'd probably present him with an inscribed coconut.

'That's very nice to hear, but I've got to go. Lots of things to pack up.'

'Of course. The boat.'

She made it sound silver-sailed and nutmeg-scented, but a very long way away. He knew it was throbbing with all the force of its diesel engines much too close for comfort.

'I'll let you know when it's dinner time.'

Out on the balcony, things were much as before. Toby was still writing, Russ was leaning against a wooden pillar and watching him, Mal and Henry were sitting with their elbows on the table, pretending not to look at Birdie when he reappeared. Debbie had returned to her usual place on the edge of the balcony, one leg hanging over, and Annabel was standing not far away, looking out into the trees with an absorption that suggested to Birdie she might have tried talking to Debbie and been snubbed. Soon afterwards, Helena came out of the dormitory, sleepy-eyed. She said in reply to their questions that no, her headache wasn't better, it was worse, only it was too hot to sleep in the dormitory and she felt awful, awful. Usually this would have been the prelude to collapsing onto Mal's receptive chest or shoulder, but this time it didn't happen. Mal had joined in the general murmur of concern, but no more than that, and kept chest and shoulders square on to the table, uninviting. Helena glanced that way, gave a pathetic little sigh, then padded heavy footed across the balcony to Annabel, who whispered something and put an arm around her shoulder. As predicted, with home and family imminent, Mal's sympathy for Helena seemed to be cooling.

Everybody but Toby seemed to sense they'd been witnessing a piece of emotional brutality, because the strained atmosphere became even more so. For a few minutes the only sounds were the buzzing of insects and the soft strokes of Toby's pencil across his notepad. Not expecting any takers, Birdie wondered if anybody fancied a farewell stroll in the rain forest. The verdict, among those who bothered to reply, was unanimous.

Mal said, through clenched teeth, 'I think we've all had enough of your rain forest.'

Russ said, meaningfully, 'Don't you think we should all stick together, Birdie?'

Henry groaned.

'Couldn't we go down to that shelter place by the harbour?' Mal suggested, 'Wait for the boat down there?'

'It's only a cargo shed,' Birdie said hastily. 'There's no room for all of us to sleep.'

'It'd be better than another night in these damned trees. I don't want to lose a minute getting on that boat.'

He glanced around at the others, looking for agreement, while Birdie hoped he didn't have another rebellion on his hands. The plan he'd made wouldn't be helped if they moved themselves the few miles down to the sea. As far as he was concerned, the thing had started around the Devil's Bath Tub and it was going to finish there. The others tossed the argument around for a while but, to Birdie's relief, Mal's side lost. Helena said she'd just die if she had to sleep on a concrete floor and Ellie, coming out in time to add her voice, insisted that Simon wouldn't possibly be well enough to leave before morning. Having seen Simon, Birdie doubted that, but supported her enthusiastically.

For Birdie's plan to work, it was essential that they should all be there to hear what he had to say. They'd decided on a high tea around five o'clock, because the scrag ends of the store cupboard hardly rated as dinner, even with the morning's harvest added to them. He managed to persuade Ellie that Simon in his convalescent state should be allowed to get up and eat with the rest of them.

The avocados, yellow and buttery, helped down the remains of the biscuits and the last few tins of corned beef. Birdie waited until they were all chewing before launching, casually he hoped, on his attack.

'Have you all done your packing, then?'

A few impatient sounds over the munching. He knew very well they'd done it hours ago.

'I've nearly finished mine. Only a few books to put away.'

No reaction at all. Birdie's packing didn't even come a good second to inferior corned beef.

'I thought nobody would mind if I took a few of Morton's books away with me. After all, he won't want them any more.'

That got them, or some of them. Russ turned to look at him. Simon put down his fork and stared at him.

'Some of them are very interesting. There's one on witchcraft and one or two on geology. I'm learning quite a lot about this place.'

Mal said, 'I'd have thought the only thing anybody wanted to know about this place was the time of the next boat out.'

'What sort of things?' Ellie said. She sounded no more than politely interested.

'Rock formations, water courses and so on.' He didn't need to be more specific than that. The one who mattered would know what he was talking about already.

'It sounds really boring,' Helena said sulkily, and Mal gave her a quick glance across the table.

Russ cut in, 'Don't you think you should leave those books here, Birdie? They might be evidence.'

They all looked daggers at him for that. The day had been a conspiracy not to talk about it, and now he'd broken it.

'I can't see it makes any difference if Birdie wants to take a lot of boring old books. I mean, we shall probably never know, shall we?'

That was Henry, sounding massively unconcerned. There was silence at first, then Ellie said, 'Of course we shall know.'

Her voice was louder and higher than usual. Henry was unperturbed.

'It's all very well saying that, but I don't see how. I mean, I dare say the powers that be will want to question us, but we'll be taking off for Barbados, then home, and I don't suppose there'll be much they can do about it.'

'That's a thoroughly neo-colonialist attitude,' Ellie said.

'You can call it neo whatever you like, it's a fact of life. Anyway, why should they be worried about Justin?'

'There's Morton, too,' Debbie said, but nobody took any notice of her.

Russ said, 'I think Ellie's right. The police on Saint Lucia will want to question us, and they'll have powers to keep us there if they want to.'

'Then we just telephone the ambassador,' Henry said. 'They can't keep us against our will.'

'Of course,' Russ said, 'it would be easier if it had been an accident.' There was a clatter all around the table as forks were put down and people turned towards him. Birdie suddenly thought he knew now where the conversation about Debbie had been leading. Russ was proposing no less than an eleventh-hour conspiracy of silence about the two deaths and what more effective way could there be of getting Birdie's co-operation than hinting that his daughter might have some awkward questions to face? He wondered, looking around the table, if Russ had been playing the same game elsewhere, whispering into a few more ears that, on the whole, it would be better if certain questions never surfaced. It looked as if it had shocked them but had it surprised all of them?

'It might,' Henry drawled, 'have certain advantages.'

'Henry!'

Annabel's gasp had a shocked giggle behind it, but she didn't sound entirely disapproving.

Ellie said positively, 'That's impractical, patronising and simply morally wrong.'

Something moved around the table, but Birdie couldn't tell whether it was a sigh of disappointment or relief. Russ let it take its course before speaking again.

'All right, Ellie. I don't suppose Simon will mind explaining how he tried to kill me with a machete. You saw it, didn't you, Birdie?'

'I'm not having Simon brought into this.'

Ellie's response was prompt and furious, while Simon just sat beside her looking worried. If he hadn't witnessed the tender scene in the dormitory, Birdie would have been amazed to find her defending Simon in public, but apparently there was a difference between Simon as present husband and Simon potentially ex. After a moment's thought, it struck him what it was. If Simon had to go to prison for murder, Ellie would be stuck indefinitely with the role of caring wife, a prospect she clearly found unappealing. So he was less surprised than Russ might have been when, having issued her protest, she took no further part in the argument.

'What do you think, Birdie?' Mal asked.

This was a difficult one. Birdie reckoned he'd just managed to spread enough bait before Russ lobbed in his suggestion, but this proposal had muddied the waters. Perhaps that was the intention. The question was, if they agreed on their pact of silence, would the murderer find that reassuring enough to cancel any further plans for hiding the evidence? Birdie could only guess, but his guess was that the murderer was thorough, a belt and braces character. The pact might make him bolder in swallowing Birdie's bait. He had just a second or two to decide while they watched him and waited, and he made the wrong decision.

'I'm inclined to agree with Russ.'

He didn't look at Debbie, but he heard a little intake of breath. He wished there was a way of signalling to her that he wasn't reneging on his promise, that this was only part of his way of keeping it. He'd have to sort that out with her afterwards. For now, he must keep his attention on how the others were reacting, which of them looked most relieved at the idea of leaving the whole mess behind on Diabola. Henry looked relieved, there was no doubt about that. Mal, on the other hand, looked decidedly doubtful. Ellie was frowning, but then she usually did, and Simon was glancing round the table as if the question had nothing to do with him. Annabel looked, if anything, rather amused and Helena was watching her, waiting to see which way her friend jumped.

Having taken the plunge, although he already half regretted it for Debbie's sake, Birdie could do nothing but flounder on. 'Accidents do happen. After all, whatever we do isn't going to bring Justin and Morton back again.'

Henry said, 'We'd have to make sure nobody dug them up for a look. Say they were decomposed when we found them, maggots and so on.'

Helena groaned 'yuck' and put her face in her hands.

Mal said, 'Steady on, Henry.'

'That's all very well, but we've got to face up to things. I mean, if we're going to do it, we've got to do it properly.' Henry had cheered up remarkably since the start of the discussion and was showing signs of treating it like a board meeting with polished mahogany and green blotters in place of warped timber and crumb-strewn plates. 'What we've got to do is take a vote on it. We've heard what Birdie and Russ think, and I agree with them. What about the rest of you? Mal?'

Mal shook his head but said nothing.

'Is that no, or abstain?'

'Abstain.'

Mal grabbed the word like a lifebelt.

'What about you, Ellie?'

'We can't not tell them. It will come out anyway.'

'I'll count that as a no. What about you, Simon?'

'I agree with Russ and Birdie.'

It was the first act of his new life. He sounded positively chirpy about it.

'Toby?'

'I don't know what everybody's making the fuss about. Man isn't an endangered species.'

'I'm counting that as another one on our side,' Henry said. 'What about you, Annabel?'

'Do I have to?'

It might have been a go at snakes and ladders.

'Yes, you do. Come on and make up your mind.'

Henry's eyes, whether accidentally or not, went to the ring of creeper around Annabel's engagement finger. She saw where the glance went and laughed.

'I'm on the other side, Henry. I mean, you can't let people get away with murder, even if it's Justin.'

'I see.'

From his expression, Henry obviously regarded it as an act of disloyalty and Annabel's chances of getting her diamond had slipped considerably. But perhaps she didn't find the prospect of marriage to Henry so attractive after all.

After that, getting Helena's vote was no more than a formality. She said she agreed with Annabel, without giving any clear sign of knowing which side Annabel had chosen. Henry had been keeping a tally by knife blade on the table. He announced the result with due solemnity.

'For accident, five votes. For murder, three votes. Accident has it, gentlemen.'

Annabel said, 'You didn't ask Debbie.'

All eyes turned to her, sitting there with bowed head, fingers tearing at a piece of green tangerine peel.

'She's not eighteen yet. She hasn't got a vote.'

'She's got an interest. I think you should ask Debbie.'

'All right, then. Which way are you voting, Debbie?' Henry's tone was bored and avuncular.

She raised her head and stared at him for a moment before replying. 'It doesn't matter which way I vote, does it? It'll still be the same result.'

'Annabel says you've got to vote, so you'd better bloody well vote. She seems to be the party whip around here.'

Unquestionably, no diamonds for Annabel.

'Abstain,' Debbie said.

Her head was down again and she was picking the tangerine peel into smaller fragments.

'That was a fuss about nothing, wasn't it? Anybody got anything else to say?'

Russ said, 'Yes. The three who voted against; are they bound by what the rest of us decided?'

'They should be,' Henry said. 'It was a democratic decision.'

'It's conspiracy to commit a crime,' Ellie said.

'That's under English rules. We're playing away.'

'I don't want anything to do with it.' She got up and stalked to the far side of the balcony, leaning out over the rail, although Birdie suspected she could still hear what was going on.

'She'll be all right,' Simon said vaguely. He was still the most cheerful person around the table.

'What about Annabel and Helena?'

Annabel answered for both of them. 'If you mean, are we going to shop you all to the local police, I don't suppose so. It just seems wrong, that's all.'

Henry's sidelong glance showed he didn't trust her and Birdie agreed with him. If he, like Russ and Henry, had really wanted this cover-up plot to work, he'd have been worried about Annabel. He certainly wouldn't, as Russ and Henry did, go on with the meeting in her presence.

'That's the principle of it, then,' Henry said. 'The point is, what are we going to do about the details?'

Birdie thought it was time he showed interest. 'They just had accidents and drowned.'

'We'll have to do better than that, Birdie,' Russ said. 'How come we didn't report it at the time?'

'Morton's radio was broken.'

'Yes, but how did it get broken?'

'Fell over?'

Both Henry and Russ snorted at that. Russ, warning him again that he had to do better, came up with a plan of his own with a promptness that showed he'd been thinking of it for a long time.

'What we've got to do is knit it all together. The point is, Morton was drunk that night. We all know that, because it's the truth, right?'

'Right.'

'Well, suppose he's really roaring drunk. So drunk he wrecks his own place, smashes up his radio then comes in here and starts shouting insults at us.'

'I didn't hear him do that,' Toby protested.

Russ ignored him. 'He storms off, in the direction of the Devil's Bath Tub. Some of us follow because we're worried about him. He's dancing about on the edge, shouting at us to come and get him, then he trips and falls in.'

He paused, looking around the table for their approval.

'Sounds good, Russ. If you want a lie well told, call in an expert,' Henry drawled from the end of the table.

Russ glared. 'Care to explain what you mean by that?'

'Nothing, Russ, nothing. Just a joke in bad taste, that's all.'

'Save them for your City friends. As I was saying, Morton trips and falls in. Before we can stop him, Justin goes in after him to try to save him, and drowns in the attempt.'

'Justin!' Annabel gave in to a fit of the giggles, choked and had to be thumped on the back by Mal.

'All right,' Russ said. 'We all know it's unlikely but other people won't. Or, if they do, it'll make it a better story.'

'"Playboy redeems himself trying to save friend."'

'But he couldn't stand Morton,' Annabel objected.

'Nobody outside knows that. And his family won't mind. From

what I can gather, they'll be only too pleased Justin did something right for once in his life, even if he is dead.'

Silence fell around the table and they looked at each other, except for Toby who was watching a lizard on the ceiling, and Debbie, who still had her head down. Birdie had the impression that up to that point the thing had been half a joke for most of them; that they'd never intended to go through with it. Russ's carefully detailed fiction had taken them further than they'd intended.

'I . . . I suppose if it saved a lot of trouble . . .' Helena said.

Annabel shushed her, 'You abstained, remember?'

Henry took it up, with another glare at Annabel. 'It'll save a lot of trouble all round. I mean, I don't suppose the police and the consular people would want the bother of it.'

'I suppose Justin's people would be quite pleased,' Mal said. 'Justin being a hero, and so on.'

Henry said briskly, 'So that's settled. We'll have to polish it a bit tonight, decide who're going to be eye witnesses and so on, but we've got the outline all right.'

He plumped two pudgy fists down on the table in front of him. 'Meeting over. I don't suppose we've got any cognac hidden away, have we?'

Debbie spoke, surprising them all, especially Birdie, who'd been watching her all the time Russ was talking, noticing that she neither moved nor made a sound. She'd seemed so deeply slumped in depression that he wasn't sure she even realised what was going on. And, now that she did speak, the lack of connection between what had been under discussion and what she said seemed to confirm it.

'What about those photos?'

Henry sighed gustily and leaned back on the bench.

'Those photos again. What about them?'

'He wanted them published.'

Mal said, under his breath, 'All he wanted was a lot of money.'

Henry said, with forced gentleness, as if talking to a difficult child, 'I think we forget about them, Debbie. It hardly goes with the image. You'd like Justin to be a hero now, wouldn't you?'

'Not that way. It's all hypocrisy. He hated hypocrisy. That's why he was . . .'

Birdie cut in hastily. 'You'd better give the rest of the photographs to me. 'I'll look after them.'

He couldn't stand the idea of her walking around with them, cherishing them like perverted icons that showed that the rest of the world was wrong and Justin was right.

She shook her head. 'I'll keep them.'

'It doesn't matter you keeping them,' Henry said, 'as long as you don't do anything with them. You don't want to cause a lot of trouble for your father, do you?'

Birdie couldn't stand this. 'That's between Debbie and me. You're not helping things, Henry.'

All he wanted to do now was to get Debbie alone and explain to her that this hideous half hour hadn't been his idea, that he'd gone along with it for reasons she'd approve when she knew them. All it would take was a few minutes alone with her, without the rest of them interfering.

But he couldn't get those few minutes. It seemed as if Debbie was determined not to be alone with her father. First she made a great business of doing the washing up, with the help of Mal, Annabel and Ellie, then she took herself off into the women's dormitory and, when he looked in, Ellie was in there too changing her underwear so he had to beat a hasty retreat. He shouted through the door to ask her to come out and have a talk with him, and she yelled back, 'Later Dad,' in a voice that suggested it wasn't a high priority in her scheme of things. He took himself off to the deserted men's dormitory and had Morton's geology book out of his pack, poring over the graphs of underground water courses. The more he looked, the more certain he was that he was right, that his trap had been well baited. It was just a case now of walking off into the forest having dropped some casual hints about where he was going, and waiting to see which of them followed him. Not that he had many doubts. But Debbie wanted more than suspicion, she wanted proof. Well, if that was what she wanted, she should have it. But he couldn't go off and get it for her before he'd had a chance to explain, to let her know that he was still every bit as anxious to find Justin's killer as she was.

After a while, he put the book away and, from the bottom of his pack, took the two carefully wrapped machetes. They were evidence, but it was in his mind that one of them at least might be more immediately useful than that. If he was right about who'd rise to his bait, he had a real fight on his hands, training and experience on his side, youth and desperation on the other. Although, when he thought of Debbie, he felt his share of desperation as well. It was that idea that made him decide to leave both machetes behind when he went into the rain forest. If he took one, he might use it, and if he used it he'd do it with all his force. He stowed the pack away in a cupboard and, deciding that twenty minutes was enough time for Ellie to finish shifting her underwear, went back to the door of the women's dormitory.

'You in there, Debbie?'

No answer. He pushed open the door and found an empty room, littered with clothes and toilet bags. Some instinct made him look for a message on her pillow but there was nothing. He breathed a sigh of relief at that. She must be out on the balcony with the others. But when he went out there seemed to be fewer people around. Ellie was there, standing by the balcony rail. Simon, Mal and Helena were sitting around the table at some distance from each other, not talking. There was no sign of anybody else.

'Where is everybody? Where's Debbie?'

When they turned towards him he was aware of a tension about them, matching the sharpness of his own voice.

Ellie took a step or two towards him.

'They've all gone,' she said. Her arm swept in a stiff arc over leaves silhouetted against a sinking sun. 'All out there somewhere.'

CHAPTER SIXTEEN

'When? Why?'

He spluttered questions, still not believing it. All day the party had huddled away from the rain forest. Now, with night coming on, half of them had disappeared into it. While he was checking his bait, the fish had swum away.

Mal said, sounding worried, 'Basically, Debbie went off, and Henry and Annabel have gone after her.'

'Gone off where?'

Ellie said, 'She seemed to have this obsession about going back to the place where Justin was murdered. She said she couldn't leave the island without seeing it again.'

It was the first he'd heard of this obsession. He didn't believe in it.

'She told you that?'

'She told all of us. After we came out of the dormitory, all the others were sitting around the table. She came out with it quite suddenly.'

'Who was she talking to?'

'Not to anyone in particular. To all of us.'

'I thought she was being a bit hysterical,' Mal said. 'That's why I didn't do anything about it.'

Birdie suppressed an urge to shake him. 'But what exactly did she say?'

'I told you. She stood there where you're standing and she said, "I keep thinking about the place where Justin was killed. I can't leave till I see it again."'

'Then what did she do?'

'She just sort of swept off down the steps. Annabel wanted to follow her to see if she was all right, but Henry said, Not to worry, she'd just gone off on her own for a good blub, she'd be all right later. Then five minutes ago she still hadn't come back and Annabel said she'd better go and see if she was all right. Then Annabel didn't come back so Henry's just gone to look for her.'

They were scared, though; far more scared than the events they'd just described would justify. They'd agreed, or most of them had, on a cosy little arrangement. Now the forest had opened its sulphurous mouth and started swallowing people again: Debbie and Annabel and Henry. There were two others as well not accounted for in the story.

'What about Russ and Toby?'

Mal said, 'We think Toby must have just slid off again while we were doing the washing up – you know the way he does.'

'What about Russ?'

Mal said, 'That's just what we were asking when you came out. Nobody saw the going of Russ.'

'Was he here when Debbie was talking about wanting to see where Justin was killed?'

'Yes, definitely. When Debbie came out, Russ was sitting here giving all of us the third degree about where Toby had gone – as if we knew. I told him, Toby's not in the same world as the rest of us. He just comes and goes, and that's it.'

'So he heard what Debbie said.'

'Of course he did. That's why he was going to look for you. We thought that's what he'd done.'

Birdie felt as if a lump of ice had hit him in the stomach. 'Well, he didn't.'

'That means he'll be out there somewhere too, looking for Debbie. Or Toby. Or both of them.'

Birdie sat down heavily on the end of the bench, cursing himself for not seeing what was coming. He'd been so busy baiting his trap that it hadn't entered his head that Debbie would be doing just the same thing. Only she was using different bait, and Russ's absence suggested that hers had been the more effective. Up to now he hadn't believed in her theory of the photographs. Now it came to him in a cold sweat that she might be right after all. He still found it hard to believe in Justin's father as a hirer of killers, but he'd been wrong often enough in the past, and might have got it disastrously wrong again. He'd been blaming Debbie for her stubbornness, then matched it with his own, driving her to a course of action that was all but suicidal. She'd made sure everybody knew she had the photos. She'd made sure everybody – with the possible exception of Peter and Toby – knew where she was going.

'She said "the place where Justin was killed". You're quite sure about that?'

Ellie nodded. 'Her exact words. That was near the waterfall, wasn't it?'

He was on the point of saying something, but stopped himself. Still as far as most of them were concerned, the pool under the waterfall was Justin's place of death. Only three people knew otherwise: himself, Debbie – because he'd told her his theory – and the murderer. So, assuming he'd got it right about what Debbie was trying to do, and he was sure of that, she'd be making not for the waterfall but for the Devil's Bath Tub, and the person who knew that and followed her there could only be Justin's murderer. But that was assuming Debbie believed his theory about where the murder was done. He thought she did, but he couldn't read her mind any more. He stood up.

'Where are you going?' Mal asked.

'Where do you think? To find Debbie.'

'I'll come with you,' Mal offered, echoed by Ellie.

'You stay here!'

He spoke roughly, not bothered about anyone's feelings or the twitterings of Simon and Ellie. Without waiting to collect his jacket or pack he slithered down the steps and let the rain forest close over him.

There was nobody at the Devil's Bath Tub, no trace of anybody. In the last of the light he stood looking for a long time at the yellow-grey swirl of water as it started its journey underground, heart pounding at every large bubble that might have been a foot or head. He daren't let himself think that it had already happened, that another body had been launched on its way through the system. There'd be some trace, surely; signs of a struggle, blood trails. He crawled around every inch of the hot rock on his hands and knees, choking in the rising fumes of sulphur, sniffing like a dog for the faintest trace of butcher's shop odour that might be underlying it. He found nothing and, when a particularly bad fit of coughing forced him to stop and think, realised he'd been wasting his time. Both the machetes on the island were back at the lodge in his pack so the murderer would have to use some other method this time. He imagined Russ's big hands around Debbie's throat and it was all he could do to stop himself abandoning his last remnants of sense and start tearing the forest apart with his bare hands. It was useless, worse than useless, to go blundering around in the dark. If it hadn't happened already – and he refused to let himself believe it had happened already – then Debbie's plan demanded that she should come to the Devil's Bath Tub, and the murderer's plan surely demanded he should meet her there, as he'd met first Justin then Morton. After an hour of patience so painful that it nagged at the very marrow of his bones, it began to occur to Birdie that he might have got it wrong again.

Debbie, baiting her trap, had said she wanted to go to the place where Justin was killed. She'd seemed to accept Birdie's theory that the murder place was the Bath Tub and not the waterfall, so it would follow that the murderer knew it, too. But there was a next stage, a stage that Birdie hadn't reached but Debbie might have: Debbie might know, the murderer might know, but the murderer wouldn't know that Debbie knew. He groaned as he followed the logic through. That meant that when Debbie issued her challenge, she'd think the murderer thought she was talking about the waterfall. All this time he'd been crawling about looking for bloodstains, waiting for something to happen, Russ might have been trailing her down through the forest to the pool. And here he was, two miles or so of dark forest away, two hours or more since both of them had left the lodge. He groaned again, beating his fist against his forehead.

'You shouldn't take it as hard as that,' said a voice behind him. 'After all, it's not as if he was the only man in the world.'

'Henry!' Birdie gripped him by the plump shoulders. 'What the bloody hell are you doing here?'

Henry wriggled and tried to get away from his grip, unsuccessfully.

'I didn't know it was you. What are you shaking me for? Stop it, Birdie. For goodness sake, will you stop it? You're out of your mind.'

Birdie hadn't been aware he was shaking him. He stopped it,

but still kept a firm grip on his shoulders. Henry's plump face was as smooth as lard and he reeked of sweat.

'What are you doing here?' he repeated.

'Trying to keep an eye on your daughter, which is more than you seem capable of doing.'

'Keeping an eye on her, is that what you call it? What made you think you'd find her here?'

'I didn't. I was trying to find Annabel, then I got lost, so I just followed the path. Then I saw somebody sitting there, watched for a bit and heard groaning, and I naturally thought it was your daughter.'

'Why naturally?'

'Who else would sit around groaning over Justin?'

Birdie released one shoulder to get a better look at him.

'I don't believe you.'

Half-free, Henry gathered up some of his shredded dignity.

'I don't care if you believe me or not. Personally, I think you were a bit mad when we started on this and got worse as we went along. Annabel told me about you attacking her.'

'Me attack Annabel!'

'Practically raped the poor girl. She was quite upset about it.'

Birdie resisted the temptation to get side-tracked.

'Why choose this particular path?'

'I told you, I didn't choose it. I got lost in all these bloody trees. Now if you'll kindly tell me the way back to the lodge . . .'

'I'm not having you wandering off again. You're staying with me.'

Clumsily, Henry tried to wrench himself away from Birdie's grip and found himself plucked backwards. He stumbled, lost his footing and fell heavily against Birdie, yelling as he went.

'So, that's the game, is it?'

The manoeuvre had taken them several steps nearer the sulphur pool. It nearly caught Birdie off balance but he managed to stay on his feet, pinioning Henry with one hand on his shoulder and the other across his well-padded ribs. Henry kicked him on the shins, wriggling and farting fit to challenge the sulphur fumes.

'Trying to get me in there too, are you?' Birdie snarled at him. 'Done anything like this before, have you?' He tightened his arm across the other man's ribs. Disconcertingly, Henry collapsed like a frosted dahlia, and slid out of his grip to sprawl at his feet. His voice, though, was as pompous as ever.

'Since you ask, I have not done anything like this before. Sumo wrestling was not on the curriculum, and if you lay a finger on me again you'll be hearing from my solicitors.'

'You tried to pitch me into that bloody pond.'

'I did not try to pitch you into the bloody pond. I was showing a kind concern for your daughter and you leapt on me like a deranged ape. I really am beginning to wonder about you.'

'You're wondering about me, are you? Well, I've got a few questions for you, my lad.'

'They can wait till we get back. I think you've sprained my elbow.' Henry got to his feet unsteadily.

'We're not going back. I'm staying out here till I find my daughter and you're staying with me.'

Logic had dictated that the murderer would be the one to arrive at the sulphur pool and although Birdie wasn't convinced yet, he had no intention of letting go of Henry.

'If you're asking me to help you look for her,' Henry said coldly, 'I can hardly refuse, even if my elbow's hurting like hell. But perhaps you'll be kind enough to tell me where we're supposed to be looking.'

The moon was rising, past fullness, but still enough of it to give a useful light. As it came up, the forest sounds got louder until the croaks and rattlings and throbbings were as clamorous as by day. The grey rock ridge turned silver in the light, rising from the dark forest on either side.

'She's somewhere down there,' Birdie said.

That was when it came, the sound he'd hoped he'd never hear again, a long drawn-out scream of pain and terror that ripped through the night and lasted half a lifetime, cutting off all the normal sounds of the forest. When it stopped at last, there were the same few seconds of total silence as there'd been on the morning when he found Justin's body, more terrible in their way than the scream itself, before the usual clicks and croaks and rustlings started up again.

Henry's body went rigid. 'What the hell was that?'

But Birdie was already on his way along the path that led off the rock plateau and down beside the ridge towards the waterfall. He ran blindly, desperately, aware that Henry was following him but not caring now whether he did or not. He'd got it wrong, wrong, wrong. She hadn't gone to the sulphur pool after all, she'd gone to the waterfall and the murderer had followed her there while he'd been sitting and waiting. Once the idea had got into his mind he couldn't bear to think about it any more, or what he'd find at the waterfall when he got there. The only thing that mattered any more was getting to the source of that scream.

He was about half way down the track, with Henry some hundreds of yards behind him, when the scream came again, shorter this time. Instead of dying away it was cut off at full blast, then there was another shorter scream, then nothing. Birdie stopped dead, unbelievingly. Unless his ears were giving out on him, those screams had come from somewhere much closer than the waterfall, somewhere not far from where he was standing. Debbie's fear that Justin might have recovered consciousness, and screamed while he was being drowned in the underground river, came back to him as a choking horror, because it sounded as if the screams had come from somewhere inside the ridge, as if the rock itself were screaming. And the rock was doing more than screaming. It was glowing. A dull, wavering light was spreading out of it and illuminating the trees, not more than a hundred yards below him. Heavy breathing told him that Henry had caught up.

'What is it, Birdie?'

'The cave. He's got her in the bloody cave.'

And Birdie took off again, launching himself down the path towards the source of the light.

A few steps above it, he stopped and listened. He could hear the sound of voices inside, two voices. One of them, a male voice, sounded angry, the other was no more than an indistinguishable murmur. Without waiting to hear any more, he bent double and burst in through the cave mouth. The first thing he was aware of was Peter's face, cadaverous in candlelight, and Peter's hand upraised to stop him. The hand looked wet and shiny but before he could think about that everything was in darkness and the Devil was on him, in a rush of noise, smell and hot gasping breath.

It was the smell he was aware of first when the light went out, a rank, sweet animal smell, hitting like a blow. Then the scream blasted his ears at close quarters, a scream as if one of Hell's teeth were being torn out by the roots. He pitched forward and, as he fell, there was a clattering sound, something trampled over his hands with cloven feet, something ripped into his shoulder then tore away out of the cave and into the open air. But the smell was still there and, although the screaming had stopped, there was clamouring. Somebody from inside the cave was yelling like a mad thing: 'Stop him. Stop him,' and somebody outside the cave – Henry presumably – was making different noises, incomprehensible noises. It took Birdie some time to make out what Henry was yelling and when he did he still couldn't make sense of it.

'Yoicks!' Henry shouted. 'Tallyho.' Then a long, wavering, 'Gone a-wa-a-ay.'

The voice from the back of the cave stopped shouting and said tragically, 'Why didn't you stop him?' It was Toby's voice.

'What are you doing to her?' said Birdie into the darkness. 'Let her go.'

'It wasn't a her, that's the whole point. We've already got a female.' A match scraped, illuminating a hand that wandered around the cave floor, located and lit a fat camping candle.

'Oh, it's you is it, Birdie? Why did you have to come bursting in at a time like this?'

'Have you got my daughter in here?'

'Now what in the world,' Toby said, 'would we want with your daughter?'

He was crouched at the back of the cave, beside a pile of tins and camping gear. The blue ice box stood open beside him. His brother was on his knees peering out through the entrance of the cave. In the candlelight Birdie saw that his hands were shiny, not from wetness but because he was wearing rubber gloves.

'What are you two doing?'

Henry's voice came from outside. 'Is there room for another one in there?'

He squeezed in cautiously, wrinkling his nose at the smell.

'I'm afraid you'll have to cross pork chops off the menu. Your little pig'll be half way across the island by now.'

'Moustached peccary,' Toby corrected.

'Hamilcar,' said Peter sadly.

'Morton's peccary,' said Birdie, with the idea that things were flying apart again.

'Yes, Morton's.'

'And what were you two doing with Morton's peccary?'

Peter picked something off the floor and showed it to him. As far as he could see it was nothing more than a short plastic drinking straw. Henry, though, let out a whinny.

'Oh, I see. You were trying to get Hamilcar to donate a sperm sample. Was that what all the noise was about?'

Toby nodded, his shadow moving on the cave wall.

Birdie said, 'How long have you been keeping him here?'

'Since early on Thursday morning. We thought you'd guessed when you found the cave. Luckily Peter was out at the time, giving Hamilcar some air.'

'So that scream the other morning, was that Hamilcar too?'

'I'm afraid so. I wouldn't want you to think we were hurting him. It was just he seemed to object to the process more strongly than we'd allowed for.'

Henry said, 'Why did you want it?'

'I told you, we've got a female, but we're having serious problems finding a mate for her. The conservation organisations don't seem to approve of Peter and me. They say we're unethical. I can't think why.'

'I can,' Birdie said. 'Just for a start, you stole that peccary.'

'Not at all. Morton was going to release him soon anyway. We only wanted a few days with him beforehand.'

Birdie's shoulder throbbed and smarted from the animal's tusk.

'Was it you two who broke up Morton's bungalow as well?'

Toby looked shocked. 'Of course not. Why would we do that?'

'What time did you take the peccary?'

Toby glanced over to his brother.

'Soon after two o'clock,' Peter said. 'We thought Morton would still be out on your exercise.'

'Did you see anybody else there, hear anything?'

'No. The place was in darkness. We tried the door in case Morton was inside, but he wasn't.'

'What was his room like?'

'Quite normal, as far as we could see. We didn't go inside.'

'So you just took the peccary and went?'

Henry said, 'What I can't understand is how you got it across the island.'

'Tranquilliser dart. They're quite humane.'

'Jolly interesting,' Henry said. 'Jolly interesting. My old man kept pigs once as a tax loss, except they went and made a profit.'

He'd crouched down against the cave wall and seemed happy to go on discussing animal husbandry all night.

'How did you get the dart into the creature?'

'Dart gun,' Toby said.

At that point, Birdie was wriggling towards the cave exit, deciding to leave them to it. As far as he was concerned, the case was closed now that he knew for certain that the scream had nothing to do with Justin's death. It had been the only point against his theory of the murder time and now he'd been proved right. The only question left was how the murderer had managed to find time to vandalise Morton's bungalow between two o'clock and sunrise – assuming Toby and Peter were telling the truth – but that was a detail. What mattered was he knew now who killed Justin and Morton, and he must find Debbie first. He stopped though when Toby said, 'Dart gun'. He was regretting already leaving the machete behind, and even anaesthetic darts would be better than nothing.

'Have you got it with you?'

Peter said sourly, 'No. If we had, Hamilcar might not have got away. We could have had another go.'

'Where is it, then?'

'Toby forgot it.'

'I did not forget it. I told you, I couldn't find it.'

The brothers glared at each other across a reeking pile of peccary droppings.

Birdie said, 'Couldn't find it where? When did you have it last?'

'In the dormitory this morning, when I was showing it to Russ.'

Birdie straightened up suddenly and hit his head on the wall of the cave. His shadow towered over the brothers as if it wanted to tear them limb from limb, and as far as he was concerned it could go ahead.

'What do you mean, you were showing it to Russ? Why for God's sake were you doing that?'

Toby said calmly, 'Because he was interested. He'd guessed about Hamilcar, or most of it, so I said I'd tell him the rest as long as he didn't pass it on to you.'

'And you showed him the tranquilliser gun?'

'Yes. He seemed to know quite a lot about them.'

'He would. Then what did you do with it?'

'I put it back in my pack. What else would I do with it?'

'And Russ saw where you put it?'

'I suppose so.'

'And when you went to get it this afternoon, it wasn't there. Didn't you ask Russ about it?'

'Of course I did. He said he didn't know anything about it.'

'Did you believe that?'

'I don't know. I couldn't press it, because I didn't want to cause an argument.'

'You've caused something worse than an argument.'

The two brothers and Henry started asking what he meant, but he wasn't staying to explain. Their questions followed him as he squeezed out of the opening into darkness that seemed complete at first after the candlelight in the cave. He stood blinking, straining his ears for anything that wasn't bird, beast or insulted peccary, but there was no sound at all that he could identify as human and, even when his eyes adapted to the thin moonlight, nothing to tell where Russ or Debbie might be. From inside the cave he heard scramblings and Henry calling to him to ask where he was going, but he'd no attention to spare for that. Up or down, that was the question. Back up to the Devil's Bath Tub or down to its outlet at the waterfall? No time to waste and no second chances if he got it wrong; probably no chance at all even if he got it right, but he couldn't think like that. By no process he could understand, his feet made the decision for him, carrying him down the path towards the waterfall where he'd found Justin's body, falteringly at first, then faster, then running and lurching, tripping over roots with branches clawing at his face and eyes, the rock face itself reaching out to batter hip and shoulder, his knee protesting but getting no response from the brain beyond a command to shut up and get on with it. Another irritant at first was the sound of Henry, crashing and twittering behind him, but he soon outran that, outran everything but the sense of urgency and the enemy in his brain insisting that it was too late, too late already, that there was nothing to be gained by hurrying.

First the thin sulphur smell of the falls came up to meet him, then the sound of water pouring out of the rock rib and into the pool. But there was more than that, something he became aware of while he ran, not just water falling but water splashing, something in the pool under the waterfall, something still alive in the pool under the waterfall.

'Debbie!' he yelled, louder than anything in the forest, louder in his own ears than even Hamilcar's squeal. 'Hang on, Debbie. I'm coming.'

Round the last corner to the awful lilies, white as neon under the moon, snapping and squelching under his feet, then mud up to his knees, holding him so that he fell forward into the pool with a final agonising wrench of the knee. And, somewhere above his head, a voice that was shaky but still had a trace of amusement in it.

'Oh, dear, Birdie. I can't save you as well.'

Annabel stood there in the pool, face pale but standing as firm as a statue of a broad-hipped nymph in a fountain, holding a soaked figure horizontally in her arms.

'Can you get up and take her, Birdie? I think I got to her in time.'

In the long half hour while they were waiting for her to recover from the anaesthetic, after Annabel and Birdie had taken turns at mouth-to-mouth resuscitation, Birdie found the dart gun, tossed into the water near another clump of lilies. He showed it to Annabel, holding it carefully by the end of the barrel. There weren't going to be any mistakes this time.

'There'll be his fingerprints on this. When I think of him waiting for her with that thing, pretending he's going to look for her and waiting to do that to her, I could . . .'

Every muscle in his body was screaming and twitching to get at Russ, but his voice couldn't say it.

'I know,' she said, bending over Debbie. 'I think her breathing's getting better.'

'And then just pitching her in. You know what we were meant to think, don't you?'

'What?'

'That she'd drowned herself. Drowned herself out of grief for that little sod Justin, that's what we were all supposed to think.'

'We might have, too.'

'I wouldn't. I'd never have accepted that, not of Debbie.'

He wasn't even going to give Justin that shade of posthumous satisfaction.

When Debbie started coming back to consciousness, Annabel tactfully drew aside to let Birdie be with her.

'Dad? Dad . . .'

'It's all right, love. Don't worry about anything. It's all over.'

'I was sitting there waiting, then I got so tired. I must have fallen in.'

'We'll talk about it later, love.'

'Something stung me through my sleeve. Have you got any of the insect stuff?' She rubbed her arm. 'Is there a spot?'

He gently rolled back the sleeve. 'Only a little red mark. You'll be all right.'

Nothing to the red marks he'd be putting on Russ.

'Thank you for getting me out. I shouldn't have gone off like that. It wouldn't have worked, anyway.'

'Annabel got you out. It worked in its way, but you shouldn't have done it.'

Later, when she was well enough to walk, she insisted they should find her jacket. It turned out to be by the rock where she'd been sitting before she fell asleep and she wouldn't move until she'd turned out both pockets.

'They're not there, the photographs.'

She looked from one to the other, a fear that hadn't been there before spreading over her face.

Birdie said, 'We'll explain later. Don't worry about it now.'

On their slow way back up the path they collected, in succession, Henry, who'd fallen by the wayside with a twisted ankle, and Toby and Peter plus ice box. When they stopped for a rest by the Devil's Bath Tub the sun had risen and, far below, they could see a white boat making for Diabola's harbour.

CHAPTER SEVENTEEN

What happened next was entirely Birdie's fault. At first, on automatic pilot, he'd played the party leader, rounded up the rest of the flock from the lodge, kept explanations to a minimum and got them all down to the jetty to meet the boat. On the way down Ellie propped up Simon, Debbie protested that she was all right but accepted Birdie's arm to lean on, and the rest trailed after them in a slow crocodile, burdened with packs. All of them except Russ. He wasn't at the lodge and none of the others had seen anything of him. Birdie had expected that. Russ would have been watching somewhere, would have seen how the thing had misfired. His plan after that, Birdie guessed, would be to stay on the island escaping and evading in earnest. The others, all except Annabel, twittered about his absence, wondering what would happen if he hadn't turned up by the time the boat was ready to sail. Birdie got them settled on board, Debbie and Simon on bunks in a cabin, the rest under awnings on the deck, then went back to the jetty, pacing up and down it, nine steps one way, nine steps back.

'Birdie.' Annabel was looking down at him, face tired and anxious. 'The captain's getting fussed. He wants to go.'

'Tell him to go, then. You look after Debbie. Book her into a hotel at Barbados. I'll pay when I get there.'

Goodness knows how.

'What do you mean? Aren't you coming with us?'

'No. I'm going to find Russ.'

She'd started arguing when a shout went up from somebody on deck. 'Here he comes.'

Birdie looked up the track, not believing it, but sure enough there was Russ marching along, shoulders square, face serious. When he saw Birdie he started running towards him.

'Birdie, did you find her? I've been looking all night.'

Birdie didn't answer. He waited until Russ got within arm's length, still talking, then let go with a right hook that lifted his heels clean off the jetty and pitched him backwards like a dynamited chimney. Russ, groggy but full of fight, scrambled to his feet and came back at him. By this time people were shouting and screaming from the deck and some of the crew arrived on the jetty to separate them. In the melee, Birdie, quite accidentally, hit the captain and laid him out cold. Which was how he came to spend the next two days in a prison cell on Barbados.

It was Henry who got him out; Henry and his bloody influence, strolling in with the man from the Consulate at midday on day two in new white yachting trousers and a shirt printed with tomato slices.

'Don't worry, Birdie, you're going home. I got the old man to have a word with the FO.'

The man from the Consulate didn't look too pleased with Henry, far less so with Birdie.

'Only you've got to apologise to the captain and give the police your statement about Justin and Morton's accident.'

'I keep telling people it wasn't . . .'

He must have bunched his fists in frustration. The man from the Consulate moved as far away from him as the small cell allowed and appealed to Henry, 'Don't let him start again.'

'Come on, Birdie, no more incidents, not after that business with the warders.'

'I didn't touch the warders. I just wanted to speak to the prison governor.'

'I think the less he has to do with the governor the better,' said the man from the Consulate. 'We've managed to book him on a plane at two-thirty.'

'I'm not going. If you think I'm going to be stuffed on a plane and leave Russ here to give his version, you can think again. I don't care if I have to stay here till bananas grow on me. All I want . . .'

Henry said, 'Russ has gone already. They all went last night.'

'All of them?'

'All except Debbie. She wouldn't go. Annabel tried to persuade her up to the last minute, but she said she'd stay here till they let you out.'

He thought of Debbie alone in a hotel room with nobody but

Henry to tell her what was going on. He couldn't do it to her. He'd have to sort it all out at home.

'You've booked a seat for her, too?'

'Of course he has. Now do be reasonable, Birdie.'

He was, up to a point, reasonable. On the flight back, with Henry asleep and snoring in the seat on the other side of her, Debbie asked him, 'So you think Russ shot me with that dart thing?'

'Yes.'

'And took those pictures out of my jacket?'

'Yes.'

'Then I just fell asleep and toppled over in the pool, I suppose.' But there was doubt in her voice, the same scared doubt that had flickered over her face when she found the photos had gone.

'I'm afraid not, love. I think he put you in that pool. He meant it to look as if you'd drowned yourself.'

'Because of Justin?'

'Yes.'

She was silent for a few dozen miles of Atlantic, then: 'I didn't think it was Russ.'

'Who did you think?'

She glanced across at the sleeping Henry.

'Or Mal. I wonder how much Justin's father paid Russ to . . .'

'To kill Justin? I'm not sure he did. I think he was paying Russ to get those photos back – only he'd pitched on a psychopath who threw in a couple of murders for free. Nearly another one, too, if Annabel hadn't been there.'

'Yes.'

He'd noticed that she didn't like any reminder that she owed her life to Annabel. They weren't being forgiven for that episode in a hurry.

'Do you think they'll get married?'

Another glance across at Henry's gaping pink face above the tomato slices.

'I don't think so.'

'She was very rude about him in the dormitory, talking to Helena. She said he was a typical TMF and he slept like a walrus.'

'TMF? Don't you mean MCP?'

'No, I asked them. Helena giggled a bit then told me what it meant. Annabel didn't want her to.'

'What does it mean?'

'Two minute fuck,' said Debbie austerely.

Henry caught that, waking up with a volcanic snore just as a stewardess was bringing a trolley.

'No, thanks. I'll just have the coffee.'

Birdie spent the next fifty five miles turning hot and cold at the thought of what Annabel might be saying about his performance.

He got back to find himself sacked by Tooth and Claw and forgiven, more or less, by Nimue. There was a note waiting for him from Justin's father. No mention of anything that had happened, just a businesslike three lines hoping Birdie would find it convenient to telephone his personal assistant and make an appointment. No malt or social chat this time, only Justin's father sitting the other side of a leather-topped desk behind a telephone that probably wouldn't ring for anybody below the rank of chairman. He invited Birdie to sit down. On the expanse of desk was just one piece of paper turned round so that he could read it: a Coutts bank cheque made out for a thousand pounds, payable to himself. Birdie put beside it one of his own, rather crumpled, five hundred pounds made out to Justin's father, who looked at it as if wondering whether to ring for a deodorant spray.

'What's that supposed to be?'

'Refund.'

Justin's father smiled coldly. Birdie noticed he was wearing a black tie.

'You did your best. I'm paying you the balance, as agreed.'

If he thought that was Birdie's best, goodness knows what the worst would be.

'It's too much, anyway. It was only supposed to be another five hundred.'

'I was hoping you'd see the balance in the nature of a retainer for further services.'

'Retainer?'

Birdie was on the point of asking if there were any more sons he wanted killed, but stopped himself. He had his own strategy and wouldn't allow himself to be bounced out of it. He'd been too impulsive already, two days in prison had taught him that, and now it was time for patience.

'I'm hoping you'll help me organise Justin's memorial service.'

Birdie was struck dumb by visions of St Paul's or Westminster Abbey.

'On the island,' Justin's father said. 'On Diabola. I want you to get all of them together again, all of you who were with him in the last few days of his life.'

Birdie stared. His plans had made no allowance for this.

'Two weeks from now might be convenient. I've provisionally booked the boat and flights to Barbados. The tablet's being made here. We'll take it with us.'

'Tablet?'

'Westmorland slate. Quite simple. Names, dates, "Greater love hath no man than this, that he lays down his life for his friend."'

'But he and Morton couldn't stand each other.' Birdie couldn't help it, and got a look as if he'd burped in church.

'I don't think we need to go into that. Henry has told me the details.'

But what details? The story of Justin's heroic end, as approved by democratic vote, or the story behind that? Birdie stared across the desk, trying to find some clue in the bland face and tired eyes, but found nothing. To all appearances, Justin's father was waiting politely, given all the calls on his time, to see if Birdie would accept his offer. When Birdie didn't reply he asked, with just a touch of impatience, 'Will you take it on?'

'They'd had enough of the island. They won't want to go back.'

'Naturally I'd pay them for their time and trouble. Say five hundred pounds each, expenses.'

'I'll try.'

It suited him far better than anything he'd planned, but he wouldn't let Justin's father see that.

'Good. Have a word with my assistant on the way out. She's got details of bookings and so on.'

Birdie stood up but didn't go. He took something out of his pocket. 'I thought you might like to see this.'

Justin's father stared at the transparency in its plastic mount. 'What is it? Justin?'

'No. Something Justin had with him.'
He passed it over.
'I daresay Russ will have given you the others already. This got separated.'

'Russ?'

The name seemed to mean nothing to him. He still hadn't held the transparency up to the light.

'How much are you paying him for extra services? The likes of Russ come more expensive than me.'

'I don't know what you're talking about.'

Birdie walked out, leaving the two cheques and the photograph lying on the desk.

He wrote notes. Toby replied by return, accepting the invitation and offer of expenses but regretting that his brother couldn't be present because the gorilla was about to give birth. Henry and Mal had already promised Justin's father to be there, so they were no problem. Ellie replied several days later in a long handwritten letter, reluctantly concluding that it was her duty to be there. A scrawled postscript announced that Simon would not be among those present because it turned out he'd been having an affair with the girl from the prescriptions counter at the chemist's and he'd moved in with her as soon as they got back. She was very glad about it, Ellie said, because the discounts would be so useful to him.

That left Russ and the Helibels. Birdie went, for the third time since his return, to call on Russ's mother in her neat terraced house on the Isle of Dogs. The news was the same. Russ was still with his friends in Newcastle or possibly other friends in Glasgow. No, she didn't have names or addresses. No, she didn't know when he'd be back.

'Doesn't he write to you?' Birdie asked.

'Write? Oh, no!'

She sounded quite shocked at the idea. Her sideboard was landscaped with pictures of Russ: Russ in sub-aqua gear, Russ with boat and dead sharklet, Russ weight-lifting, Russ with alsatian dog. She seemed to find it quite natural that Birdie was impatient to renew acquaintance with her wonder-man son and would have been more helpful if she could. She promised to pass on the message about the memorial service as soon as he got back.

The Helibels didn't reply to his note. After two days, he phoned the number Annabel had given on the booking form and invited himself round. It was midday but she sounded sleepy, asked what time it was and said, Oh God, he'd woken her up. Still, he could come round if he wanted to, only give them time to get decent for goodness sake. When he got there everything was as decorous as a vicarage with the two of them waiting for him in their big comfortable living room, blinds filtering sunlight onto striped wallpaper and watercolours, wing chairs on islands of sheepskin rugs.

'She doesn't want to go,' Annabel said.

Helena, sitting hunched on what looked like a camel saddle, nodded and gave a little shudder.

'Justin's father will be disappointed.'

Annabel gave him a long look. The ball of one brown foot rubbed against the arch of the other.

'Does he want us to go?'

'He wants everybody to go.'

'And are they?'

'Everybody except Peter and Simon.'

'I think we should go,' she said. Helena groaned. 'No, really. If Justin's father wants us, I think we should go.'

And, as usual, once Annabel had decided, that was that. They poured coffee, asked after Debbie, agreed with him that it wouldn't be fair to make her go back to the island. Anyway, Birdie pointed out, term had started and she had a lot of work to do. As Annabel showed Birdie out she asked if the expenses from Justin's father would be payable in advance. She supposed they'd have to buy something black.

The sulphur smell came to meet them while they were still out at sea. Justin's father wrinkled his nose when it got to him and so did the clergyman and photographer they were bringing with them from Barbados. They and the seven members of Birdie's original party were standing at the rail watching the mass of green forest coming closer until they could pick out individual trees and see the red roofs of Morton's bungalow and the lodge. Henry and Mal were standing on either side of Justin's father and Henry was pointing to the dark grey crags that overlooked the Devil's Bath

Tub. Throughout the long flight to Barbados and the voyage to Diabola nothing had been said to contradict the official version that they were there to commemorate Justin the hero. That suited Birdie. He'd go along with it until the right time came. His confidence was growing as they got nearer the island. It was more his territory than the office with the leather-topped desk.

Russ was standing a little apart from the others, hand on a fender rope, still doing his scout act. When they'd met at the airport he'd held out his hand to Birdie and smiled his broad, open smile. The message was clear – he was man enough to forget that fracas on the quay and hoped Birdie would do the same. Birdie, biding his time, had shaken the hand but not managed the smile. He'd watched throughout the journey for contacts between Russ and Justin's father. They'd been introduced to each other by Henry and shaken hands like strangers. Russ offered decent commiserations for Justin's death and that was that. From then on, as far as Birdie could see, there'd been nothing but the routine politenesses of two people travelling together.

As he watched Russ, Birdie was aware that Ellie was looking in the same direction, although Russ gave no sign of noticing her. She'd been as tense as a trap on the journey, saying as little as possible to the rest of them. Any mention of the memorial service or the plaque that was lying below, wrapped in sacking, brought a stiffening of her neck and shoulders as if she was getting ready for a fight. Birdie wondered why she'd gone along so far with the fiction of Justin's death and wondered whether she was planning to explode the other version at a moment of maximum drama, like the memorial service itself.

Toby and the Helibels had moved to the bows to watch the arrival at the jetty. Helena was wearing a black trouser suit vaguely Chinese in style, set off by a white artificial chrysanthemum in her hair, Annabel a black silky skirt and top. Even to Birdie's eye, they must have cost a fair amount of the expenses money Justin's father had paid but, judging from the looks he'd been giving the two of them, he was at least getting his money's worth from that part of his investment. When he'd seen Annabel at the airport his eyes had widened and the handshake he'd given her had lasted some seconds longer than necessary. Now, as the boat tied up, Annabel's skirt blew up in the sea breeze, revealing her long brown legs. He noticed that the hand smoothing it down had no twist of creeper on the engagement finger and no diamonds either. That reminded him that Annabel, like Ellie, had voted against the hero scenario, but she might not share Ellie's taste for a fight.

Once landed, they arranged themselves for the long walk to the Devil's Bath Tub. Justin's father went in front as chief mourner, accompanied by Mal and Henry, hot and incongruous in suits and ties, then the clergyman and photographer, both of whom seemed slightly puzzled about what they were doing there. Birdie could have told them. If Justin's life had cost his father a few thousand votes, then the manner of his death might pick them up again. After them came Ellie and Toby, saying nothing to each other, then the Helibels who'd changed into black track shoes for the walk and stuffed wedge-heeled sandals into shoulder bags. Some way behind them came two crew members sweating under the weight of the memorial tablet, ostentatiously assisted by Russ. They stopped at the bungalow to collect Morton's successor, a young St Lucian whose white shirt and trousers were so far undimmed by sulphur. At this point too the tablet was transferred to a creaking handcart and the cortege wound its slow way uphill in heat that turned clothes into damp cardboard.

There was at least a breeze on the plateau around the Devil's Bath Tub, coming off the sea. It cooled Birdie and Russ and the two Hoorays as, under instructions from Morton's successor, they manoeuvred the tablet into the slot he'd hacked out for it. It was, as it happened, more or less exactly in the place under the rock wall where Birdie had stayed awake all night waiting for Justin to attack him. When it was done the clergyman read some prayers and they joined in embarrassed murmurs, while the sulphur pool provided its own glutinous base line. Henry, as the nearest thing available to friend of the deceased, read something inappropriate from the psalms as if delivering mid-term company results in a disappointing year. All the time it was going on, Birdie was waiting for Ellie, or just possibly Annabel, to say what a mockery it was, but nothing came from them except the occasional dutiful Amen.

When it was over, the photographer wanted them grouped around the clergyman with the sea in the background. Birdie stayed where he was, staring at the inscription on the plaque, wondering how long it would be before it was rubbed out by the sulphur fumes. As soon as this nonsense was over it would be time to get Russ on his own. In the pack he'd brought with him was a collection of things that had kept him sweating when they went through customs: two machetes, two warning notes, an anaesthetic dart gun and a battered thesis on underground water courses. He thought about the book and the mind that had traced its way through a maze of graphs and footnotes, and reacted so swiftly to what it had found. As he stared down at the plaque, visualising the book's pages, he was aware of somebody standing beside him. A tightening of his muscles told him, a split second before he heard the voice, that it was Russ.

'What does it say, Birdie?'

At first he didn't understand the question. In spite of his determination to keep calm this time, his mind was fogged with anger.

'What's that?'

'What does it say on the inscription?'

Birdie stared at him. 'You can read.'

Russ shook his head. 'Didn't my mum tell you? I'm dyslexic. She does the reading and writing for me.'

He was still smiling, still talking, while Birdie was sinking fathoms deep in deprivation and bewilderment.

'I'm surprised she didn't tell you. She was quite proud when they found out. Up till then they thought I was just thick.'

'Can't read? Can't read at all?'

Against his will, some memories were coming back to him: Russ's apparently arrogant refusal to use maps, his indignation when Mal accused him of getting something out of a book.

'Not a word. Still, I'm doing all right, aren't I?'

Birdie thrashed around. 'You can use a dart gun though, can't you? You can use that all right.'

Russ took a step backwards, watching Birdie's hands warily, but his voice was more sorrowful than angry.

'You really think I did that, Birdie? You still think I used Toby's gun on Debbie? I like that kid. Honest, I like her.'

There seemed nothing but hurt and puzzlement in his eyes.

'You took that gun away with you, didn't you, Birdie? Toby's

been asking me about it. He thinks I took it.'
'I wanted to get it finger-printed.'
'And did you?'
'Nothing. It had been wiped.'
'Well, then.'

Birdie went on staring at Russ while his mind went through the convolutions of trying to reorganise itself.

'You really can't read, you mean that?'
'Ask Ellie. She was trying to teach me. Didn't get very far, though.'

While Birdie wondered whether to believe him, he remembered another reason to get angry.

'What did you think you were doing, telling my daughter about me and Annabel?'

Either Russ was the best actor he'd ever met or those eyes were registering surprise. More than that, alarm even, as if the question changed his view of Birdie.

'What were you doing with Annabel?'

Birdie's snort of anger brought glances in their direction from the photograph line-up.

Ellie called out, 'Birdie, you mustn't start on Russ again.'

Henry tried some diplomacy. 'Got enough photos? Right, a drink — that's what we all need. This way, Reverend.'

Some more of the boat's crew had been directed to organise refreshments at the lodge before the trek back to the harbour. Henry ushered them in a straggling line past the memorial tablet, the clergyman first, then Justin's father deep in conversation with the Helibels, then the subsidiary mourners. Ellie, at the end of the line, was inclined to linger.

'Are you two coming?'
'Don't worry about us. He's not going to hit me again, are you, Birdie?'

Don't depend on it, Birdie thought.

He said to Ellie, 'Is it true Russ can't read?'

Instantly she was on the defensive. 'Don't you start on that. He had enough of it from Simon.'

'Is it true, though?'
'Yes, but . . .'

Russ interrupted. 'Ellie, I told you it doesn't bother me. Birdie made an issue out of it because I asked him to read the tombstone to me. But we're getting on all right, aren't we, Birdie?'

Birdie said they were. It was the only way to get rid of Ellie.

When the bushes closed behind her Russ returned to the attack. 'So what were you up to with Annabel, Birdie?'

'You know damned well. Well enough to blab to Debbie about it.'

'Birdie, I'm asking you, what am I supposed to have told her?'

Birdie said through clenched teeth, 'About her and me having it off on the balcony.'

The surprise in Russ's eyes changed slowly to amusement. 'You didn't, did you? How much did she charge you?'

Birdie could have hit him again, except the smash would have brought Ellie back.

'You think it's a joke, do you, telling a girl of seventeen that her father . . . ?'

'For goodness sake, will you listen? I didn't say anything about you and Annabel. I didn't know anything about you and Annabel.'

'You told her Annabel was a tart.'

'Yes. She is.'

'Just because she . . . '

He heard his own voice raging on while his mind was trying to come to terms with what he'd heard.

'When you say a tart . . . ?'

'Very high class, of course. Specialised too. Debbie showed you the photos, didn't she?'

'Photos?'

His mind flashed up a transparency, a woman with a cane, legs long and elegant under a black academic gown. But there was another more recent picture superimposed, a picture from only a few hours ago, long smooth-muscled legs under a black silk skirt that blew up in the breeze off the sea.

'Annabel . . . the woman in the photographs.'

'That's right, Birdie. Surprised you didn't spot it. Perhaps you were too busy reading things.'

'How did you know?'

'I worked for them once, only she threw me out because I said I was supposed to be a bodyguard, not an errand boy.'

'And when you saw them here?'

'I thought they were really after Henry and Mal. Thought they'd decided to marry money and turn respectable. Then I worked out they must have come specially to meet Justin and hand over those photographs.'

'No.'

While Russ was talking, Birdie's mind had cleared. The anger and the sulphur fumes of the past weeks had lifted, leaving a conclusion stark as the rock they were standing on.

'No, that wasn't it at all.'

And he ran off, followed by Russ demanding to know what he thought he was doing this time.

The eruption of Birdie and Russ, dishevelled and sweating, spoilt the decorum of the funeral party. They were all there on the balcony drinking gin and tonic or tea, all except the two Birdie wanted. When he asked about them Henry said, 'Justin's father wanted to be alone for a while.'

'He did, did he? And I suppose he needed Annabel to help him?'

He didn't wait to see how Henry took that. He knew the pair of them couldn't be far away and, sure enough, found them at the point where an uprooted tree slanted close to the path, a few hundred yards below the lodge. Annabel was sitting sideways on the tree, swinging an ankle, feet restored to their black sandals. Justin's father had a foot on the tree trunk and was apparently listening to her politely.

'I should be careful,' Birdie said, 'or she'll kill you as well.'

They'd been too absorbed in what they were talking about to hear him coming. They froze, staring, but Justin's father recovered in seconds.

'I don't think so. In my case it's only blackmail.'

'And now he's blackmailing me,' Annabel said.

There was a giggle in her voice, but a scared one. She gave Birdie a sidelong glance, like a child caught out in a game, signalling for rescue.

'She killed your son,' Birdie said. 'And Morton. And she tried to drown my daughter.'

He wanted to say a lot more but his voice gave out on him when he thought of Annabel in the pool with Debbie in her arms.

Justin's father shook his head. 'You saw the inscription.'

'You're going along with that story to stop her publishing those photographs. That's the price, is it?'

Neither of them said anything.

'They must have been running a nice blackmail game, her and Helena. I daresay you were only one of dozens. But if Justin had sent those photos to the papers it would have blown it all wide open. They didn't want them published any more than you did.'

Justin's father said, sounding weary, 'I didn't even know of the existence of those photos until you dumped one of them on my desk.'

'That's true,' Annabel said. 'We hadn't got round to him yet.'

Birdie said to her, 'You wiped the finger prints off that dart gun right under my nose, while I was looking after Debbie. I must have been out of my mind.'

'No, just worried,' said Justin's father consolingly.

He battered on at them, trying to get some reaction. 'That was why you and Helena were late back at the lodge the night we did the walk. You'd already killed him then. It must have been a disappointment when you found he didn't have the photographs in his pack. You found the messages he'd written, though.'

Annabel had turned away from him. The ankle swung hypnotically.

'And to make the alibi work you had to kill Morton, too. But that was even easier, wasn't it?'

No response. He appealed to Justin's father. 'Did she tell you how she drugged Henry so she could go out and kill Morton? She'd even practised it on me.'

He'd no embarrassment left, nothing but anger and determination to drag a reaction from them.

'Then they had to lose Morton's books, but she left that to Helena. "Your turn now." I remember her saying that to Helena, but I thought she was talking about getting engaged.'

She was smiling at that, had turned just enough towards him to let him see she was smiling.

He turned on Justin's father. 'And you're letting them get away with it. They did all this and you're letting them get away with it rather than face a bit of bad publicity.'

Justin's father said quietly, 'Do you think I want people to remember my son like that – trying to do that to his own father?'

Annabel at last turned full face towards Birdie. When she spoke her voice was silky and sympathetic.

'And Debbie would have to give evidence in court about how she went off with him, about seeing the photos. You wouldn't want that for your daughter, would you, Birdie?'

'It's all hypocrisy,' Debbie said. 'If you're rich and important you can get away with anything.'

He'd told her about it when she came to stay with him and Nimue at half term. Nimue had insisted on that. For three days now, in between her visits to the Tate and the National Gallery, he'd been listening to variations on the same theme. He wasn't arguing any more, not that he'd been able to argue much in the first place. At least today, though, the accusations of hypocrisy weren't coming in such a barrage, just fired off in salvoes here and there as she dashed around their little flat changing to go out. She sounded happier than she'd been for days, borrowing Nimue's hair dryer, tights, trying on half her wardrobe. She came out of the bedroom, bizarre but striking, and flashed Birdie a great grin before she remembered she was supposed to be fighting him.

'Nimue, you don't mind if I borrow the jade silk blouse, do you? And I think I've used up your French scent.'

Her hair was still spiky, but copper coloured. He was getting used to it.

''Bye Dad. Don't wait up for me.'

He said the usual things about being careful and back before midnight, adding casually, 'Who're you meeting?'

She stopped for a second on her rush to the door and replied, equally casually, 'Russ. 'Night, Dad.'

He wailed to Nimue, 'He's a loudmouth. He's been a brothel bouncer. He's a bloody dyslexic.'

'Well, at least her taste is getting better.'

There were times when he thought Nimue might have more sympathy.